EX
ON THE
BEACH

D1714290

EX ON THE BEACH

Cover Design by Melissa Williams Design

Coconut Cocktail by sabelskaya on AdobeStock

Yellow Flip Flops by krissikunterbunt on AdobeStock

Hanging Lights by Amanda with A.J. Reid Creative

Chairs by Melissa Williams Design

Umbrella by ylivdesign on AdobeStock

Published by Garden Ninja Books

ExtraSeriesBooks.com

First Edition: December 2020

0 9 8 7 6 5 4 3 2 1

EX ON THE BEACH

THE EXTRA SERIES *Book 11*

MEGAN WALKER & JANCI PATTERSON

For Heather Clark
Our judgiest superfan

ONE

Kim

've got a plan for this.

Okay, that's not entirely true, given that I don't know the reason my agent needs to meet with me "today, if possible," but telling myself that helps loosen the tension in my chest a bit. I've been with my agent, Josh Rios, for long enough to tell by the tone of his voice that the news isn't great. Probably the Sofia Coppola project next year is getting pushed back—that kind of thing is common, but Josh knows how much I hate my schedule getting messed up. Not just because I've got a stronger emotional attachment to my intricate, color-coded calendar system than most of LA feels for their favorite Botox provider, but because The Schedule is in careful balance with my ex-husband as we manage our time with our kids in between both of our busy film careers.

Messing with The Schedule often means a domino effect of epic proportion, which requires me to actually converse—even if only via text—with Blake.

I pace in the entryway of my house, my sandals clicking against the tile floor. One of my cats, a Maine Coon named Roz, has her huge girth balanced precariously on the stair banister, watching me with her single eye. I pet her on the one spot on her back where she likes to be touched and think through what my plan could be if the Coppola project gets stalled.

I may have to cancel the trip to Australia for the World Surf Championship—which was supposed to be a surprise for my daughter, Ivy. While I'm not particularly sad to miss out on days of watching a sport I don't have any interest in, I was looking forward to seeing her enjoy it. Sharing the part of her life that she normally only shares with her father. Blake is the fun parent. I've long since resigned myself to that fact—I'm the parent that counts the number of vegetables they've eaten and charts their screen time.

I was really excited to be the fun parent, for once.

Not that the kids don't enjoy their time here on the ranch. I know they do. Lots of animals and outdoor space—I have that going for me. And Ivy will be just as excited when the championship comes around in another year, so I could still—

The gate comm buzzes; I glance at the camera and see Josh's sleek Porsche, and I press the button to open the gate. While I wait for him to make his way down the drive and park, I breathe in and out slowly.

Whatever the news is, whatever changes to The Schedule and family plans it entails, I can handle it. No doubt I've handled far worse. Or survived, at least—even if it felt like just barely.

There's a knock, and several dogs begin barking and howling from behind the closed door to the bedroom areas. Their barking sets off more from the dogs outside. It's a familiar chain reaction that never fails to make Luke giggle. He calls it the "Twilight Bark," like from *101 Dalmatians*.

I miss my kids, even though they're just at school right now. No matter how many animals and ranch workers are here at any given time, the house feels a little empty without them. It's worse when they're at their dad's, which they generally are about half the week, unless one or the other of us is off filming on location.

I open the door. Josh Rios is standing there in a nice, fitted suit, his dark hair styled back, looking, as always, every inch the professional. We used to have our business meetings at a restaurant, but the paparazzi are ruthless, attempting to lip-read video footage or sneak in long-range mics to get the scoop on my future projects—or to suggest that my agent and I are having a torrid lunchtime affair over Cobb salads at Angelo's. Now I usually meet him at his office.

His offer to drive all the way out here might mean that the news is worse than a shift in schedule.

He greets me with a handshake and a smile that looks a little tense. Roz greets Josh with a hiss, her back arched, and her lone ear—on the same side of her head as her lone eye—flattened against her head.

"Don't worry about her," I assure Josh, who shoots a wary look at the large ball of angry cat. "She's all talk."

Josh laughs. "I deal with that type a lot." Still, he gives Roz a wide berth as he steps into the sitting room. I feel better about my decision to keep the dogs out of this part of the house. Josh has been to the ranch a couple times over the years, and overall seems to deal well with the animals, but I doubt he'd appreciate the enthusiasm of the roaming pack of house dogs—especially our new short-haired Chihuahua, Urkel, who gleefully humps every pair of men's dress shoes he encounters.

I'm working on getting him to stop, and while I'm not unused to training challenges—most of the animals at my sanctuary here have special medical needs or training problems that make them difficult to place in normal homes—his passion for Italian leather Oxfords might be one of the epic love stories of our time.

"Can I get you anything?" I ask as Josh settles in on the sofa, taking in the view of the ranch from the big picture windows. This room is probably my favorite in the house—the vaulted, exposed timber ceilings and the way the sun streams through the windows, warming the tile. But the best part is definitely the view of the land, dappled with fruit trees and yew pine, with the sunlight sparkling off the duck pond in the distance.

In addition to the land itself, the view also includes numerous buildings I've added—stables, supply huts, chicken coops, medical stations, that sort of thing. One of my ranch workers is driving by on a golf cart loaded with bags of dog food while being chased by about a dozen dogs. There are goats climbing over my patio furniture, chewing on the already ragged edges of my rattan chairs.

I'm usually out there with the animals myself when I can be. Administering meds, training, playing with them. This sanctuary is still my dream come true.

Even if it somehow feels a bit hollow.

Josh starts pulling paperwork out of his briefcase. I'm dying to leap into the reason he's here and get to figuring out a solution, but there's this small-but-persistent part of me that hopes the problem will disappear if I front-load it with enough small talk and caffeine. "Some coffee? Something to eat?"

"No, thanks," he says. "I actually just had a brunch date with Anna-Marie." He smiles when he says his wife's name, like he always does—that reflexive smile of a man deeply in love. I wonder if Blake ever did that when he thought about me, even in the early days.

"Nice," I say, shaking off the thought. It doesn't matter anymore; it hasn't mattered for six years. "Celebrating anything?"

"Just an hour in which our schedules line up. We've learned to steal every chance we get."

I remember how that used to be. Between film schedules and kids' schedules and industry events, some of the best alone time Blake and I had were those midnights we'd order from that all-night Thai place not far from our old house and sit out on the backyard patio under the stars. We'd eat, and talk, and laugh, and toss rice noodles to our pet pig, who'd be snuffling around by our feet.

Sometimes those nights feel so long ago, so out of reach, that it feels like I imagined them entirely.

I sit on the chair across from Josh. "We've still got to arrange a time for you to bring Anna-Marie and your little girl here to see the ranch—what is she now, two? Three? My kids would love to show her around."

Josh's grin widens. I've met Anna-Marie a few times at agency functions, but I've only seen pictures of their gorgeous, dark-haired daughter. Josh Rios can be a shark when it comes to contracts and protecting his clients, but he has an equal reputation for being an unabashed family man—his wife and daughter are the top priorities in his life, and he makes no excuses for that. It's one of the reasons I signed with him. It's rare to find someone in this industry who gets what's really important.

"Riony's two," he says. "And they would love that. Ri's been obsessed with horses lately. Dragons, too, but I'm guessing you have fewer of those."

"Horses we have. I'll work on the dragons." I smile, then let out a breath. We've done enough small talk to make me feel socially competent, and I know the problem—whatever it is—is still waiting for me. "So, what's the bad news?"

Josh nods and sits forward, slipping right into business mode. "In the grand tradition of most things in life, there's both good news and bad news. The good news is that the new Hemlock movie's been green-lighted, and they definitely want you back. They're willing to pay very, very well for this one."

My eyes widen in surprise—this is about Hemlock? After my last two movies playing the comic book character exceeded box office expectations, it was pretty much guaranteed they'd make a third. Playing Hemlock hasn't exactly been the artistic pinnacle of my career, but it's been fun, and I've already told Josh I'd be up for another movie. I can't imagine how this would lead to bad news.

"Okay," I say slowly. "So, what, are we going to be filming in Siberia or something?"

"Close. Miami. In July and August." He pauses. "This July."

My brow furrows. "But that's—"

"Only two months away, yeah. Apparently all the secrecy around this project, all that stuff *I* couldn't even get them to

9

breathe a word on—well, what they've been working on came together all at once, and they want this done fast."

Miami in July sounds a little miserable, but I can handle it. I technically don't have any projects for the next six months. We can tinker with The Schedule to give me more time with the kids before that. Maybe I'll take most of June and—

"That's not the important part," Josh says, his expression reluctant. "This project is a crossover with a romantic subplot. They want Hemlock with Farpoint."

I make a choked sound I'm not particularly proud of, then clear my throat. Farpoint is a character with a rival comics company. He's had several successful box-office hits of his own, all of them starring my ex-husband.

"Farpoint," I say numbly. "So that means . . ."

Josh nods. "That means you'll be starring with Blake."

I didn't realize until that moment that my body could feel icy cold and flush with warmth all at the same time.

Starring in a movie with Blake.

It's not that I haven't done that before. That's part of the problem. We co-starred in seven movies during the eight years we were together. We used to love doing movies together. It was like being back on that very first film, where we fell in love along with our characters.

But now . . .

"That's not possible," I say. "They can't make a movie like that. Farpoint and Hemlock aren't even owned by the same comics company." The knowledge that there was zero chance these characters could ever interact was probably one of the main reasons Blake accepted the role of Farpoint, a year or so after our divorce. Nova Comics and Brigand Bay Comics are mortal enemies in the fandom world. Their fans seem to solidly line up in camps and spend most of their time piling weirdly specific hate on the other side.

This can't be happening. There's no way. They might as well announce that Batman's new love interest is Black Widow.

"I know," Josh says, and by the way he says it, I think he gets it even more than I do. I remember him saying once that he's a bit of a comic book geek. "But the studio execs don't care about fandom wars. They care about getting Hemlock and Farpoint together—especially as played by you and Blake. They stand to make a ton of money on this."

I groan. "It was that webcomic, wasn't it? That—what's her name, Hannah Ver-something, put out a couple years ago." Nobody was even thinking about Hemlock and Farpoint in the same sentence before that came out—the characters aren't even in the same literal universe. But then there was this webcomic using stills from the movies, telling the epic affair of Hemlock and Farpoint's undying love. The photoshop she did to put us together was actually really good. So good it was painful for me to read.

"Hannah Verhoeven, yeah. That got huge in the geek world. Big enough to be worth working something out with Nova and Brigand Bay to make this happen. And with you and Blake, well."

He doesn't need to spell it out. Hemlock and Farpoint together is one thing. Kim Watterson and Blake Pless back on screen together pulls in a whole other huge group of fans.

I'm standing before I even realize I'm doing it, pacing again. My chest is tight enough I feel like I'm pushing my lungs through a strainer. I force myself to be still, to breathe deeply.

"You don't have to do this," Josh says. "We can pass." He pauses, his dark eyes sympathetic. "I can imagine how difficult it would be to work that closely with an ex-spouse."

He doesn't know the half of it. He, like most of the world, probably believes Blake cheated on me with our nanny. It wasn't true, but we didn't bother to fight that rumor, because it was easier than trying to explain to the world what really happened to our marriage. Honestly, I wasn't even sure myself at the time.

It took me another few years and a medical diagnosis to piece it together. By then, it was way too late. Blake had long since moved on.

I, unfortunately, can't seem to do the same.

"But my career," I start, then squeeze my eyes shut together.

"Will be fine," Josh assures me. "You're Kim Watterson. There will be other roles. Great ones."

There will be other roles, but far fewer than there used to be. I may be Kim Watterson, former Family Network teen idol turned A-list film star, but I'm thirty-six years old now, in an industry built on the perky bodies of young twenty-somethings. The roles I'm being offered will be increasingly less "romantic lead" and more "dried-up mother of young ingenue."

"If I turn it down, they'll just replace me, won't they?" I can't keep the edge of bitterness from my tone. "With some twenty-year-old."

Josh nods. "Probably, yeah. But that doesn't mean—"

"But if Blake turned it down?" I raise my eyebrow at Josh. Challenging him to tell me the truth.

The nice thing about Josh is that he always does. He doesn't bullshit about the inequities of the industry, and he clearly hates them himself—his wife is an actress, so he gets it. "The whole project would probably fall through." Then he gives a little shrug and a half-smile. "Unless they could get Hugh Jackman."

He obviously means that last part as a joke, but I could see it. No disrespect to Hugh, who I'm actually good friends with, but it's pretty special to think that to keep me as a romantic lead I'd probably be paired with a guy in his fifties, while Blake—who's the same age as me—would get some doe-eyed starlet barely out of high school.

The Hollywood double standard makes me furious. And besides that, I don't want to see Hemlock played by someone else. Not yet, at least. She's kind of ridiculous—a genius chemist who is also a vigilante assassin in her spare time, and she dresses like a dominatrix with a plant fetish—but I've grown attached to the character. She's mine, and I want to keep her that way.

I can do this, even with Blake. I'm an actress, damn it, and a good one. I'm a professional. I can put my feelings aside.

I have to start being able to do that at some point.

"I'll do it," I say, sitting back down.

Josh blinks in surprise at my sudden turn-about, then sets a contract on the coffee table. "Here's their initial offer. It's a decent amount, but we can get more."

I eye the number on top. It's more than I was paid for the other Hemlock movies, by enough it's clear they know there's a good chance I'll refuse to work with Blake. It's not like I'm hurting financially, but the sanctuary isn't exactly cheap to run.

"Good." I think of that Hollywood inequity thing again and add, "I don't want to make less than Blake. That's important." That's not a Blake-specific demand—I've been refusing to do the same job as my male counterpart for less money for a while now. Usually I'm the more famous of the two, so it's not an issue, but Blake is a different story.

"Absolutely." Josh makes a note on the contract. "What else do you want?"

"This romantic plotline—how romantic are we talking?" I've done some pretty racy scenes with co-stars before, and it's not a problem, but the thought of doing that again with Blake . . . I feel the heat creeping up my face, like I'm some sixteen-year-old with a crush on the quarterback, and it pisses me off.

I need to stop. It's been six years.

"Well, it'll be PG-13 like the others, so any sex scene would likely be cut-away. Probably a few kissing scenes."

I try to control my spinning thoughts, keep the wall up around years' worth of memories. "No sex scene. Try to get them down to one kissing scene."

"Done." Josh makes another note. "Anything else? You've got the power here, Kim. They really don't want to replace you."

I think through all the demands I could make, but I've generally tried to not be too much of a diva. I don't need specialty cheeses imported daily from Southern France or my own personal Reiki masseuse. I shrug. "I mean, if Blake and I are both on set, we'll have our kids with us, so we'll need accommodations for them, as well as our nanny. But that's pretty much—oh."

I just remembered an email I got today, finalizing my most recent adoption, who will be arriving at the ranch at the end of next week. The rescue all but begged me to take him on. He's a total sweetheart—we bonded instantly when I flew out to South Carolina to meet him—but definitely a high-needs case. Which had been fine when I wasn't planning on shooting a movie for the next six months.

Josh is watching me expectantly, his pen poised above his notepad.

"I'm also going to need some accommodations for a blind boxer," I say. "He's got several health problems, but the main problem is that he has some pretty severe attachment issues. I'll need to have him on set with me."

Josh stares at me for a moment, blinks, then jots down some notes. "Okay. A blind boxer who will need on-set . . . assistance?"

"Yeah, someone to watch him when I'm filming. Keep him company. Clean up any messes he makes."

Josh is looking increasingly alarmed, though he keeps making notes, and suddenly it hits me what his confusion is.

"It's a dog, not a person," I say. "Boxer is the breed. Not a profession."

"Oh god, that's good." Josh lets out a laugh. "I was seriously trying to figure out how I was going to phrase this demand for an assistant for your mess-prone boxer friend."

"And yet, you were going to do it anyway." Another reason why Josh is pretty much the best agent around.

"It still wouldn't be the strangest client demand I've fought for."

I imagine not. He works in Hollywood, after all.

We work out a few more details, making a list of questions he's going to find answers for, and then Josh leaves.

I'm left alone again in the sitting room. My house-tortoise, Newman, crawls slowly across the tile and pees next to the divan, but I barely notice.

A movie. With Blake.

Can I really do that again? After everything?

I should be up and getting things done, doing preliminary updates to The Schedule. But I just sit there, numb, for easily a half hour.

My phone dings with a text, and when I pull it out of my pocket, I see the text is from Blake.

I can turn it down if you want me to, it says.

Just that.

He already knows, obviously, and by the lack of preamble, he must somehow know I've found out by now. His agent, Camilla—who used to be my agent, too, until I decided to switch after the divorce—has an ability to suss out information that the NSA would be jealous of, so I'm not really surprised by that.

Or by his offer, really. It speaks volumes in only a few words. He gets the position I'm in—if I really don't want to do this and bow out, I'd take a lot more heat than he would for doing the same thing. And it would have a lot less overall effect on his career.

It's a kind offer, but it also flares up that old anger—at Hollywood, at the differences in treatment of us by both the public and fellow industry professionals.

At him.

No need, I text back. *I'm fine doing it.*

I consider saying more, but put the phone down instead. I was needlessly curt, just like I always am with him. I know it. But I can't seem to be any different. Every time I talk to him, every time I text, I feel that bitterness I hate so much—the anger that he moved on so easily, that he got over me so fast, and I can't seem to do the same, no matter how much time has passed. The hurt that he wanted out of our marriage, that he walked away without ever turning back.

I don't blame him for any of it, not really. I made his life hell. I didn't mean to, but I did anyway. Knowing that, though, doesn't make the hurt less. It doesn't make my feelings for him go away.

15

I drop my head in my hands, my heart squeezing tight.

I'm going to be starring in a movie with my ex-husband, the father of my children, a man who I am still, after all this time, desperately in love with—a man who doesn't feel the same way about me, if he ever did.

I definitely don't have a plan for *this*.

TWO

Blake

'm still stinging from Kim's response to my text message as I'm waiting in the entry courtyard of my condo complex for Kim's driver to drop off the kids. I always wait inside until I see them through the gated doors. Through the slats, I can see the ever-present car parked across the street—a Miata this time. This particular paparazzo is doing well.

I settle my sunglasses and sit down on the edge of a large planter filled with six-foot palms. It's not like Kim being short with me is unusual—the opposite, in fact. And this was far from the height of snappy, irritated things she's texted at me in the six years we've been divorced.

She's *fine*. Fine doing a movie with me. Fine with me playing her love interest. Fine walking onto a movie set with me like that doesn't bring back all the memories in the world.

But having a conversation with me about it? *That* is clearly out of the question.

I shake my head, glad that the thick, wide gate bars shield me from photos. Not that there aren't about a million pictures of me in cargo shorts and t-shirts and sunglasses outside this place. The security within was the main reason I bought the condo—it's nice to be able to take the kids to the pool or run around with them in the interior courtyard gardens without having to tread beyond the iron gates that keep us in and the many photographers out.

It's about the only way I can spend time with my kids without security, and I'm grateful for it, even if I do envy Kim her ranch and the privacy it affords.

I was supposed to run it with her, once upon a time.

A slick, black car pulls up outside the gates. I see the Miata's window drop as Lukas bounds out of the car, hauling along the plastic case he uses to store his latest Lego set. I unlock the gate and swing it open as Ivy follows her brother out of the car.

I swear my daughter gets taller every time I see her—which is usually every couple days, so it can't actually be true. She's only twelve, but she's almost as tall as her mother, though she's still got a long way to go before she catches up to me. She's also starting to fill out, and I'm sure getting no shortage of attention for it—attention she complains about and attributes to being *Ivy Pless*, which she says in the most condescending tone possible.

"Dad!" Luke throws his arms around me. I hug him back and pull Ivy in with us, then wave a hand at the photographer across the street, who's snapping away. As long as they stay over there and don't start harassing my kids or trying to get past the gate, we're good.

The photographer waves back and keeps on snapping.

I usher the kids through the gate. I'd swear that the press has worked out our entire custody schedule, but I know they don't have to. Most of the major entertainment news places have at least one photographer permanently on Blake Pless duty, especially since they haven't been able to pin down who I'm dating lately. It's been a year since Simone and I broke up, and whoever gets the first scoop on my next longterm girlfriend stands to make a lot of money.

Joke's on them, because I'm not going to settle down like that again. Swearing off marriage was clearly not safe distance enough.

"So," I say when the gate locks behind us. "I'm thinking we head up to the condo, change, and then hit the pool. Who's in?"

"Me!" Luke yells.

Ivy, who is too cool for childish outbursts, gives me a calm smile. "Sounds good," she says. I sling an arm around her—thankfully she hasn't gotten too cool for that, at least when we're locked away from the public eye—and we follow Lukas as he races out of the entry yard and across the lawn, which is flanked on both sides by large, multi-level town homes.

Luke comes running back when it's clear we're not following fast enough. "Guess what!" he shouts, more as a statement than as a question. "I got a job!"

I smile. "Really? I didn't know they gave those to seven-year-olds."

"They do to seven-year-old actors," Ivy says.

She has me there. "True. Are you an actor, Luke?"

He wrinkles his nose. Thankfully neither of my kids have expressed any interest in going into acting. It might be hypocritical, but I have enough trouble shielding them from the effects of the Watterpless fame. I don't need them stepping out on their own to add to it.

"No," Luke says. "I meant a job on the *ranch*."

I'm pretty sure he has lots of jobs on the ranch. To listen to the two of them whine, you'd think Kim was working them both to the bone. "A new one?"

"Yes!" Lukas shouts. "I'm feeding Susan the chicken."

I'm trying to figure out who Susan is named after—Kim names all her animals after characters from classic television shows—when Ivy leans over to me confidentially. "It's a bigger deal than it sounds. Susan's beak is broken, so she has to be fed through a dropper."

I smile. "Of course she does. That sounds like a big job, buddy."

Luke beams at me. "Mom says I'm very adept at it."

I laugh. "Sounds like your mother."

Ivy gives me that look she gets when she thinks I might be insulting Kim. Which I never do, and not just when they're around. Besides that she clearly can't stand me, I don't actually have many complaints about Kim.

"So how did Susan break her beak?" I ask.

Luke rockets off ahead of us again, apparently already done with this conversation.

"Susan came from an abusive home," Ivy says. "The place Mom got her from thought her beak was clipped with wire cutters."

I wince. "Ouch."

Ivy nods sagely. "Yeah. It's pretty bad. But she's getting some weight back on her through the dropper."

Anyone else would be fattening up the chicken for the slaughter, but Kim is a staunch vegetarian. With help from Kim's staff of animal handlers—and Lukas, apparently—Susan will get to live to a ripe old chicken age. However old that is.

"Any other new animals?" I get the update whenever the kids come over, and even though it's often only been a few days since I last saw them, there's usually one addition or another.

"Nothing new," Ivy says. "But Mom's getting a blind boxer next week. His original name was Lazyboy, so Mom is renaming him Costanza. It's more distinguished."

I laugh. Susan must be named after George Costanza's late fiancée. Kim usually picks a show and mines it until she runs out of characters, but she's doing that faster lately than she did when we were married.

"A blind dog, huh," I say. "Think you could teach him braille?"

Ivy rolls her eyes. "He doesn't need braille. What he needs is a seeing-eye person."

I bump her with my elbow. "Sounds like fun."

Ivy doesn't admit that it will be, but I can tell she's looking forward to it. She has also recently become too cool for looking forward to things.

We climb the stairs to my condo, with its terrace view overlooking the garden. We are in the door less than three seconds when Ivy announces, "Lukas got in trouble at school for karate chopping a girl."

I turn to him. I haven't heard about this, so I'm guessing it couldn't be *too* much trouble. "Seriously? You know you're not allowed to use karate outside of class."

Luke looks offended. "She jumped on me and was *kissing* me! My lips were in danger!"

I smile. I bet they were. "She shouldn't have done that, but you didn't have to karate chop her."

Luke pouts. "I know. Later when I used my words, I told her never ever to kiss me again, no matter how handsome she thinks I am."

"I bet she loved that," I say.

"She cried," Ivy adds.

Luke opens his mouth to argue, but I beat him to it. "But she shouldn't have kissed you without your permission. No matter how handsome she thinks you are."

"Besides," Luke says, grinning gleefully at Ivy. "Ivy has a boooooooyfriend."

I raise my eyebrows. This is the first I've heard of this. Ivy flops down on my leather couch and slings her feet over the arm. "I do *not*."

"Yes, you dooooooooo," Luke shouts. "She got her phone taken away for talking to him too much."

Ivy folds her arms and glares daggers at Luke, who cheerfully runs off to the Lego room clutching his case, which he uses to bring his current favorites back and forth between Kim's place and mine. I'd feel bad for the kid that he needs to do this, but he's getting two Lego rooms out of the deal, so I think he's doing all right.

"Is that true?" I ask Ivy.

"Yes," she says grudgingly. "Can you talk to Mom and get it back?"

I'm willing to bet if Kim took Ivy's phone away, there's a good reason. "Maybe. Tell me about this boy."

She sighs. "His name is Chris, and he likes to surf."

"Okay. And how'd you meet him?"

Ivy gives me a dark look that tells me she knows I'm not going to like the answer. "Online."

"So you don't have any way of knowing who this kid really is, right?"

Ivy sinks down on the couch.

Oh, great. There's clearly more to this story. "Ives?"

"I met him at the mall," she says sullenly.

Shit. "Does your mom know about that?"

"No," she says. "I told her I was going with friends. And I did! My friends were there the whole time and so were his. I wasn't alone with him. I'm not stupid."

I know she's not. Clearly, because she's been executing all of this without her mother or me knowing. "How old is this boy?"

She gives me another side-eye, and my stomach drops. "Fifteen," she says.

I watch her for a moment. It could be worse, but I still don't want my twelve-year-old hanging out with fifteen-year-old boys. I was one of those, once, and Ivy isn't ready for that. "So your mom took your phone away for talking to a fifteen-year-old boy, who you had also met at the mall."

Ivy gives me a sulky look. "She didn't know I met him. But he's really nice! And he talks to me every day."

"Until you got your phone taken away."

Ivy looks away.

Great. "You're still talking to him?"

"On my computer," she says. "We video chat."

Oh. My. God. I try not to freak out visibly. It's good that she's telling me this, and I don't want her to stop feeling like she can talk to me.

But I also can't let my twelve-year-old video chat with strange teenage boys over the internet.

"He's really cool!" she says, clearly anticipating my objections. "He's never asked me for naked pictures or anything!"

I try not to let my eyes bug out of my head at the lowness of *that* bar. "Has someone else been asking you for naked pictures?"

"*No*," she says. "But it's happened to some of my friends."

Thank god for that. Not the part about her friends, of course. It's times like these that I think maybe we shouldn't have agreed to give Ivy a cell phone, but Kim and I both want her to be able to communicate with us when she's with the other parent, and us being who we are, we also want her to have a way to contact us instantly if she ever gets in a bad situation with fans or paparazzi.

At least Kim found out about it first and took away her phone. "You know I'm going to have to take your computer, right?"

Her face contorts in horror. "*Why?* I swear, he's super nice. And I didn't do anything wrong. That's not *fair*."

I care very little about what's fair, and yet my children both continue to find this argument airtight. I shake my head. "It's not a punishment, but I'm your dad, and it's my job to protect you."

"You don't need to protect me," Ivy says. "I can handle it. I'm mature."

She is, especially for her age. This is precisely what I'm worried about.

"He's never sent me any dick pics either," she adds.

I close my eyes. "Have other people been sending you those?"

"A couple times," she says. "I told Mom, and she installed a filter, but it doesn't work."

Oh, god. Of course it doesn't. There is no filter in the world smarter than the dirty mind of a teenage boy. "I'm glad you told your mother. And I'm glad you told me about this. But I still have to take your computer, because you can't be video chatting with older boys."

Ivy flops her hands down at her sides. "He's not even that much older!"

"It's a big gap when you're so young. Fifteen-year-old boys have different expectations than twelve-year-olds."

She scowls. "I thought you'd be more reasonable than Mom."

Because I don't have as many rules and expectations as Kim does, she thought I would just let her do whatever she wants. Kim's accused me of the same more than once, both before the divorce and after.

Coming from my daughter, this stings.

"I love you, Ivy," I say. "And that's why I'm taking your computer. I'll talk to your mom about the phone, and we'll decide what to do from there."

Ivy's eyes widen, and her body flattens. "I might have told Mom that Chris is thirteen and a half."

I raise an eyebrow. "So you lied to your mother." She'd already admitted to as much by sneaking around to see this kid at the mall and chatting with him on her computer, but those weren't—as far as I know—things she'd been expressly told not to do. Telling Kim an outright lie seems worse. More concrete.

"If I didn't, I knew she'd freak out. You know how she is."

I do, and I don't like what Ivy's insinuating. "Your mom wants to protect you, just like I do. So if you knew she would freak out, you also should have realized you were doing something wrong. Didn't you?"

Ivy heaves a sigh. "Yeah. Maybe you don't have to tell her."

I certainly do. "Were you going to talk to Chris again today?"

"Yeah," Ivy says. "Around nine."

Of course. When she's expected to be in bed reading.

Her face lights up. "Hey, maybe you could talk to him! Then you'll see he's not dangerous."

"Oh, I will be talking to him. Don't worry about that." I imagine the boy turning on his camera to see the father of the girl he's sniffing around will be startling enough, but I also hope he's seen at least a few of my more violent movies.

I move over to her backpack by the door and extract her laptop. Chris and I are definitely going to have a little chat.

Ivy whines. "You're so mean. I wasn't doing anything wrong. I just want to kiiiiiiss hiiiiiiiim."

I take solace that if she's whining about wanting a kiss, probably nothing scarier has happened.

Yet.

"Why don't you kiss a boy your own age?" I ask.

She glares up at me. "Twelve-year-old boys are so gross."

"Can't blame you there. What about Ty Mays? He's thirteen. I bet he'd want to kiss you." Ivy's friend Ty has been adorably enamored with her since they met a couple years ago at a party at Kim's agent's house. He's probably the only boy I'd encourage my daughter to kiss, because he's even more innocent than she is. We've had him over to swim in the pool a couple times, and the way he follows her around like a puppy dog is ridiculously cute.

Ivy gives me a look like I am terribly foolish. "I can't kiss *Ty*. He's my *friend*."

Ouch. Sorry, Ty.

"Well, eventually you'll be fifteen, and then you can kiss fifteen-year-old boys all you want." I don't add *as long as that's all you're doing*, even though I want to. I was going further than that at fifteen, and I'm determined not to be one of those fathers who shames his daughter about her desires.

I am, however, going to protect her from them until she's of reasonable age, and twelve ain't it. I leave her moaning on the couch like she's ruptured her appendix, secure the laptop in my bedroom, then shout to both of them to put on their swimsuits. Ivy drags herself through this chore like she's preparing for a painful trip to the dentist. Luke and I are waiting for her at the door before she's even changed her clothes, at which point I realize I'm not sure they even know about the film.

"Hey Luke," I say, loud enough for Ivy to hear. "Did you hear your mom and I are going to do a movie together?"

Luke looks surprised, and Ivy appears around the corner, wearing her t-shirt over her swim bottoms. "What?"

"Yeah," I say. "They're doing a Farpoint/Hemlock crossover,

and we're going to film it in Miami in a couple of months."

Ivy puts her hands on her hips. "You can't work with Mom. You guys hate each other."

I give her a warning look. "That's not true. You know I love your mother." I tell her this often enough, but she never believes me. Probably because she assumes any normal person who got a divorce would be angry with the person they were married to. Kim certainly has that part down.

She has every reason to be angry with me. I failed her.

"Yeah," Ivy says. "Because she's our mom, duh. But you guys don't like each other."

I don't correct her. It's easier to let her think that, just like it was easier to let the public believe we split up because I had an affair with the nanny. Sometimes the ugly lie is less painful than the truth.

"Your mom and I will be fine," I say. "Plus, we'll be in Florida, so maybe I can take you guys to Disneyworld. Or Legoland."

Luke cheers at this news, as I knew he would.

"Dad," Ivy says, "we live right next to both those places here."

"But this will be a *different* Legoland!" Luke announces, spinning in a circle while making crazy robot arms.

I smile. At least one of them is excited. "We can go surfing," I tell her.

She perks up at this but still adds, "We can also do that here."

"Maybe you can find some sort of animal to rescue in Florida. God knows your mom probably will."

"Yeah!" Luke says. "Like an anaconda!"

"Those are in South America," Ivy says.

"They have alligators in Florida," I say.

Ivy opens her mouth to protest, probably that an alligator would be too dangerous to keep on the ranch, but I beat her to it. "Hey, maybe your mom could find an alligator with no teeth."

"I could feed it through a dropper!" Luke announces. He

26

leaps and karate chops the air, which I hope is not what he would do with a toothless alligator and a dropper.

"You'd need a turkey baster," I tell him.

Ivy rolls her eyes at me, but she finally finishes changing, and we head to the pool. As we all try to squish on one floaty raft and end up submerging it entirely beneath us, I try not to think about how I really do need to call Kim to talk over this Chris thing. I shouldn't be happy about that; Kim certainly won't be.

But having a reason to hear her voice, even a concerning one, is always something I can't help but look forward to.

I call Kim after dinner, while the kids are watching a movie. I've slacked majorly in the homework department today, but it's Friday night, and they have all weekend.

I'll make them do it before tomorrow night's drop-off, though. I know Kim hates it when they play all day with me, and then she has to make them work on her time. I can't change that I was a complete failure as a husband, but I make it my business now to be the best possible ex-husband I can be, as if that could ever atone for what I did to her.

It's her Friday evening without the kids, so she's probably out doing something, but I call her anyway, figuring she'll call me back when she can. I'm surprised when she answers.

Her voice is sharp. "Blake? What's going on? Are the kids okay?"

"Yeah." I guess I probably should have texted a preamble. It's not like we *never* have to talk, but Kim likes to keep it to a minimum. I can't remember the last time I just called her. "The kids are fine. Mostly, anyway. I took away Ivy's computer because she's been using it to chat with a boy named Chris?"

"*Oh*," Kim says. "God, Blake, I should have told you about the phone. I meant to text you about it, but I forgot. I probably overreacted, but—"

This is more words than Kim has uttered to me in a long while. "No, you didn't," I say. "Ivy said that she told you this boy is thirteen, but he's actually fifteen, and she's met him in person at the mall."

"*Seriously?*"

"Yeah." I hate being the bearer of bad news, but I guess it can't hurt how she feels about me. That hit bottom long ago. "I told her having her phone and computer taken away aren't a punishment, just measures to protect her. And I'm totally going to scare the hell out of this kid when he contacts her over her computer in an hour. But there should definitely be some consequences for her lying to you. I figure that's yours to decide."

Kim is quiet for a moment. "But she told you."

"Yeah." I hate admitting this part, since I know Ivy and Kim share the opinion. "I think she assumed I'd let her get away with it. She's not thrilled with me." I realize then that I don't actually know if Ivy told me the whole truth. "What prompted you to take the phone away?"

"I saw some texts that worried me," she says. "Nothing really horrific, more like 'I'd love to see you surf, I bet you look good in your wetsuit,' that kind of thing. But it was definitely enough that I didn't want it going any further."

Oh, hell no. "I'm glad you did that." I pause. "I was going to scare him anyway—is it bad that I want to take it up a notch for him saying that to my daughter?"

"I'm not going to argue with it," Kim says.

I smile and consider quipping back that she generally does argue, but decide against it. We've had a civil conversation, which I have to take as progress. I know we'll never get back together, but a part of me still hopes that one day we'll be the type of friends who sit together at the kids' events and laugh like we used to. "I'm starting to empathize with your father," I say, and Kim does laugh.

Her dad never liked me, partly because Kim broke her policy against dating co-stars for me, and partly because he couldn't stand not being the most important influence in Kim's life anymore. I wait, hoping she's going to have a comeback for that, but all she gives me is silence.

My heart twists. I want to ask how she's doing with the film, or with the fact that Ivy lied to her, which I'm sure is eating at her.

But I don't, because before I can decide what I can safely say without her snapping at me, her tone turns crisp. "Well, thanks, Blake."

"Yeah, of course. I'll keep you posted if I hear any more."

"And I'll do the same. Goodnight." This last is said quickly, like she can't wait to get away from me. Then the line goes dead and she's gone.

My chest aches with the hollowness that's been there since the day I moved out of the house we used to live in. The day I finally gave in to what I'd known was coming—I was a terrible husband, and I was slowly driving Kim insane with my inability to be what she needed. When I left, I'd leaned into the one hope I still had—that by giving her up, she'd be able to find someone who would make her happy in all the ways I couldn't. Six years later, it still hasn't happened, and the idea of starring in a film with her makes me happier than it should, happier than I'll ever let on, because it means I'll get to spend time with her.

Even though I know it'll never mean to her what it does to me.

THREE

When I wake up at five-thirty AM on day one of shooting, the first thing I do is tell myself this is going to be like every other movie. It's a job like all the others. There will be people I enjoy working with and people I have to endure. There will be incredible days—where the scenes go better than expected, where there's this energy on set and everyone can feel it—and miserable days, where things go wrong and everyone's tired and we all remember we're filming in Miami in July.

Working with Blake won't make any of that different.

I can do this.

I let out a breath and sit up, which wakes the huge dog curled on the pile of blankets next to my bed. Costanza lets out a snort and a loud fart and swings his head in my direction. His brow furrows, like he's confused as to why I'm waking up so early and what on earth that nasty smell is.

I laugh, swinging my legs out of the bed and scratching him behind his ears. "Good morning, cutie," I say. His tongue lolls out happily, and he licks my arm. His cloudy eyes gaze up at me. His face is so trusting, even after all the abuse he's been through, and it breaks my heart. "It's going to be a bit of a weird day. Maybe even a weird couple months. But you and me, we're tough, right? We're going to be okay."

He makes another snorting sound I take as agreement, and I give him a kiss on his furry head and get ready for the day. I take my shower and get dressed but don't bother doing anything with my hair—my stylist will undo it all, anyway. I put on the barest amount of makeup to make it so I don't look like a sleep-deprived zombie in the dozens of photos that will be taken of me on the walk from the hotel lobby to the car that will be waiting to take me to the film set.

Then I take my meds. I pause, staring for a moment at the newly refilled prescription bottle. Only one other person knows about my diagnosis, other than, of course, my doctors.

I know I shouldn't be ashamed. I know mental health is a thing that often requires intervention and treatment. But my OCD—and how late I learned about it—has cost me so much. It's this part of me I know I have to accept, and so I do, but only enough to keep it from ruining my life any more than it has.

One day, I'll find the words to tell the kids.

One day, maybe, I'll even be able to tell Blake. It won't change anything, won't undo the past, but I feel like I owe him an explanation for the way things turned out between us.

One day. But there's no way in hell it's *this* day. This day I just need to survive.

It's six o'clock by the time I knock on the door to the adjoining room, which is where my kids and their nanny, Marguerite, are staying. The kids' room has a little living area with a couch and table, and then three beds on the other side, one for each of them and one for Marguerite. On the *other* side of the kids' room is the room where Blake is staying, with his own adjoining door. It wasn't easy finding a nice hotel with these exact specifications, and the rooms aren't as posh or spacious as usual because of it, but that's fine. I figure it's more important that the kids have fairly equal access to both of us—and that we can still do our approximation of The Schedule, wherein Blake and I should only have to interact while actually filming. I definitely wasn't going to do a traditional suite with a shared living space. I can not share a living space with Blake.

Lukas opens the door, blue eyes shining and a wide smile on his face even at this hour. My kids are both early risers, but Luke has always done so with joyous gusto. "Mom!" he says, giving me a big hug, as if I wasn't the one he had to spend all day at the airport with yesterday and who tucked him in last night.

"Good morning," I say, returning his big smile. Luke's joy is always infectious, his smile like sunshine.

He takes after his father that way.

He pulls me into the room, which smells deliciously like coffee, and I see Marguerite sitting at the table drinking some, reading a textbook that I'm guessing is for her online marketing class. One day we're going to lose her to some amazing marketing firm, a day I am selfishly dreading, as she is incredible with the kids. She smiles at me, though she looks a little tired. I don't blame her; it's not easy to sleep in with two kids in the same room.

This next couple months are going to be intense for her, too. Luckily, she'll have lots of free time when Blake or I take the kids after work.

"Coffee?" she asks.

"No, thanks," I say. "I'll caffeinate up on set. I'm sorry the kids woke you up so early."

"I was being quiet!" Luke protests, and Marguerite grins.

"He was, actually," she says. "But I needed the study time. Big test later this week."

I grimace in sympathy. I never went to college, but I can imagine how stressed out I would be over tests. "Well, we'll make sure you get plenty of time to—"

"Mom, Mom." Luke tugs on my hand, clearly done with being patient. "You have to see the tower I built." He leads me toward a surprisingly intricate Lego fortress nearly as tall as the the couch it sits next to. He must have gotten up even earlier than I thought, because this sure didn't exist when I put him to bed last night. Costanza follows me, short stubby tail wagging so hard his whole back end shakes, and I hold him back so he doesn't keep walking right into Luke's tower. No matter how sturdy Luke has built it, I don't see it withstanding the attack of the seventy-pound boxer.

"That's fantastic, Lukey," I say, crouching down to examine it. "You're a regular Frank Lloyd Wright."

Luke throws his arms around Costanza, who licks him happily. "Who is he?"

"A famous architect." I straighten again, ruffling the soft curls on the top of Luke's head. "But I bet you could show him a thing or two about how to make a flying catapult." I pick up the catapult, to which he's attached two big Lego wings, and flap them.

Luke grins. "It's so the knights can fly their catapult over the walls and shoot *from the inside.*" This last he says in a near-whisper, like he wants to keep his battle plans secret from imaginary enemies.

Or maybe his sister.

"Mo-om," Ivy says as she emerges from their bathroom, turning my name into that two syllable whine that means she's about to tattle on Luke. "I heard Luke running water when he woke up, and I found him filling up all the cups in the room. He was going to make a moat for his tower."

I raise an eyebrow at Luke, who looks slightly abashed. "I was going to put towels in a ring around it to hold the water in."

"A moat, Mom! In a hotel!" Ivy folds her arms.

"I was definitely still asleep for that part," Marguerite says, holding in a grin.

I'm holding in my own laugh at the thought of how the people in the room below us might feel about Luke's moat idea. "Luke, honey, while the towel idea was smart, we can't build moats in a hotel. That's more of an outside activity—maybe at the beach, when Marguerite takes you guys."

Luke pouts a little, but then sees something to adjust on his tower and happily occupies himself with his Legos.

"Thanks for keeping the room from being flooded," I murmur to Ivy, pulling her in for a hug.

She smiles at me, always grateful when her responsibility is appreciated.

"But," I continue, "go easy on your brother, okay? It's not super easy living out of a hotel."

She purses her lips, then nods, and her gaze drops down to her massive-headed Hello Kitty slippers, which she scuffs against the carpet. She's gotten rid of almost all her stuffed animals and toys she deems "for little kids," which makes me sad, but she's still kept some favorites.

God, it's not easy to see her growing up.

"So, Mom," Ivy says, scratching Costanza behind his ear. He leans into her, thumping his leg against the ground, a big doggy smile stretched across his face. He loves the kids almost as much as he loves me. He'd probably be all right staying here with them, but the kids aren't going to be spending their days in the hotel. And the hotel staff wouldn't appreciate the disaster they'd find if this dog was left alone in an unfamiliar place for the day.

"Yes, hon?" I can already tell by her long pause what she's going to ask.

"Can I get my computer or phone back? It's been a really long time."

"It has," I agree. "And you've already earned back the privilege of using your computer when your dad or me or Marguerite is in the room with you."

Frustration furrows her brow. "But—"

"Remember what we agreed on for the lying? Three months without the phone."

"I didn't agree," she mutters, in what I assume she thinks is under her breath.

"Lying is—"

"—a really big deal, I know." She frowns at Costanza but keeps scratching him.

34

I sigh. It still hurts that she lied to me. I'm trying hard not to take it personally—kids lie to their parents, right?

Except Ivy's always been so much like me, a stickler for the rules. Mature beyond her years. And though I know this is probably the exception to the typical parent-child relationship, I never lied to my parents. Honestly, throughout all my simultaneous childhood and career—starting with that first Chef Boyardee commercial as a marinara sauce–covered toddler and through my years long, major-hit stint as a teenage spy-in-training on *Spy High*—I generally trusted that they knew what was best for me.

At least until it came to Blake. They never thought he was good for me, and I stopped listening to anything they had to say on the matter. I'm sure they felt vindicated by the divorce, but they had it all wrong.

I was the one who wasn't good for *him*.

"But I already had my phone taken away for a week—" Ivy starts again.

"For talking to a boy you met online that I didn't know. That doesn't exactly count towards your penance."

What I'm sure she hasn't quite internalized, even though we've definitely talked about it, is that once she gets it back, the rules on phone use will be much tighter than they were before. Maybe it's harsh, but she's my daughter, and I have to protect her.

At least I know Blake is on board with that.

A knock sounds from the door leading to Blake's room, and my heartbeat speeds up. I know I'm going to see him a lot now, but if I can keep it on set, I can view him solely as a co-star, nothing more. I know this is insane, but I'm used to having to play these games with my brain.

"We'll talk after work, okay?" I squeeze Ivy's shoulder.

She looks like she wants to protest, but then glances over at Blake's door and sighs. "Okay. Love you." Even after that, she sounds like she means it.

"I love you too. Both of you," I say, though Luke isn't paying the slightest bit of attention and has bounded over to Blake's door. "All three of you," I say with a quick smile to Marguerite, who laughs.

Then I make my escape with Costanza back into my own bedroom just as Blake's door opens. I let out another breath. Costanza whines at me. He needs to go outside, and I need to get to set.

I give him his meds and attach his leash. He walks into a bedpost before I manage to guide him toward the door.

In the hallway, two guys in suits greet me. They're from the local private security firm hired by the film as part of my contract. There are also a couple who will be accompanying the kids and Marguerite on all their outings, though they aren't arriving until later.

The hotel isn't busy at this hour, but I get some stares and people pointing in the lobby. Where the security really come in handy is the moment we step outside, and they have to push back the throngs of paparazzi waiting for the appearance of me or Blake.

What they'd really kill for is the sight of both of us together.

I put on my big sunglasses right before we head outside, even though they clearly know who I am. The security guys can keep them from touching me, but not from shouting at me. I try to ignore them as Costanza lifts his leg on the base of the nearest palm tree. That should make for a good picture.

"Kim! Kim! What's it going to be like working with Blake again?"

"Kim! Why were you out with Roger last month? Are you two an item again?"

"What do you think of Blake's new girlfriend? Is it true you called her a Kim wannabe?"

"Did you get in a fight with her, Kim?"

I don't answer any of these questions; it never does any good. I knew the questions about Blake and me working together again were a given and that my meeting my ex-boyfriend Roger for a friendly dinner was sure to come up, but I hadn't heard anything about a new girlfriend of Blake's. And I certainly haven't fought with said girlfriend or called her anything, let alone *that*.

Honestly, I think sometimes they just make this shit up on the spot to get a rise out of us. A paparazzi-punching celebrity meltdown is tabloid gold.

Costanza and I are ushered into the idling black town car, and I settle into the soft, leather seats and try not to wonder if Blake does have a new girlfriend. I try not to care.

We make it to the set, though Costanza whimpers and shivers and clings to me the whole way there. He doesn't like car rides much. I use some calming training techniques on him, which seem to help a tiny bit, but which will hopefully work better each time, as he realizes he's not going somewhere he'll be hurt, and he's not being abandoned again.

Maybe these techniques will help me feel the same.

Security ushers us in, and Costanza and I exit the car and are led to my trailer. There are several trailers set up next to each other for the major stars, and I have a fleeting memory of that first movie Blake and I were on together, *Over It*, a romantic comedy that became one of those movies with a passionate fan base who still watch it over and over. I still get more fan mail about that movie than any other, except maybe the Hemlock ones.

I remember Blake's trailer next to mine. Before we started dating—that whole two weeks when I thought I could still stick to my rule about not getting involved with co-stars—we'd each sit on our steps long into the night, him making me laugh louder and more genuinely than anyone ever had in my life. Neither of us wanting to say goodnight.

It wasn't long before we were spending nights in each other's trailers, sneaking back the short distance in the wee hours of the morning. Not long after that, we decided we couldn't go back to living more than ten feet apart and moved in together when the filming was done.

It's not likely that Blake's trailer is next to mine now. The film people will have made sure of that.

I walk into my trailer, and there's a guy in his mid-twenties setting out packets of sugar and some creamer next to a Starbucks cup. He straightens when I enter and smiles. He's got a nice smile and wavy blond hair. Colorful tattoos spill down his arms from under his sleeves to his wrists.

"Hi, Ms. Watterson," he says. "I'm Aaron Destin. I'll be your assistant." He glances down at Costanza, who walks right into his leg. "And your dog's, too."

"Call me Kim," I say, shaking his hand. He's got a firm grip and doesn't seem nervous to meet me, which is a nice quality in an assistant. I've had assistants before who could barely speak to me for the first few days. "Thanks so much for being willing to take on Costanza here. He's a sweet boy, but he can be a handful."

"I'm happy to do it," Aaron says.

I imagine he's less happy than he lets on, but he's being well compensated for this. Not to mention, most assistants have dreams of acting or directing or producing one day. Taking care of Kim Watterson's dog on one film could lead to the perfect introduction at some industry event later. I try my best to be a helpful cog in the Hollywood Networking Machine.

So I don't feel too bad when I start running through the detailed list of care for my special-needs dog. The number of daily walks he needs, the way to calm him if he starts getting nervous, how to stop the howling when I first leave him behind, his proclivity for bolting if he smells a squirrel and then running right into a tree.

Aaron's eyes are widening more with each new instruction, but he nods along as I talk.

" . . . and the vertigo shouldn't be a problem, as long as he takes his pills three times a day," I say, pulling Costanza's pill bottle out of my purse and handing it to Aaron. "I've given him his morning pill, and I'll give him one at night, but you'll need to give him one at noon. If he won't take it from you, you can wrap it in some meat—he loves bologna. If you haven't given him the pill by about one, you'll notice he's starting to get dizzy and—Costanza, no!"

Aaron swears and drops the pill bottle, jumping back—but not soon enough—as Costanza lifts his leg and pisses right down the leg of Aaron's jeans and onto his Vans.

"I'm so sorry," I say, cringing. "I just had him out, and he usually doesn't—"

"It's fine, Ms. Watterson," Aaron says, clearly trying to stifle a grimace as he shakes excess urine from his pant leg. "Really, it's—I'll take him out and then come back and clean this up."

"No, Aaron, I'll get this." I give him an apologetic smile. "Cleaning up piss is something I do more often than you'd imagine."

Aaron laughs at this, but I can tell by the way he runs his hand through his hair that he's realizing Costanza duty may be more than he bargained for.

I take a deep breath. Costanza will get used to Aaron, and the two will be best buddies by the end of this shoot. I'll buy the kid new pants.

It'll all be okay.

"Oh," Aaron says, as he heads to the door with Costanza's leash in hand. "There's a new call sheet on the vanity. You'll want to look it over. They switched the order of your first two scenes since the email last night."

Great. My first scene initially didn't involve Blake. I'd been glad I could get through that always nerve-wracking "first scene" without adding him to the mix.

But I keep my expression even. "Sounds good. And my M&Ms?"

"All taken care of."

It's a stupid thing, and probably comes across as a diva move—maybe it is, a little—but on my first day filming *Spy High* at fifteen, the caterer left me a bowl filled with a mix of regular and peanut M&Ms. Ever since, I've considered that snack to be a good luck charm on the first day of any new project. I always have a little baggie or bowl right before I run my first scene. Two-to-one regular to peanut, exactly.

I'd had a coffee mug full of them in hand the day I met Blake, right before our first scene. He looked so nervous, sitting on the edge of the dilapidated rowboat in which we were about to make out. Flipping through his script, chewing at his lower lip.

He'd only been in two other films before that, both of them smaller roles. He'd never done a kissing scene before, I was pretty sure—though a guy as hot as him surely had plenty of real-world experience.

I introduced myself and offered him some M&Ms. "It's the perfect mix," I said, explaining the ratio.

He paused, like he was considering, and then said, "It can't be the perfect mix without peanut butter."

"In your extensive experience with perfect candy mixes."

He smiled, and my heart did a backflip in my chest. "Because I have a sense of taste, Watterson. You should try it."

I told him I'd never dilute my perfect mix by adding a lesser M&M.

"We'll see about that," he said, that mischievous gleam in his eyes I grew so quickly to love.

From then on, every film we were in together, he'd find some way to sneak a handful of peanut butter M&Ms into my bowl. And every time, he'd deny being the one who did it, those gorgeous blue-green eyes flashing at me.

Will he do that again, for old times' sake? Or won't he?

I feel a hollow ache at either thought.

"Thanks, Aaron," I say, feeling tears starting to well up. *Tears.* Over stupid candy mix. I clear my throat, forcing the emotion back down. "If Costanza gets to be too much—"

"It'll be okay, Ms. Watterson," he says, and tugs the leash to guide Costanza forward and out the door, leaving a urine-lined footprint in his wake. Costanza whines at being pulled away from me, and Aaron has to all but haul him out. "I've got this,"

Aaron says, just before he closes the door.

His words sound much more assured than his tone.

I've got this, I tell myself. But I'm even less convincing than Aaron.

FOUR

Blake

'm in my trailer waiting for wardrobe to bring in my costume, going over the call sheet and script changes for the day, and sweating about not having seen Kim yet. I thought maybe we'd run into each other in the kids' room, but given how quickly her adjoining door shut when I opened mine, I gathered Kim was hoping we wouldn't.

I squint at the script, not that it helps. I'm dyslexic, so I need more time with the script than most actors, and when they change the lines on me at the last minute, I'm always scrambling to keep up. I wish I'd brought Ivy to set today—she's my go-to scene-reading partner, and she's been reading scripts to me since she was five.

Sadly, today, I'm on my own.

My assistant, Cassie, pokes her head in to tell me that she's working on her super-secret assignment, and I smile. At least that's going right.

She ducks out again just as the wardrobe assistant arrives—a blue-eyed girl with blond corkscrew curls who looks to be in her early twenties. "Mr. Pless!" she says, "I am such a big fan . . . of your costume."

I laugh. "Please. Call me Blake. Also tell me that you've

somehow convinced the director that I don't need to wear a visor with tiny holes in it in every shot."

"Oh, no," she says. "Your outfit wouldn't be complete without it." She reaches into her garment bag and extracts my nemesis—a golden semi-circle that will soon be attached to my face above my eyebrows. It's full of pencil-width holes so that under the right lighting—and man, do the gaffers have to work on that lighting—the shadow casts pinpoints of light all over my face. The fans say it's supposed to look like a constellation. I say it makes me look like an idiot.

I shrug. "You can't blame a guy for trying."

"I'm Kelsey," she says. "And *this* is Farpoint's new and improved wardrobe."

The pieces are familiar, though wardrobe has clearly made improvements, including sizing down the strange leather loincloth over the black leather pants to make it look more decorative than functional.

Farpoint doesn't have a secret identity, and at the beginning of this film, he's being catapulted into Miami from his home dimension of Astra Vel. We'll do all the Astra Vel scenes back in LA at the studio during the second block of filming, so for the entire duration of the Miami shoot—all six sweaty weeks of it—I'm going to be wearing the iconic suit. Long-sleeve shirt, leather overcoat, knee-high boots, leather bracers, and all.

"Any chance this version will be any cooler than the last two?" I ask.

"In Miami? Ha! This thing is going to be an oven. But we did line the shirt with a water-wicking layer. And it could be worse. You could be wearing a silicone prosthetic suit or face mask. At least Farpoint looks human."

"And he teleports, so I don't have to run in it."

Kelsey nods. "Exactly. Totally the editor's problem."

She sets about explaining to me the hazards of my costume—the loincloth on the front and the strategic butt covering on the back are now near-identical, so it's easy to put the damn pants on backward. I imagine I will do this several dozen times, even after the warning, but I nod dutifully. Kelsey, true to her first statement, seems more in awe of my costume than of me, which I appreciate. I sort of fell into this whole acting thing, and I have Kim to thank for both the variety of my career and its longevity. Yeah, I've worked hard for roles, especially the ones I took to expand my range and evolve my brand.

But I've always felt like I'm just along for the ride.

"But hey," Kelsey says. "At least it's not a pair of underwear over fishnet stockings, am I right?"

I smile. I'm sure Kim doesn't complain about her costume on set, but I'm equally sure she hates it.

Kelsey cringes. "Oh, sorry. I shouldn't have mentioned her."

I blink. "Kim?"

The cringe deepens. "Yeah, Troy said not to mention you guys to each other, like, ever."

Ah. The director is already trying to shield his set from potential drama. He doesn't need to worry. Kim and I are professionals. "Don't worry about it. I think it's a lot more awkward if we pretend she doesn't exist."

"Oh good," Kelsey says. "Then can I ask you all the forbidden questions? What's it like being here with her? Is it weird? I bet it's weird."

I shake my head and fake a laugh, which I think sounds natural. It's times like this I'm grateful for fifteen years of acting experience. "No. We have kids together. We have to talk all the time. It's not really a big deal."

I can see Kelsey bubbling with more questions, so to avoid continuing to lie, I turn it around on her. "What about you? Any exes lurking around the set?"

"No, thank god," she says. "I have a thing for bad boys. Waaaaaay awkward when I have to work with them after. Especially the last one. He stole a bunch of money from me to buy drugs."

"Yikes. That does sound like a bad guy."

Kelsey shrugs. "Par for the course, really. Okay, you put on your costume and I'll come back and check to make sure you're good. Meanwhile I'm going to check out Ms. Watterson's assistant. *Mm mmm. He's cute.*"

She bounces out of the trailer, leaving me with the many parts of my costume to wrestle into and script changes I've only half memorized. I decipher the new dialogue and repeat it to myself as I dress, get wardrobe checked, and submit to makeup, which consists mostly of heavy eyeliner so my eyes don't completely disappear under the ridiculous visor.

I run into the director, Troy, on my way to the beach where we're shooting. We met before back in LA when he first got assigned to the project. He's dressed casually in a t-shirt with an open button-up over it and a pair of cargo shorts—a look I've seen a lot from directors that clearly says "I'm the most important person on set, and you have to do what I say, no matter how I dress."

Troy smiles and waves at me. "Blake!" he shouts. "Good to see you. You ready to go?"

"Sure am." I'm still running through the new lines in my head like a kid expecting a pop quiz, and I hope it doesn't show. At my level of success, no one expects nervousness, but especially with a new director, I never know if they're going to expect me to get the lines word-perfect or if it's okay if I say what feels natural as long as I catch the important bits. I work far better with the second kind.

"Good to hear it." He gestures to a woman beside him. She looks pretty enough to be an actress herself, with long blond hair and chiseled features. In fact, she looks like one of the Kim-clones I've dated, all lined up in *In Touch Weekly* to prove the point. She smiles at me, but it's made out of plastic, and I can tell that it's not her usual expression.

"This is Sarah Paltrow," Troy says. "My assistant. She'll show you to your chair while the set people finish up with the beach."

I recognize the name—we've emailed about the project in

depth. I've wondered if she's any relation to Gwyneth.

"Right this way, Mr. Pless," she says in a crisp British accent.

I force another smile. "Call me Blake." I'm going to say this a hundred times today.

Sarah leads me to a chair out on the sand, covered in a pop-up canopy. The staff has set up water bottles and a makeup kit to fix my face between shots. I can see Kelsey across the way, huddling under the wardrobe tent, keeping the backup supplies from blowing away.

On the other side of the tent, Kim sits in her chair—on the exact opposite side of the crew set-up. I so rarely see her in person that I almost feel like I'm celebrity sighting. *Oh my god, there's Kim Watterson, drinking from a water bottle as she's about to start her first scene.* She's beautiful as ever—by far the most gorgeous woman I've ever met, and I've met a disproportionate number of lookers. She's ready in her Hemlock costume—a corset over tiny green shorts, fishnet pantyhose, and knee-high boots—which I swear gets skimpier with every film. I've seen the first two, of course. I still watch all her movies, though I stream them instead of going to the theater. No need for the tabloids to report about *that*.

Kim runs a hand through her loose hair beneath the crown of silver branches affixed to her head. My heart is pounding, like I'm seeing a ghost. Unlike your average celebrity watcher, I have a good idea what's going through Kim's head right now. She's always nervous the first day of a shoot, because she doesn't yet know what the set culture will be like. This is especially true with a new director and new co-stars. She and I have worked together a ton, but never since Lukas was born.

She's probably thinking about how much she's dreading working with the man who let her down.

I sit back in my seat and shift my gaze to the ocean. The waves roll in—not big enough for good surfing, so Ivy and I will have to find out where to find better waves when we go.

I glance back at Kim, wishing she wasn't so far away, so I

could talk to her and make it look casual. They've done this on purpose, of course, to give us both separate places to retreat to. I should be grateful, and I'm sure Kim probably is, but it all just makes it more awkward, like we're not adults who can speak to one another.

We aren't, but I wish we were, and if this film is going to work as a stepping stone to get us there, someone has to break the ice. Kim shifts in her chair, reaching for a bowl on her side table, beside her water bottle.

Her M&Ms. Kim always gets nervous on the first day of a shoot, and the M&Ms—the perfect mix—is her way of calming down. I've snuck peanut butter M&Ms into the mix on every project we've ever done together, and I bribed a staffer to do it for me on a few that I wasn't present for, back when we were married. I catch the eye of my assistant Cassie, talking to Sarah on the other side of the sprawl of beach where we're about to shoot. She gives me a thumbs-up.

Her secret mission is complete, which means Kim's perfect blend of M&Ms has been spiked. I wait for her to notice and either shoot me a death glare or smile. Either would be progress from the way she's pointedly ignoring me.

Instead she pushes the bowl across the table to the far side, her face hardening in disgust. She shivers, wraps her arms around herself, and looks down at the sand.

My stomach sinks. I debated about those damn candies for weeks. Should I sneak them in? Should I not? I only meant it as a joke, to make her smile.

She's not smiling now. God, we've been on set together less than ten minutes, and I've already managed to screw this up.

I sit back in my chair and take a sip from my water bottle.

I need to get a grip. Kim and I are divorced. I shouldn't care what my ex-wife thinks of me. I shouldn't care if something I did annoys her or if she wants to ignore me. It's been six years, and she must expect me to have moved on by now. God knows she has.

I watch a wave crash on the beach. It's warmer here than it was on the beach where we first met, filming our first scene for *Over It*. We'd sat on the edge of the boat where we were about to make out, and I, newbie actor that I was, had the nerve to ask her if she wanted to rehearse.

I *meant* it—damn, was I nervous, and I just wanted to run the scene and kiss her once there on the set before the cameras turned on, to get the jitters out of the way. Kim decided I was hitting on her and told me that she doesn't get involved with co-stars, and therefore she was never, ever, *ever* going to sleep with me.

We used to laugh at the memory, but now it stings. *I can do this*, I tell myself. I'm one of the top ten highest paid actors in Hollywood, and I've been pretending to be okay with my breakup with Kim to every news publication, co-star, and girl-friend I've had over the last six years, not to mention Kim herself.

I remember vaguely that I wanted to do this film, wanted to be around Kim and see her smile, even if it's never directed at me anymore. I stare down at my water bottle. This morning on this beach, Farpoint is going to save Hemlock from an attack by a sea hydra, the first scene of their slow-burn romantic arc.

That's when I realize what I really wanted. Kim's going to look at me like she sees something in me, something that excites and attracts her. The way Hemlock has to look at Farpoint. The way Kim Watterson used to look at me.

My heart aches, because I know I'm going to get what I wanted, but it will never be real again.

Imagining that it could is just torturing myself.

FIVE

Kim

I spend a ridiculous amount of time trying not to care about whether Blake spiked my M&Ms, but in the end, I can't bring myself to find out. It's not even like I would need to bite into them to tell—the peanut butter ones are smaller than the peanut, but rounder than the plain, so a careful look into the bowl would answer that question. But when I do glance in, the colors all blur together, a dark wavering rainbow, and I realize that the tears are back in my eyes. God, what is my problem?

I push the bowl to the other end of the table, hating myself.

Being on this beach certainly doesn't help. Remembering again and again that first time I met Blake, like a movie scene set in some constant loop in my head. Right away, I could tell he had this sunny, sincere quality about him that felt so different from the type of people I often met in my line of work. It hooked me instantly, as it soon would millions of fans.

He asked to rehearse the kiss before filming, and maybe it was how even just talking with him was already making me feel, but I blurted out my rule about never dating co-stars. That should have made things awkward between us; he claimed he wasn't hitting on me, and though it wasn't the first time a co-star had used a line like that on me, I think in that case he really wasn't. But somehow it was never awkward.

Not until much, much later.

I dig the toe of my black leather thigh-high boot in the sand, shifting in my chair. Which, like pretty much every other movement I make, has the unfortunate result of sending my shrink-wrap-tight green booty shorts—worn over fishnet stockings, for some ridiculous reason that some male comic artist thought necessary—farther up my ass. I swear these things get shorter and tighter with every Hemlock movie.

Maybe it's good I can't bring myself to eat my M&Ms. I'm not sure the fabric could handle the strain.

My gaze lands on Blake, sitting across the way under a canopy matching mine, and my breath catches. He's not looking at me, of course, but focused on the ocean. He's always loved the water—loves surfing and swimming—and something about the ocean always reminds me of him. The color of it, blue-green and shifting in different light, like his eyes. The scent of it, fresh and cool and with a hint of salt, which always seemed so Blake. Sunlight sparkling, bright like his smile.

Except he's not smiling now. Judging by the multiple leather layers of his costume, he's probably more miserable in this heat than I am in my ever-shrinking shorts. And I know Blake must hate that gold visor thing stuck in his hair. I'm not sure what on earth—or wherever Farpoint is from—those little dot shadows are supposed to be for, but there's probably some crucial comic book reason for them. Just like the pantyhose firmly wedged up my crotch.

I want to laugh with him about our costumes. I want to hear his commentary—because I know he has some—on that weird loincloth thing over his pants. I want to tell him how many hours I've spent practicing walking in high-heeled boots in the sand, because apparently Hemlock prizes sex-appeal over common sense and arch support.

I want to tell him everything. But I can't. My feelings aren't his burden anymore, and I'm sure he's much happier for it.

"Kimberly!" A familiar, British-accented voice calls, and I stifle my startle reflex, hoping no one saw me blatantly staring at my ex.

"Bertram, hi." I smile as my former co-star from the first Hemlock movie approaches. My smile widens as he gets closer, and I can see that my costume isn't the only one becoming increasingly more ridiculous. Bertram O'Dell—or should I say, *Sir* Bertram O'Dell, multiple Oscar winner and dear friend of the queen, which he brings up repeatedly after a few drinks—is shaved completely hairless, from his head and eyebrows all the way down his bare chest. Possibly even the rest of him under his puffy, white silk harem pants. He was always one to fully embrace a role.

The new aspect to his costume is a long, trailing red coat lined along the collar and wrists with a fluffy, red feather boa.

"God, Bertram, what have they done to you?" I ask with a laugh. I would hug him, but we're both already in makeup, and I don't want to face the wrath of wardrobe after my costume gets coated in his white body-powder.

"Don't take your jealousy out on me, Kimberly. You know you wish you could pull this off." He pats the fluffy collar, and one of the feathers floats off to stick to his lips. He spits it out with a grimace.

"You're absolutely right," I say. "Hemlock bows to the fashion sense of Naked Mole Rat." His villain name, I remember being informed by the director on the first movie, is not a joke. I have yet to be able to say it outside of filming, however, without making it sound like one.

Bertram raises an eyebrow. "Don't bow too low in that corset, my dear. Those things will pop right out."

"I think there are other people who might appreciate that sight," I say.

"Such as your ex?"

I'm not able to hide my wince, and Bertram's saucy grin drops. "Perhaps I shouldn't have—"

"No." I cover with a laugh that is all too shaky. "No, it's fine. Blake and I are good."

"Really?" Bertram sends a frosty glare over to Blake that I'm pretty sure is on my behalf. "Because working with exes can be trying. When Marcus and I performed in that *La Cage* revival—"

"I know, but we're good," I assure him, before he can launch into his usual rant about Marcus—a rant I heard no fewer than six times during the filming of *Hemlock*. A rant I once clocked at twelve minutes, discreetly using my phone as a stopwatch. "Our divorce was six years ago. We've moved on."

Well, one of us has.

Bertram looks dubious, and I think he's about to call me out on my total lie, but then he makes a face. "Dear god, it's that Dryden fellow again."

I follow his gaze to see a man of a similar age to Bertram, probably in his late fifties, who was heading towards us but has been stopped by Troy, the director. "Is that the new Guidepost?" I ask.

Guidepost is Farpoint's arch-nemesis. The original actor playing Guidepost died of an overdose last year while in a three-way with two underage prostitutes. It shocked the public; he was a beloved actor usually known for his family-friendly "wise mentor" roles.

From what I understand, it didn't shock anyone who actually knew the guy. I was dying to get Blake's thoughts on all of it, but of course I couldn't bring myself to call him.

Bertram sighs. "Yes, unfortunately. The chap did some cop show years ago and is pretentious as hell. And he won't leave me alone. I've never had a straight man so determined to affix his lips to my ass." He gathers up his long coat, which is already dusted with sand. "I'm going to flee before he escapes Troy. I will see you on set for our scene later, dear."

"Bye, Bertram," I say, laughing at his attempt at a dignified exit while scurrying away with an armful of coat and feathers.

I'm trying to both avoid looking at Blake and also figure out how to adjust my shorts without getting caught picking them out of my ass crack when the AD, a British woman named Sarah Paltrow, approaches with an assistant at her side.

Sarah smiles as she walks up to me. "Has everything been set up to your liking, Ms. Watterpless?"

I blink, wondering for a moment if I misheard her, but her pale cheeks turn a bright pink, and her crisp facade cracks a bit. "I'm so sorry," she says, clearly flustered. "I meant Ms. Watter*son*."

She's not the first person to inadvertently call me by our old couple moniker, and I doubt she'll be the last. When I first suggested we get our agents to feed the name "Watterpless" to the press soon after Blake and I started dating, it was because I knew otherwise the press would go with something horrific like "Blim." Blake thought my attempt to create our own couple name was hilarious, but it totally worked.

Maybe a little too well.

"Everything's great." I figure she'll be less embarrassed if I don't call any more attention to the slip. I grab the bowl of M&Ms from the table; I still can't bear to look closely enough at them. "You can take these, though," I say, handing the bowl to the assistant at her side.

The assistant, a kid who looks barely out of his teens and is clearly starstruck, fumbles the bowl as soon as he takes it, spilling M&Ms all over the sand.

"Gary!" Sarah's eyes flash, but I jump in before she can rip into him. I hate on set power trips.

"It's okay," I say, mostly to Gary. "It's really fine. I wasn't going to eat them, anyway." I stand up to help clean the M&M mess, but Sarah's gaze hits something behind me.

I know it's Blake before I turn around, and my chest tightens.

"Well, I'll let you two catch up," Sarah says briskly, grabbing Gary by the shoulder and pulling him away from where he's crouched, picking candy out of the sand. "We'll be ready to shoot in five."

I turn, and yep, there's Blake. Right there. My palms begin to sweat.

You'd think that over six years of being divorced and sharing custody of two children, I'd have been within five feet of my ex-husband often enough that this wouldn't seem so strange. But the kids always get driven to and from his house by the nanny or a driver, and while I've certainly seen him at industry events, I do my best to steer clear and avoid being introduced to his latest gorgeous girlfriend.

"Hey," he says. He looks strangely sad, almost resigned. "I'm sorry about—" He gestures at the little specks of bright candy in the sand.

"You didn't have anything to do with spilling them," I say, confused.

"Yeah, not that. About . . ." He makes a little motion with his hand, and suddenly I get what he means.

My eyes widen. "You *did* put the peanut butter ones in! I didn't know if—I mean—"

I thought before that it would hurt equally either way, and that's why I couldn't know. But now I realize that's not true. I was really worried he wouldn't. That it wouldn't even occur to him to anymore, that he wouldn't give me or my damn candy a second thought.

He did, though. There's a fluttery feeling in my stomach I know I'm going to regret.

Blake's sad expression disappears, a slow smile appearing in its place. "*I* didn't do anything," he protests, as he always has. He gives me a look of mock concern. "So weird that person is still following you, trying to mess with your perfect M&M mix."

I find myself smiling back. "I really do need to launch an investigation. This has gone on far too long."

"Seriously. Whoever this stalker is clearly has deep, unresolved feelings for you."

There's this little skip of my heartbeat, a flush of warmth, but my rational brain knows he's joking.

The fact that he can tell a joke like that might even be a good sign. It means he doesn't know the truth about my feelings for him. A silver lining, I suppose, but it doesn't take the pain away.

There's a reason I had the rule about not dating co-stars. My parents were the ones to first suggest it, but it was sound advice. I'd been in the industry practically my whole life, and so I knew how common it was for co-stars—especially ones in romantic roles opposite one another—to confuse their characters' feelings for their own. It never seemed to end well.

But Blake . . . It wasn't long before I knew, deep down, that this was something different. Something real. Something I felt for him that had nothing to do with the characters either of us were playing.

What I didn't know was if it was different for him. He hadn't had the experience in romantic roles that I'd had. What was real for me could easily be acting runoff for him.

He convinced me otherwise, but the thought has nagged at me over recent years. Maybe that's all it ever was for him. Maybe our relationship was the high of the role, and then inertia, and then he was trapped with me and my problems and the mess I made of our marriage.

My gaze has dropped back to the sand, and before I can think of something witty to say, before I can fake a smile or nonchalant laugh—god, I don't know if I've ever had a laugh with him that could be described as *nonchalant*—he clears his throat, and I look back up.

"So, how's Roger doing?" He adjusts his visor, tucking back a lock of his hair that has escaped to hang nearly into his eyes. He's got this great, natural reddish tint to his brown hair, especially in the sunlight.

I blink in surprise. "Good, I guess. I mean, last I heard, he's opening up a new gallery in—"

"Oh, so you two aren't back together?" He seems to realize he cut me off, and his cheeks redden.

I remember the paparazzi shouting at me outside the hotel, the story of Roger and me being together again on the cover of *Us Weekly* several weeks ago.

I also remember the mention of Blake having a new girlfriend.

"No," I say. "We met for dinner when he was back in town last month, just, you know, a friends thing." I don't know why I felt the need to qualify that. I shift awkwardly. These boots are the worst, and standing in sand isn't exactly helping. "How's . . . whoever the latest one is?"

The second the words leave my mouth, I regret them. God, that couldn't have sounded bitchier or more obviously jealous. The way he winces makes me feel even worse.

This is why I shouldn't ever talk to Blake. I can't keep my emotions in check, not around him. I've never been able to.

"There's not anyone, actually." He smiles, but I can tell it's forced. It's missing that spark of joy or mischief that characterizes a Blake smile. "I guess we both should know not to believe everything we read, huh?"

Troy shouts that we're ready to run the scene, and I'm spared further conversation that will inevitably lead to me hating myself even more.

There's a twinge of sorrow, though. I've avoided talking with Blake for so long, especially face-to-face like this, but now that it's happened, part of me doesn't want to stop.

The scene we're shooting takes place in front of a sea cave that they've constructed on this beach especially for this. The cave looks realistic enough, if you can ignore the fact that it's jutting out on the middle of a beach with nothing else around it in a way that I'm pretty sure is geologically impossible. But that'll get taken care of with the right camera angles and some CG wizardry.

Blake and I run our lines smoothly, dropping right into our roles without any awkwardness, and I'm glad that my years and years of acting experience are finally deciding to help me out.

Troy has us run this several times, even still, and I find myself admiring how Blake finds these tiny nuances in the lines to make each take something slightly different and special. Giving me something new each time to play off, to give him something new back.

He never used to believe me when I'd tell him how good he is at this. Even from the very first time I acted with him—when he'd only done two movies, having just sort of fallen into this career—I could tell how much raw talent he had, how much potential. The fans and the industry always made such a big deal about how gorgeous he is—and I certainly won't deny *that*—but it took them awhile to see what I did from the very beginning. That underneath that breathtaking smile and leading-man sexiness is a seriously gifted actor.

They know now, though. Farpoint and similarly commercial roles aside—hey, we have to keep our fans happy—he's done some challenging and impressive roles over the years, both during our marriage and after. He's been incredible in each and every one of them.

Hurt and regret aside, I'm so proud of him. I always have been.

Working with him like this, slipping back into the natural chemistry that made us one of Hollywood's favorite pairings—it's like recapturing this little bit of magic I thought was forever lost.

Maybe most of it is, all the parts of it that really matter, but it's nice to experience that again, even if it's just for the film.

The next part we run has no dialogue, just action. Apparently Farpoint's nemesis has not only sent *him* from Astra Vel to Earth, but also a hydra, which the script notes also refer to as a she-dragon. I'm not sure why the fact that this dragon is female actually matters, since neither Farpoint nor Hemlock is conducting any kind of gynecological examination of the thing, but whatever. The she-dragon—which for our pre-CG purposes is a tennis ball attached at the end of a long pole being held by a guy with giant, sweaty pit-stains—is going to attack us with a spray of acid, and Farpoint is going to save me.

I have some issues with Hemlock, who is a badass fighter, being unable to dodge one little spray of acid venom, but she saves him several times during this movie, so at least the random bursts of incompetence aren't always one-sided.

Troy yells action, and Blake and I watch the tennis ball as it rises into the air with expressions of stunned shock. When the tennis ball reaches its apex, I shift into Hemlock's signature pissy determination. The she-dragon launches her venom spray, which is marked by a long piece of string tied between weights, and Blake pushes me out of the danger zone, stumbling with me.

Troy yells cut. Blake's arm is still around my waist, and my whole body tingles.

"Good, good," Troy says, and Blake's arm drops away. Its absence carries even more weight than its presence did. "But this next time, I want you to really grab her. Just hold on tight."

I swallow past a lump in my throat. Next to me Blake nods, not looking at me at all.

We run it again. As soon as they call out the spray, Troy is yelling "Grab her, Blake! Grab her!" and I have to fight to keep from laughing, thinking back on the first sex scene Blake and I ran together, way back on *Over It*, with the director calling out similar directions when he wanted Blake to grab my boob.

We get out of the splash zone, and Blake's arms are around me—he definitely grabbed me—and I'm a little breathless, and Blake and I meet eyes. His are sparking with that mischief again, and I know he's thinking the same thing as I am, and I can't help it.

"Cup it! Cup it, Blake!" I say quietly to him, mimicking our *Over It* director.

He laughs, and then I'm laughing, and god, it feels so good, laughing with him, and his arms around me, and—

"Okay, that was great," Troy says, and it's like being yanked back into cold reality, remembering that this is all fake, that we're filming a movie and tons of people are watching us. Blake's arms drop again, and the laughter dissolves into a pit in my stomach.

Especially now that the memory of that first sex scene is inevitably leading to the memory of later that night. The first time Blake and I made love for real. The first time I really knew that sex could be so much more than I'd ever experienced before.

"This time," Troy says, leaning forward on his chair so that his elbows rest on his knees, "I want you guys to fall when he grabs you, Kim. Like, roll a bit so Blake is on his back and Kim on top. Yeah?"

Oh, god. My whole body flushes, between that memory and what he wants us to do.

It's nothing, I tell myself, nodding that I understand, unable to look over to see if Blake is doing the same.

It's definitely nothing to him. So it needs to be nothing to me.

I ball my hands into fists. I'm a professional. I can do this.

We run it again, and Blake grabs me, and we fall to the sand and roll, and suddenly I'm on top of him, my body pressed up against his, my knees on either side of his hips, and my sand-speckled hair hanging down onto his chest. His eyes are so green right now, his mouth just slightly open, looking a little stunned, and my pulse pounds in my ears.

"Great, keep going," Troy calls out. "Now Kim, ride up on him a bit."

I can't breathe, but I shift up, and god, Bertram was right, my boobs are practically falling out of my corset and right into Blake's face. His hands are on the backs of my thighs, this familiar, amazing feeling, and my heart is slamming against my ribcage. My whole body is aware of every place it's touching his.

Aware of every place it desperately wants to touch his.

"And, cut," Troy says. "That was great, guys. I think we got it."

Thank god we got that in one take. Thank god Blake's such a good actor, while I'm still in love with him and hardly needed to act at all.

I meet eyes with him, and everything in me aches and aches. I want him, and I love him, and I can't stop either of those feelings. I feel the tears about to come back.

I push myself off him and get to my feet with as much dignity as I can muster in these heels in this sand, and I walk off without turning around.

Because when it comes to Blake, I already know I'm going to spend the rest of my life looking back.

SIX

Blake

I'm lying on the futon in my trailer, a thin layer of sand still dusting the back of my costume, my entire body on fire. I suppose I'm glad we started with this scene—got it over with, as it were. I can still feel Kim's hands on my shoulders as she was lying on top of me, her thighs where they hugged my hips. The body rush when she rode up on me is still burning, my mind returning to all the times that she touched me because she wanted to. Because she loved me and not because some director was yelling at her to do it.

Until I ruined it.

I groan and sling my forearm over my eyes. Thirty minutes, and I have to be back on set. My trailer is air conditioned by the humming window unit, but it's not enough to cool down, and I sure as hell can't shower. There's not enough time for makeup and wardrobe to reassemble me.

I hate myself, most of all because Kim could just get up and walk away dispassionately. She feels nothing more for me now than resentment. It's over, and it has been for years, and I don't know why I can't finally accept that. We've still got the scene where I kiss her to film—later this week, unless the schedule changes—and I'm not sure how I'm going to survive it.

"Knock, knock," Kelsey says as she opens the door. "Just here to find out how your costume is fitting. It looks great, but—" She stops short as she spots me lying on the futon in a miserable heap. "Oh, man. We haven't given you heatstroke, have we?"

"No." I wipe the sweat off my forehead, and I'm sure makeup will need to touch that up. "The costume is fine. One of my bracers keeps slipping, but I think we just need to use some tape."

Kelsey doesn't respond about the tape. "You look sad. Is it Kim?"

I take a deep breath. I shouldn't be talking about this on set. In fact, I never talk about it at all. Even my family thinks I'm at peace about the divorce—except my mother and my sister, who seem to psychically know the truth, which is the reason I rarely go home anymore.

But right now, if I don't vent this tension somewhere, I feel like I'm going to snap. Kelsey might not be my best friend, but she's here. "Yeah," I say. "It's Kim."

"Hard working with the ex, huh? You guys looked really happy to be rubbing up against each other."

I wish that wasn't acting on her part. "Was I that obvious?"

Kelsey shrugged. "I just call it like I see it. Maybe you guys should just have sex to cut the tension."

I shake my head. "Kim hates me. That's the last thing she wants."

"My ex stole money from me to buy drugs," she says. "I'm no fan of his, but we've hooked up a couple times since."

The father in me wants to tell her what a terrible idea this is, but I'm pretty sure Kelsey isn't going to listen. The rest of me is returning to all the thoughts of the things I'd like to do to Kim, the things she used to do to me.

She has a rule, though. She doesn't hook up with co-stars. She broke that rule for me back on the set of *Over It*, and I think the way that turned out was enough to ensure that she's never done it again.

"Yeah, well," I say. "Kim and I have kids together. We have to be responsible."

"Right. Because exes with kids never do anything spontaneous."

I laugh—for real this time—and Kelsey gives me an odd look. I'm remembering the night after the first sex scene Kim and I ever filmed together—the first sex scene I ever filmed at all. We were all up against each other on a lounge chair, naked except for a thong for her and a taped-on plastic "privacy shield" for me. I felt completely exposed, less because of the nudity and the cameras and the director yelling the infamous "Cup it, Blake!" at me, even though I clearly had my hands all over her bare breasts.

More because I was already falling in love with Kim, and touching her, being with her like that—it stirred all kinds of feelings I knew I wasn't supposed to have. Not with a woman who had already expressed that co-stars tend to confuse their characters' feelings for their own, and because of that she was never ever *ever* going to sleep with me.

Then later that night, we went out to eat and laughed off the tension from the day, after which Kim announced that she'd planned for us to go back to her trailer after dinner and have "spontaneous" sex. I mocked her a bit about her definition of *spontaneous*, and then we did just that.

"I don't think it would help," I say. "Because I'm still in love with her."

I immediately hate myself for admitting that. Kelsey seems nice, but also chatty enough to spread this news all over the set. Not that the tabloids don't report it every time one of us dates someone new—complete with pictures of the other glaring in the direction of the new couple photo on the cover—but people I work with generally know better than to believe tabloid news.

A firsthand account is another thing entirely.

"Awww," Kelsey says. "Are you really?"

I shrug. "No. I'm just being dramatic."

I think I'm usually a pretty good actor—especially when playing the part of the easygoing ex. It's been a steady role over the last few years, even if it doesn't pay.

But I'm apparently off today, because Kelsey ignores my denial. "If you still love her, why don't you try to get back together?"

"Because there's a reason we got divorced."

"Was it the nanny?" Kelsey looks at me with this open expression, like she's not about to judge the answer. She just wants to know.

I'm clearly too upset to make judicious choices about who I talk to. Kelsey's nice enough, and she's here, and if she spreads rumors, well—

I'm sure they were going to start anyway, even without my help.

"I didn't cheat on her," I say.

Kelsey's eyes widen. "Did she cheat on you?"

"No," I say. "I'm the one who filed for divorce, but it wasn't her fault. I was a shitty husband."

Now Kelsey looks confused. "You didn't cheat on her. And I'm guessing if you were an addict or a pathological liar that would be all over the news."

I laugh, but it's bitter. "Yeah, not any of those things."

"So how bad a husband could you have been?"

Those are her standards? "Jeez, you really do date bad boys, don't you?"

Kelsey smiles. "What can I say? I have a type."

"Yeah, well, it turns out I really suck at meeting a woman's emotional needs. Just ask any of my ex-girlfriends. It was the worst with Kim, though. We fought all the time because I couldn't make her happy, and I just couldn't stand doing that to her."

Kelsey scrunches her nose. "*You* filed because you couldn't make *her* happy?"

I wave a dismissive hand at her. This is why I let the nanny story fly. It's so hard for people to understand why I had to do

64

what I did. "She kept saying how much easier life would be if we weren't together. I gave her the divorce because I wanted her to be happy, even if I wasn't. I've never gotten over her. Hell, all my girlfriends look just like her."

Kelsey nods sagely. "So you're aware of that."

"It was in *In Touch Weekly*," I say. "And yes, it took me that long to clue in. Right after the article came out, I dated Catherine Peyton. She has black hair. It lasted three weeks."

Kelsey shakes her head at me. "You are so pitiful. Is this an act that you use to seduce women?"

"Sadly, no. Also, you're closer to my daughter's age than mine."

"Good. I'm not into this, either. You are way too nice a guy for me." She rifles around in her wardrobe kit and pulls out some double-sided duct tape. "Let's get that bracer fixed. And get the makeup people to touch you up before Troy realizes you're not ready for your next scene."

I nod and extend my arm to her, but I remain slumped on the futon. After the bracer is taped, I head over to makeup in an attempt to not behave like a self-absorbed diva, get my makeup fixed, then go back to the beach for my next scene. This one's later in the film, after Hemlock has disappeared, and Farpoint goes searching for her. Instead, he finds her nemesis, the Naked Mole Rat, played by Shakespearean actor Sir Bertram O'Dell, who happens to be plotting at the time with Farpoint's own mentor-turned-nemesis, the infamous Guidepost.

The old Guidepost was kind of a douche, but I've never worked with his replacement or with Bertram, so I was looking forward to meeting both of them. But when I step past the gaffer crew readying their boom mics to catch our voices above the roar of the ocean, Bertram gives me a condescending look, mutters something about how he always expected Kim to have finer taste, and makes a show of engaging Sarah in conversation instead of me.

That's fair, I suppose. He worked with Kim on her first Hemlock film, so it's not surprising he has a low opinion of me.

What I didn't expect is for the new Guidepost—Peter something—to also find me wanting and follow after Bertram like his snobby shadow. O'Dell has been making movies since I was in diapers; he has no need for my approval. But I figured the former star of some cop show might at least give me some respect.

Whatever. I'm always wishing people would stop treating me special just because I'm *Blake Pless*. I'm not here to be liked. Not by Bertram, not by Peter, and especially not by Kim.

I'm just going to play the damn part, then go home to Los Angeles, get completely wasted, and pretend this whole thing never happened.

SEVEN

Kim

We're five days into filming when Josh calls to see how everything's going. I tell him that it's been great, which is a bit of an exaggeration, but the truth is, things have been fairly smooth since that first scene on the beach. Blake and I are doing our jobs, which consist of a fair number of scenes that we aren't even shooting together, and the rest of which don't require us to roll around on each other in the sand. We alternate nights with the kids, and while I'm sure he's getting at least as much of Ivy's wheedling for her phone back as I am, we haven't discussed any changing of the rules yet.

It's the kind of thing we normally would work out via short texts, but that feels strange to do now, when we see each other every day. Talking feels strange, though, too. We avoid each other whenever possible. It's what I thought would be ideal when I first took this job—as much as the situation could be, anyway—but there's nothing that feels ideal about it. It feels like my chest is hollow and cracked, and I'm only being held together by Hemlock's too-tight corset and boob tape.

I worry he knows how I feel. I worry he pities me. Worry worry worry.

I don't tell Josh about any of this, or that today we're filming the movie's now-lone kissing scene. He's a fantastic agent and might have been willing to secure accommodations for any professional boxers I add to my entourage, but there's nothing even he can do about my real problems. Which I hope won't become worse after today.

Shortly after the phone call from Josh, I make my daily call to Helene, who's my CAO—Chief Animal Officer—to see how my charges back on the ranch are doing. She's telling me about how the iron treatments seem to be helping Niles the goat's chronic anemia, but I'm only half paying attention, my gaze flicking over and over again to the call sheet with the script attached.

Suddenly, Kelsey arrives back at the trailer with today's wardrobe.

"All fixed!" she proclaims, holding up the shredded post-battle #5 corset. "No more left nipple exposure—oh, sorry." Her round cheeks flush when she sees I'm on the phone.

I smile to let her know it's totally fine and quickly finish the call with Helene. Costanza, hearing Kelsey's voice, lumbers over to greet her and ends up enthusiastically licking the leg of my vanity instead. Kelsey giggles and gives him a hug, receiving a big slobbery kiss in return.

"Thanks," I say, taking the corset from her. It looks just as ripped as it did when I first put it on, but all it needed were a few extra stitches to keep me from gracing our family friendly PG-13 film with an R-rated wardrobe malfunction. I take off the towel I'd been loosely wearing over the remainder of Hemlock's costume—my hair and makeup were already done, and I wasn't about to screw up the several hours' worth of bloody wounds and burn marks by throwing on a *shirt*—and Kelsey helps me into the corset. It's not strictly necessary to have help for this, but after she spotted my nipple making a cameo appearance when she helped me in earlier this morning, I'm pretty much never getting dressed again without her.

She eyes me and grins. "Awesome. Totally hot."

"Yeah, I'm sure this charred look is really working for me."

I take another peek in the mirror. Hemlock might be mortally wounded, but not, of course, in a way that affects my face, other than a little residual blood splatter across my cheek.

I should be offended by this—do they think audiences wouldn't buy into Farpoint declaring his love if she looked like someone who'd *actually* been beaten all to shit?—but I'm secretly glad they didn't make me look too terrible.

Maybe for just one moment, when Blake's holding me and telling me he loves me, he'll remember the times when he thought I was beautiful. When he said those words to me and meant them.

Or at least, when he thought he did.

Kelsey adjusts the twisting-vine metal band on my right arm, and she gets a smudge of red makeup on her fingers. "I'm serious. You're totally smokin' for a girl about to be a corpse." She winks at me. "Also, no surprise nipple, and with—" she checks her watch "—three minutes to spare."

I force a smile at her. "You're the best."

Three minutes. My hands tremble, and I think I'm going to be sick.

"Are you okay?" Kelsey asks. "With the scene today?" She seems sincerely concerned, and I'm tempted to spill it all to her. But there's not time, and even if there was, I've learned from years of therapy—and one long-overdue, relationship-ending conversation with Roger—that telling someone about my feelings for Blake doesn't make them go away.

I sigh. "I don't know."

Her brow furrows. She looks like she wants to tell me something, but I can't handle any platitudes about how time will heal all things or how I really just need to get laid. None of the usual nuggets of post-divorce advice have ever produced results, and I doubt they will now. I grab Constanza's leash from the table.

"Shouldn't Aaron be here to pick up Costanza by now?" Costanza hears his name and sits up, his head swiveling eagerly in my general direction. I open my trailer door, wishing for some fresh air to help calm my nerves, but it's July in Miami, and I don't think there's been air even remotely fresh here for months.

I spot Aaron, standing in front of Bertram's trailer, busy with something on his phone. Kelsey does, too. "I'll take Costanza over to him," she offers quickly.

A little too quickly.

I raise my eyebrow. "Didn't you say before that you liked bad boys? Aaron doesn't seem to fit that mold." Today's lateness aside, he's pretty responsible and unfailingly polite—even though Costanza seems to still think he's a walking fire hydrant.

Kelsey shrugs as she openly ogles him. "I might be willing to make an exception for that one. And besides," she coos to Costanza, scratching him behind the ears as he does a full-body wiggle of sheer doggy happiness. "I love *you*, and you're a good boy, aren't you?"

"I leave him in your capable care," I say with a smile, genuine this time, handing her the leash. "My dog *and* my assistant."

She grins and heads off, her curls bouncing. Costanza tugs her along—I clearly need to train him not to pull on a leash when I get back home—and they both nearly barrel into a crew-member carrying a huge fake rock.

Seeing Kelsey with Costanza brings back a different memory of Blake, not on a film set, but in the red rocks of southern Utah, laughing his head off while walking a pack of dogs who all seemed determined to drag him in separate directions.

We'd gone on a road trip, leaving two-year-old Ivy with my parents for ten days. I'd been stressed about that, but my OCD—which neither of us had any understanding of at the time—must have been at a low ebb. I'd talked about how much I wanted to check out this famous animal sanctuary in Utah, and Blake suggested we go—just the two of us and the open road.

The whole trip was incredible, and not because of any fancy accommodations or exotic locations. We ate at greasy truck stops and went to see movies at small-town theaters, slipping in after the movies started so as to not be recognized. We drove and drove and talked for hours and still had things to say late at night in our hotel room. At the sanctuary, we pitched in with the animals, and Blake seemed to have just as great a time doing all of it as I did.

Especially during that walk.

"This is my future, isn't it?" he called over to me, a wide grin on his face, stumbling after the dogs.

We already had several special-needs animals at this point, including Ugly Naked Pig, a pig I picked out for him when we first moved in together, because he said he'd always wanted one. We'd started talking about the kind of ranch we'd run together someday, and not just in generalities.

"You still up for it?" I called back, with an equally wide grin.

"Just try to stop me," he said. Then he tripped over a rock and face-planted into the dirt as one of the German shepherds lunged forward.

We laughed so hard we were both crying.

The memory aches now. The ranch had originally been my dream, but he embraced it wholly, and it became *ours*. When I lost him, I couldn't stand to give up my ranch dream, too, and I'm glad I didn't. But sometimes I think of how it would have been if we could have done it together, like we'd planned.

I shake myself free of the image of Blake and the dogs and his happy, gorgeous smile, and hurry to the location we're shooting today. It's another beach scene, of course. My life on this set apparently wouldn't be complete without getting sand in every crevice.

Troy gives me a look when I show up; I'm a few minutes late by now, but honestly, I'm hardly the first star to miss call time.

Telling myself this doesn't make me feel better.

Nor does seeing Blake. He gives me a half-hearted smile, which I try to return. Beads of sweat drip down the side of his face. God, he must be miserable in this heat in all that leather.

Clearly he wants to get this over with quickly. That's probably better for both of us.

Troy indicates where I'm to lie down on the sand, an area marked with fake rocks with scorch marks across the tops of them from the blast of the laser weapon that Naked Mole Rat used on Hemlock. Apparently Guidepost brought some brutal tech along with him from Astra Vel.

As I lie down and makeup swoops in with a few, last-minute additions of blood splatter to my cleavage, I try not to notice that there seem to be more people milling around than usual.

This is it, the big Watterpless post-divorce kissing scene. No one wants to miss this.

My chest is so tight it hurts. I look up at Blake, but he's staring down at the sand, his arms folded. He looks almost angry, and I don't blame him.

Just try to stop me, I hear him say, laughing, in my memory.

But I did. I was scared and out of control, and I pushed him away with both hands. Then I did nothing but act like a bitch afterward, because I was hurt that he let me.

I close my eyes against the harsh glare of the sun and practice the calming breathing techniques my therapist taught me. Finally, they have us ready. Troy calls out action, and I am Hemlock, bleeding out on the sand, eyes wide into the open sky.

Blake makes a strangled sound, falls to his knees beside me. "Sabrina," he gasps, calling Hemlock by her real name. He looks in shock and horror at my wounds.

I channel Hemlock's fear, her rage. I grit my teeth and try to move, imagining the pain ripping through me, forcing a sob through my lips.

"No, don't—" he starts, putting his hand behind my head, cradling me. "Don't move." Tears well up in his eyes.

Tears.

Outside of his movies, I've never seen Blake cry. Not when we'd fight; not even when he said he wanted a divorce.

I was the one crying then. Always me.

I yell in angry Hemlock pain, seething that she should be so weak. "Leave me," I hiss. "Go. Get back to your world before he destroys it."

He holds me and chokes back a sob. "No," he says, shaking his head. "No. I can't leave you. Not like this—not ever." He blinks and looks away, and I can see the moment when Farpoint makes the crucial third-act decision. He reaches into his vest to pull out the Astran Orb, the thing we've spent the movie thus far pursuing, the key to him returning to his home world. It's this glowing blue chunk of what looks like a clump of Pop Rocks and maybe actually is. After our kiss, he's going to smash the "orb" and use the magic to save my life, which will theoretically strand him here forever.

"Don't be an idiot," I say, trying to shake my head, knowing by his expression what he means to do. Hemlock spends much of the movie calling him an idiot.

"Too late for that," he says, a tremulous smile forming through the tears, and my heart skips several beats at that smile. "I already fell in love with you."

I can't breathe, and it's not because of my incredible acting skills. It's Blake, and his face is so close, and he's telling me he's in love with me, and his eyes are my favorite shade, pale green like an antique glass bottle.

And I'm the idiot, I know it, but as he leans in to kiss me, his free arm outstretched to break the orb, I let myself believe that Blake feels the same thing I do. That he always did and always will.

His lips meet mine. Gently, softly, because I'm dying.

I don't feel like I'm dying. I feel like I'm waking up for the first time in six years. Heat spreads through me, memories washing through me in this torrential downpour. My body hungers for him, for us, for the way we used to be.

His gentle kisses quickly begin to match my need, our tongues finding each other, sunlight sparking in my vision even though my eyes are closed. My arms draw him against me, and there's a soft thump as he drops the orb, unbroken, into the sand, his hands in my hair. It's like all those years of hurt and anger and sorrow are gone, and it's just us again. It's Kim and Blake and we're together, our lips moving, our hands moving, makeup smearing all over each other.

Somewhere in the background, I hear someone saying, "Kim, you're dying. Guys, not that much."

But Blake's on top of me, and my legs wrap tight around him, and I can feel him hard against me, he wants me again, and my whole body is on fire, and the rest of the world doesn't exist—

"Cut!" Troy yells, and I realize it's not the first time he's said it. Just the loudest.

Blake seems to actually hear Troy at the same time I do. He pulls back, his eyes wide, his breathing as ragged as mine.

Oh yeah, the rest of the world exists. And is watching us, gaping, filming us with actual goddamn movie cameras that I *knew* were running because I'm in a goddamn *movie* and not with Blake in real life, no matter how turned on he seemed to also be—

He rolls off me, his face pink. "Kim," he says, barely above a whisper.

I stare at those green eyes, shame burning through me. There's no way he—along with everyone else watching—doesn't know the truth now, that I have never gotten over him. So much so that I'm apparently willing to turn this film into a porno the minute I get my hands on him.

I feel all the eyes on me, but it's his that really matter.

Was any of that real for him?

I might have kissed him like I used to, but he kissed me right back, way more than the film called for. He wanted me, if only for that moment.

I don't want to feel this tiny sliver of hope. I can't let myself feel that hope, only to lose it again.

"I—I can't do this," I say, forcing myself back to my wobbly feet. This time there's no dignified walk off set.

This time I run.

EIGHT

Blake

I run between the trailers after Kim, my heart pounding in my throat. Kissing her after all these years spun my head around, but I shouldn't have let it carry me away. She knows now—she *has* to know how I feel about her. I'd been barely passable at covering it before, but losing myself like that made it undeniable.

I need to apologize. I know that. But at the back of my brain, one thought plays over and over on repeat.

She kissed me back.

I hear the door to Kim's trailer slam and approach it cautiously.

Of course she kissed me back. It was in the damn script. Her character was supposed to be dying, and yet she wrapped her legs around me like she used to and damn well lit my whole body on fire. I'm having reactions that are all too apparent in Farpoint's skin-tight pants, and I pull the overcoat tighter around my abdomen.

Then I knock. "Kim? Are you okay?"

For a moment I think she won't answer, but then the door opens and Kim's standing there, still covered in fake blood, which one or the other of us smeared through her pale hair in a long, bright streak. She looks at me, her sky-blue eyes wide, then turns away, like she can't stand the sight of me.

But she's left the door open, and I don't want the entire crew listening, so I step inside and close it behind me.

"Kim," I say. "I'm so sorry. I wasn't thinking, and I didn't mean—I'm just really sorry."

Kim flinches and looks up at me. She's out of breath, probably from the sprint off set, but there's something so . . . vulnerable about her expression, in a way I haven't seen since before the divorce.

"You're sorry," she says. "So you're saying you didn't want that at all?"

My mouth falls open. She has to know that isn't true—we were pressed so tight together that I know she felt exactly how much I want her. Still.

Always.

I stutter an incomprehensible jumble of syllables, wishing I knew how to tell her how much I hate myself for being so pathetic, for being so deeply and irrevocably in love with her that I can't be a professional and kiss her like I'm supposed to without losing myself in things that can never be.

Kim takes a step toward me, and the stream of nonsense dies on my lips. She's so close, not a foot away, this energy crackling between us. I try to breathe; I try to think of what I'm supposed to be telling her—that I can do this. I'll do better next time.

Then Kim reaches her arms around my neck and pulls me down and kisses me. Her lips are insistent and hungry, and I'm lost like I was on the set, my body humming the song of us, the one I thought we'd never play again. Kissing Kim is like losing myself in all of my best memories, the days of my life I wish I could relive over and over again. Her hands slide up my chest and tug off my overcoat, and I groan as her lips move down my throat. My hands run down her arms, further mangling her makeup. And though there's an entire set of people waiting for us to get our act together and run the scene like professionals, I can't let go.

Kim obviously has no intention of letting go, either. Her hands are in my hair, and my visor—god, my visor, how did I forget about it, I look like an idiot in this thing—clatters to the floor. I go to pull off her crown but my fingers dig through the million pins affixing it to her hair, and then I have to stop because she's pulling my shirt off over my head. Troy is going to kill us for ruining the shoot, but I'm unhooking her corset anyway, and then Kim pushes me backward and I'm lying on her couch with her on top of me, my hands smudging bloody makeup over her chest.

I kiss her breasts, brushing my tongue over her the way she likes, and she gasps, her back arching. There's this cosmic energy between us that was always there, even before our first time together. It took me almost a year after the divorce to start dating again, and I'd been alternately terrified of discovering that the euphoria of being with her wasn't special, or that it was, and I'd never get back there again.

I'd been right about the second part. No one compared to her, to what we had. Kim runs her teeth gently down my ear—because she remembers, god, she remembers—and the world around us turns a blinding white.

Kim unbuttons my pants and pulls down my underwear. Her hands begin to stroke, and I'm suddenly reminded of the time that she tried to explain to me how to drive a manual transmission using my dick as a stick shift and we laughed and laughed and then made love on our living room floor. I want to laugh now, at the memory, but the sensation of her touching me there is overwhelming, waves of heat and pleasure rolling through me, and instead I groan, my head falling back on the arm of the couch. I've missed this so much, wanted it for so long, and the unexpected elation at finally having her with me again has shut down every part of my brain that must know this is a bad idea. I slide down her shorts and her nylons, lost in the breathtaking sight of her, all of her, and then my mind snaps back to reality.

"Do you have—" I ask, but Kim's already reached under the couch and spilled the entire contents of her purse across the floor. She rummages through it, and when she sits back up, I stare at her in awe. *Her*, here again, wanting me. "Kim," I say.

She looks down at me. Her fingers crinkle a shiny square wrapper, but we're staring transfixed into each other's eyes.

I love you, I think. *God, I love you.* But my throat closes and the words don't make it out. Instead I pull her down on me again, and my hands are roaming, desperate to take in every inch of her smooth skin, and hers are tearing frantically at the wrapper and sliding the condom on.

Then I'm inside her, and we're together like we used to be. I haven't said a woman's name during intercourse since the last time I said hers—and got slapped by my soon-to-be-ex girlfriend. But I'm safe again, here with the only woman I want to be with, and it's as natural as it is miraculous. Our rhythm builds, and her moans are so delicious, so incredible, and those waves of heat are cresting, and I want to freeze time, to live forever in this moment, where nothing in the world exists except her and me. Time seems to collapse in one bright flash, and I cry out and she cries out, shuddering around me—

And then we collapse. We lie there against each other, breathing hard, all sweat and smeared blood and the parts of our costumes we didn't bother to take off. Kim's hair hangs loose, and her crown frames her face like an angel, and my tongue is trying to find words for all the tangled thoughts inside my head.

Kim buries her face in my shoulder. "It doesn't have to mean anything," she says.

My chest constricts. God, doesn't it? I mean, yeah, we've both had casual sex, but never with each other.

But then I remember. Kim's not only over me, she hates me. I never made her happy, and nothing's changed.

It never will. This isn't a thing I can have, only a brief reminder of all that I've lost.

"Yeah," I say, though it comes out strangled. "Okay."

"Exes hook up all the time, right?" she says. "It's a wonder it never happened before now."

I can't breathe. My eyes are burning, and for one blinding second, I'm terrified that I'm going to break down and cry. The only time I've cried since I was thirteen was when Ugly Naked Pig died. I managed to be strong through the divorce, through moving into my own place, through the tabloid speculation about Kim's new loves, through discovering she was serious with Roger.

But when my pig died—the pig she found for me, the last surviving piece of our life together other than the kids—that's when the weight of losing Kim opened up like a cloudburst.

I sobbed for three days, and god, I don't want to do that now.

Kim shudders. She sits up and turns away, but not before I realize that *she's* crying. She tugs at her pantyhose, but I reach out and run a hand along her jaw, the tears soaking my fingertips.

"Kim," I say. "What's wrong?"

She dissolves. I wrap my arms around her as she sobs, not sure what I've done, but certain that, as usual, I've ruined everything.

"I know I messed it all up between us," she says. "But I just have to know, was there ever a time that you loved me?"

My arms go slack, and her words circle through my mind as I try to make sense of them. "Was there ever . . . *what?*"

"Even if it was before we were married," Kim continues between sobs. "Did you ever feel anything real for me, or did you just realize one day that you never had?"

I pull back, staring at her. Kim's face is blotchy and her eyes rimmed red. I've seen her cry like this more times than I can count, and nearly all of them were my fault. I've always been helpless to fix it, always left nothing but pain in my wake. But the words fall out of my mouth anyway. "I never stopped. I'm still in love with you."

Kim stops crying, looking first stunned, then confused. She opens her mouth to respond—

A loud knock sounds on the door, not three feet away. "Kim?" Sarah shouts. "Troy's wondering when you'll be ready to be back on set."

Kim reaches for her corset, but I get up off the couch and step over Kim's spilled purse, pulling up my pants and fastening them. No way am I making her answer the door, not like this. I stand in front of it and crack it open, so no one will see behind me while Kim dresses.

"Hey, Sarah," I say. "We're going to need a minute."

Sarah stares up at me from below the trailer steps. I know what I must look like—I'm naked from the waist up and covered in the combined makeup of two action heroes, one bleeding and close to death. I can see crew members huddled between a few of the other trailers, and no doubt at least one of them is taking pictures.

As if we hadn't put on enough of a show already. Behind me, I can hear Kim scrambling into her clothes, and I think about what she said.

Did I ever love her? God, doesn't she know?

"Actually," I say, "tell Troy we need the rest of the afternoon off."

Sarah arches an eyebrow at me. "But we're all set up, and we only have permits for—"

"We'll be back on set tomorrow, ready to go. But we're having an emergency, so we're going to need the rest of the day. Troy's just going to have to deal with it."

Sarah gives me a look that says she thinks this emergency is happening in my pants, but she takes a step back. "I'll talk to Troy," she says, and I close the door again.

I find Kim fastening the hooks on her corset. She looks at me warily, and I'm at a total loss for what to say next.

I need to tell her the truth, all of it. And there's clearly a lot going on in her head I don't know, and for the first time in six years, it seems like it might actually be my business to know.

I want to, more than anything, and I don't want to be interrupted again. "Let's get dressed and clean up," I say. "And then drive back to the hotel and meet there. The kids will be gone for hours. We can sit down and talk, okay? We can talk about everything."

For a moment Kim looks reluctant, but then she nods. "Yeah," she says quietly. "That would be good."

As much as I want to just hold her and tell her that everything is going to be okay, I realize I don't know that, and it scares the hell out of me.

So instead I open the door again and begin my walk of shame back to my trailer, praying that by the time we both get to the hotel, Kim will still want to listen to what I have to say.

NINE

Blake

I stand outside Kim's hotel room on the red and blue geometric hall carpet, trying to breathe. All I can hear is Kim's voice in my head, over and over again, asking if I ever loved her.

I get that she thinks I'm over her. It would be more reasonable if I was. But what have I done to make her think it possible that I never loved her at all?

More importantly, if she got over me six years ago and has hated me ever since—why does she *care*?

I knock, and Kim opens the door. Her eyes are red from crying, and her mouth is set in a hard line.

My heart cracks. She's going to tell me it was all a mistake, that she was just working out stress. That she doesn't love me anymore, that she just wanted to know if our whole marriage had been a lie. Kim doesn't say anything, but she lets me in, and I pull a chair out from the small table and sit down.

This time, I'm going to talk through it, even if neither of us likes what the other has to say.

"Troy hassled me while I was washing up," I tell her. "He threatened to replace us with 'professional actors.' I told him he can recast if he wants, but he won't have actors on set tomorrow if he decides to do that, and we'll be there, ready to work."

Kim sits on the very edge of the bed and closes her eyes. She hates disappointing the people she works with, so it's a testament to how bad things are that she doesn't call Troy right now and take it all back.

We're both quiet. "He's not going to replace us," I say.

"You can't be in love with me," she responds.

I open my mouth and close it again. I guess I should be glad she's going to start the conversation, because god only knows I have no idea how to.

"I am," I say. "I always have been."

Kim shakes her head in that resolute way she does when she feels she has irrefutable evidence against me. "You got over me so fast. You wanted to get divorced, and I saw the look on your face when you left. You were relieved."

There's a lump in my throat, but I choke past it. I don't want to tell her how pathetic I am, but I suppose I already have. The rest is just details. "I didn't want to get divorced. And I sure as hell wasn't relieved."

Her face hardens. "You *said* you wanted a divorce. You *told* me that's what you wanted."

"I wanted to stop hurting you. You were so miserable with me. You talked all the time about how it would be easier to split up, and I wanted to give you what you needed."

The certainty fades from Kim's face, and she stares at me blankly.

"But it doesn't change anything," I continue. "Because you were miserable, and I don't want to do that to you again."

Kim squeezes her eyes shut. "I was miserable, but it wasn't you."

That's ridiculous. "What else could it have been? We fought all the time, and—"

"I have OCD," Kim says. She winces and falls silent again.

I stare at her. I can't have heard her right. "You have . . ."

"OCD," she says. "Obsessive compulsive disorder. It isn't like you see on TV, with the hand washing and door locking. I mean, I guess it is for some people. But for me it's these thoughts that stick in my head and won't go away. It gets much worse after I have a baby."

My breath is shallow, and my heartbeat seems to slow. "What kind of thoughts?"

Kim looks down at her hands, which she's knotted together. "Like that last fight we had, when I left and went to my parents? I was sure that Luke was too warm, and you said he was fine. You wanted me to leave him with you, but I took him with me anyway, and you thought I didn't trust you."

I nod. I'm not proud of the way I handled that. I wasn't even at the time. "I was just trying to give you a break, you know? You were so stressed out, and I thought you could use it."

Kim nods miserably. "I know. What I didn't tell you at the time was that I *couldn't* leave him with you. Because I knew—I just *knew* that if I took my eyes off him, even for a second, that he was going to die and it would be all my fault."

I scoot forward on my chair. I remember pacing back and forth after she left, not sure what the hell had just happened.

I felt like that a lot.

"You tried to tell me," I say. "You told me something was wrong in your mind, and I said you were fine."

"I wanted to be fine. I wanted *so badly* to be fine for you. For us. After the divorce . . . I finally got to the point where I knew I wasn't getting over it the way that I should. So I went to a therapist to talk about that, and I ended up getting diagnosed. I told Roger, because we were dating at the time, but no one else knows."

My mind is reeling over all the fights we had over stupid little things. Me telling her that everything was fine, stop worrying, just make a choice, it doesn't matter which one. "That time you wanted me to have an opinion on which stroller to buy," I say.

Kim cringes. "Every time I looked at a stroller I imagined it folding up with Ivy inside. Those things look like the jaws of death. I knew I shouldn't be so afraid, but I wanted you to make the choice, because I was sure if I did, I'd make a mistake, and she'd die."

I'm pretty sure my heart has completely stopped. "You were sick, and I abandoned you."

Kim shakes her head. "No. I was making you miserable. I was scared and losing my mind, and instead of talking to you about it, I pushed you away. It's not your fault you left. You're right. I talked about divorce. I made you think I wanted it."

"I wasn't miserable."

She looks up at me, and I can see tears glistening in her eyes. "You were. How could you not be? I was rigid and unreasonable and constantly picking fights with you and—"

"You told me something was wrong, and I didn't listen." The words seem to echo in my hollow chest. I'm remembering all the times we fought, and I couldn't even tell what about. I was supposed to care more about minuscule things—this baby proofing method or that one, this music class, that baby gym. I always thought if the decisions were so important to Kim, I'd let her make them. She'd always been opinionated, and I didn't even stop to think why she was so fixated on this stuff.

I thought I was the problem.

"It's not your fault," she says, wringing her hands. "It's mine. I ruined everything. Of course you had to leave."

The tears have reached her cheeks now, and I want to go back to the man I was six years ago and shake him. Make him see what was happening and not make the biggest mistake of his life.

She was sick, and I left her alone.

"You didn't want the divorce," I say. She's said this, but I'm having a hard time adjusting to it. Our lives are like one of those pictures that looks like a duck, until someone points out to you it might be a rabbit, and then you can't figure out how you ever thought it was anything else. "God, Kim, I'm so sorry." The words are beyond inadequate, but they're all I have.

Kim straightens and brushes her hair back out of her face. "It doesn't matter now, I guess."

85

It does, but it takes me a minute to wrap my head around why. "Is that why you hate me? Because I left you alone when you were going through that?"

Kim looks surprised, and then she sighs. "I don't hate you. I wish I did. I've never been able to get over you, and you seemed to so easily, and—"

"I never got over you either," I say. "You said I was relieved— it's the opposite. The day we split up was the worst day of my life. I'd been dreading it so long—I knew things were falling apart, and I didn't know how to fix them. I could never do anything right, and I thought I was making you unhappy . . . I guess maybe what you thought was relief could have been the finality, you know? I didn't have to dread the day anymore. It finally came."

Kim sniffs and wipes tears out of her eyes. "I'm sorry I did that to you. And I'm sorry I've been such a bitch. I just—I was so hurt, and I could never figure out how to talk to you without all the pain seeping out. You were always so good at that, so I assumed it was because you didn't care."

"I want to say it's because I'm a good actor," I say, "but maybe it's more that I'm the suffer in silence type, which was never your strong point."

Kim laughs bitterly. "That's the truth."

We're both quiet for a moment, and I'm trying to sort through the mess in my head—the mistakes of the past, the startling revelation that Kim wasn't unhappy in our marriage—

And the horrifying conclusion that this means I've made us miserable for the last six years for absolutely no reason.

TEN

Kim

There's this silence that stretches out, and I can't think of how to break it, because I'm too busy trying to piece together fragments of this conversation into something that makes sense. Something that fits with the story I've been living with the last six years.

No, not living with. I was drowning in that story, drowning in my mistakes and pain.

But he loves me. Then and still now. He didn't want to get divorced, despite what he said at the time. Though I have six years of that other story to convince me this can't be right, I have the look on his face right now as he says these words. I have the way he made love to me in the trailer, with the same need and longing that was coursing through me.

I'm desperate to believe this and scared of it all at once. Scared of what it means we've done.

It's like a dream, this conversation and what happened in the trailer. A dream and nightmare both, the latter because I'm facing head-on all that my sickness cost us. I thought I had dealt with it as much as one could. But it's sharply bittersweet, knowing he loved me—knowing that maybe I could have salvaged things between us if I had just figured it out sooner.

Blake is leaning forward with his elbows on his knees, his face in his hands. Chunks of his auburn hair fall over his fingers, and I remember the soft feel of that hair, the scent of his shampoo. I close my eyes.

"I left you," Blake says, finally breaking the silence trapping both of us, "and it ruined both our lives."

The old hurt squeezes in my chest, and I can't help it. "You seemed to move on well enough," I say, tracing the geometric pattern on the bedspread.

He barks out a humorless laugh, looking up at me. "You mean to the long string of girls who looked like you?"

I know all too well what he's talking about. That article that lined up all the slim, blond, blue-eyed girlfriends Blake had after me, most of whom were also actresses and driven, strong-willed women. Kim clones, the article had called them. Other piggy-backing articles were less kind—one called them the Kim-bots.

People seemed to think I should be flattered by that, but I took it in a totally different way.

"I read that article," I say reluctantly, "and I cried. I was sure that all I had been to you was a type, one you kept picking because you thought that's what you wanted, but could never make you happy."

"Simone threw that *In Touch Weekly* issue at me when we broke up," he says, studying his hands before looking back at me. "And yeah, I might have been looking for a type, but that was after our divorce. I was looking for *you*. None of the others could ever make me happy because they weren't you." He rubs his forehead. "Would have been nice if I had figured that out *before* someone made a line-up of all my girlfriends in an entertainment magazine."

I swallow past a thick lump in my throat at the mention of Simone. He dated her longer than the others. No matter what he said to the press about never re-marrying, I wondered if she'd be the one to change his mind, to undo the misery I'd inflicted on him that made him despise the very concept of marriage.

Except he says he wasn't miserable. That he wanted to stay married.

"Were you in love with Simone?" I ask. My fingers find a stray thread on the comforter, and I pick at it, trying as best I can to brace myself for the answer.

But Blake shakes his head. "No. I cared about her, and I was closer to her than I was to the others." He pauses. "You want to hear why we broke up?"

"*People* reported it was because you were spending too much time apart on different projects."

He gives me one of those half-smiles. "You believe everything you read about me?"

I shrug. "I tried not to believe any of it, but when there's a dozen articles talking about how an 'inside source' says you've fallen in love and are happier than you've ever been—"

"Yeah," he says, "I read those same articles about you."

He's got a good point. But somehow it seemed so much easier to believe about him. Because surely he would find someone he could really love. Surely he would be truly happy with someone who didn't have my problems and constant fears. Someone who wasn't me.

He gets up from the table and sits on the bed next to me. I want to lean into him so badly I ache with it. But I don't. I'm not sure what is happening between us, what even *could* happen between us, and I'm afraid to hope because of how much it'll hurt if I'm wrong.

"I'd been away filming," he says. "And I came home, and Simone arranged this nice dinner in. It was supposed to be romantic, I guess."

I grimace, picturing the gorgeous spread of food on the table, the candles lit. Music playing softly in the background. Simone was supposedly an excellent cook, something I've never been. Our romantic dinners in were always takeout. "Do I want to hear this?"

"Yeah, I think you do." He draws in a deep breath. "So, then you called, something about Ivy's science fair project, and we talked over what she'd done with you, and what she and I had talked about doing. I don't even remember what—"

"She was trying to build a rocket," I say, remembering that night. "I wanted to do a bottle rocket because they don't go up in flames, but you and she had discussed getting a model rocket engine with actual gunpowder in it."

"That's right. And I was on the phone with you for, like, ten minutes. Then I hung up and turned around, and Simone was standing there with this look on her face, and she says to me, 'You're still in love with her.'"

My eyes widen. "Over a science project?"

"She said I was happier talking to you for ten minutes about our daughter's homework than I ever was talking to her."

I wince. "I'm sorry she broke up with you over that."

"She didn't," he says. "She broke up with me because I wouldn't deny it."

My heart pounds. He's already said he's still in love with me, that he always has been, but hearing it again . . . "Really?" My voice is barely above a whisper.

He takes my hand, and it feels so good, his fingers warm against mine. "Really."

We're both quiet for a few breaths, and then he smiles. "The miracle," he says, "is that Portia never talked to the press about the time I called her Kim in bed."

My mouth drops open. "You didn't."

"Yes, I did," he says sheepishly. "She slapped me and dumped me right then and there."

Not that I love hearing about his post-divorce sex life—I've done my best to think about it as little as possible—but this makes me happier than it should.

His smile slips, and he looks down at our joined hands. "What about you? Were you in love with Roger?"

I wonder if I sounded like that when I asked about

90

Simone—so tentative. I probably did. "I wanted to be," I admit. "Roger was great to me, and he really loved me. I wanted to get over you, but I never could. So no, I wasn't."

He nods, but he doesn't look particularly happy about it. Does he wish I had been? Does he want me to have moved on, even if he does have feelings for me? Maybe he still knows that ultimately he can't be happy with me, and the only thing that's changed is now he knows why.

"He asked me to marry him," I continue quietly. "I thought about it."

"Why didn't you?"

I remember the look on Roger's face when he asked me, and then later when I'd turned him down. I also remember the stark difference between how I'd felt during his proposal and how I'd felt during Blake's. "He was a good man. In the end, I decided it wasn't fair to him. I was never going to love him, not the way he wanted me to. And maybe he was okay with that, ultimately, but I never was."

"You deserve that," Blake says. "To be with someone you love."

The breath catches in my throat, and I meet his gaze. "Do I?"

His eyes are are a shade more blue than green right now, and his face is so close to mine. "Of course you do."

It takes everything in me not to lean in and kiss him. To feel again (and again) that completeness, that intense bliss of being with him.

Except I don't know if that's what he really wants, deep down. Not after what I did to us. He was the one who left, but he had good reason to.

"It took me a long time to figure it out," I say after a moment. "Why I pushed you away."

"What did you figure out?"

It was hard enough telling him about the OCD. This, somehow, is worse. "I wanted you to fight for us. I knew I was making you unhappy, even though I couldn't stop myself from doing it. But I wanted to know that I was still worth it to you. I kept floating the idea of splitting up because I was desperate for you to tell me you didn't want that." The tears start to build again. "I wanted so badly for you to want to stay together."

His face pales. "I'm sorry, Kim. I'm so sorry. I understand if you can never forgive me."

"Forgive *you?*" I shake my head, disgusted with myself. "I just finished telling you how it's my fault. How could you have known if I didn't tell you? You're the one who shouldn't forgive *me.*"

"Because you wanted me to fight for you?" His brow wrinkles. "God, Kim, I should have. I hate myself that I didn't."

"But I shouldn't have gone about it like that. It wasn't fair to you." I've gone over this time and again. With my therapist, with my own brain in the middle of the night. So many regrets, so many things I've wished I could change.

"Maybe not," he says, his tone angry. As it should be. But then he continues with, "but me walking out on you was hardly fair, either." He closes his eyes, and I know it's not me he's angry with. It's himself.

God, how did we screw this up so badly?

"I suppose it doesn't matter now," I say, mostly in answer to my own question.

Blake turns to me, and there's this vulnerability in his expression that breaks my heart all over again. "Doesn't it?"

I don't know what to say to that. That growing hope that I've been trying to avoid flickers again, and I'm so afraid to stoke it, to give it any more life than it already has.

Blake looks back at our hands. Still joined, fingers entwined. "What do we do now?"

My throat is dry, and I don't want to make any assumptions as to what he means. Clearly I've not been the expert on Blake's mind that I once thought I was. "About the film? I guess we just get through it as best we can."

He shakes his head. "No, I don't mean about the film."

"You mean, what about us?"

Could he really want something again with me? Is a second

chance possible, after all that's happened?

"Do you want anything to change?" he asks.

"It seems like it'll have to," I say cautiously. Because there's no way things can be exactly as they were. But that doesn't necessarily mean he wants—

"Do you remember when we decided to move in together?" he asks, and I blink, surprised. Of course I remember. He gives me a wry smile. "We were almost done filming, and you were asking me if I might want to move closer to where you lived, and I said that would be nice, and we started talking about me getting an apartment *in your neighborhood* because neither of us was brave enough to admit that we wanted to live together." He smiles, and my whole body warms. "We're doing it again, I think. Circling the issue."

I return the smile. "Yeah, we tend to do that."

He draws in a deep breath. "I'd want to try again. If you think you could give me another chance."

That flicker of hope turns into a bonfire. For a moment, I can picture it. Blake living on the ranch with me. Walking five dogs at once. Wrestling with the kids in the living room. Falling asleep with his arms around me at night.

But. "Would you really want that? I mean, I'm medicated now, but the OCD is still a thing. It's more under control, and I'm better at dealing with it now, but—"

"That doesn't bother me. I never would have left you if I knew that's what it was. I thought you were unhappy with me. I had no idea it was a disease, and if I had known, I never would have left."

I close my eyes, the emotions overwhelming. It's so hard to understand how it couldn't have mattered, how it couldn't have changed how he felt about me.

If he can be brave, though, so can I.

"I'd like to try again, too," I say. "If you're sure you want to. But I don't even know what that would look like, with the kids and the press and the movie." As soon as anyone outside this room gets wind of what's happening, we'll be on the cover of every entertainment magazine worldwide. And how the kids will react is hard to guess. This isn't exactly something any of us anticipated.

"What would you want it to look like?" he asks.

I hesitate, not even sure how to wrap my mind around this question.

He smiles. "We could lay out all the options and list the pros and cons."

I let out a little laugh. "You know me well."

"Okay, we could date casually. But I think the con for that is I'm not sure either of us would be capable of it. Too much history."

I look down at the floor, feeling a prickle of fear. "You're sure you wouldn't want to see other people?"

He squeezes my hand. "No. No way."

I smile in sheer relief. "Me neither, so that's a pretty big con. I'd say casual dating is out."

"So on the extreme opposite end, we could immediately get remarried." He ducks his head close to mine. "Just to be clear, those statements I made about never getting married again don't apply to you."

Remarried.

I could be married to Blake again. We'd be together like we always should have been. A family, like we were. The idea—not to mention the very fact that it's somehow a real possibility and not some dream I'm about to wake from—makes me lightheaded.

But it's not just Blake and me that we have to consider.

"If it weren't for the kids, I'd say yeah, let's just elope and fight for our marriage again like we should have the first time." I run my thumb along his, feeling his skin under mine. "But we can't do that to them, can we? We need to take it a little slower, make sure they're okay with it."

He nods. "Okay. So we'll hold off on that until our family is ready."

Until. He says this like it's certain, not something he needs to consider. "You'd really want that?"

"I never wanted to get divorced in the first place."

I press my lips together. "Neither did I."

Blake groans. "We're idiots."

He's got that right. But I'm so happy, I'm all but floating. Yet that fear is still there—a weight holding me down.

"Maybe we shouldn't tell the kids yet," I say. "I mean, what if you change your mind, and you can't deal with being with me, and then we disappoint them—"

"Kim." He takes my other hand in his so he's holding them both, and he looks me straight in the eyes. "I can deal with it. That wasn't really the issue even before."

I bite my lip. I know he really believes it. But my OCD is still a thing, and even medicated, it will still affect us. What happens if he finds he was wrong?

"If we don't tell the kids," he says, "we can't see each other much. I mean, we can sneak around here, I guess, stay in each other's rooms while the kids are asleep. But once we go home, they're either with you or with me, right? They're going to notice if we're suddenly sticking them with Marguerite constantly to sneak around together."

It's a good point. "And as soon as the public knows, the kids will feel betrayed we didn't tell them. We'd get caught eventually."

"The public will already know. There were cameras on us today. Lots of them. We're probably already all over the internet."

I sigh heavily. How could I have forgotten all those cameras on us, all those people watching? If Troy didn't release the footage himself, there are any number of crew members who probably sold photos for a tidy profit.

"Besides," he says with a smile, "I'm pretty sure I'm going to be so clingy that I'll never want to be away from you."

My heart flutters. "Me too. So we have to tell the kids and the public." I let out a long, slow breath, steadying myself, and he wraps an arm around me.

"I'm terrified," he says "You?"

"Completely, utterly terrified," I admit. Yet, the feel of his arm around me, the memory of his lips on mine—no matter how scared I am, there's no way I can give this up. Not if he really wants to try.

"I love you," he says, but there's a hesitance in his voice. "I'm still afraid I won't be able to make you happy."

I lean in closer to him. "You did make me happy. Even when I was losing my mind." I pause, thinking of something I've wished so many times that I'd brought up before. "If you want, we could try therapy. If you'd be okay with that."

He hugs me tighter. "I always regretted we didn't do that. We should find someone in Miami, not wait. God knows we could use the help."

"I like that." I smile up at him, my brain already going into planning mode. My fingers itch for colored pens to start making lists. "We'll need to get ahead of the press. Maybe we should write a press release."

"Or Twitter," he says. "We could tweet at each other and act like we're making up online. People will know that's fake, but we could give them a few details, look like we're being transparent, and maybe the coverage will be about how cute we are rather than how we can't control ourselves on set."

"They'll still say that, but getting them to root for us wouldn't hurt." Now I do groan. "I need to call my agent and get my publicist on this. I should have done that an hour ago."

He elbows me. "You would have, if I wasn't so distracting."

Distracting is right.

Blake leans into me, and we stretch out together on the bed. We're stroking each other's arms and shoulders and hair, and I'm pretty sure our hands are about to roam elsewhere and tear each others' clothes off all over again, but for this moment, we just hold each other close, breathe each other in.

"The sexy outfit you had on before wasn't helping," I say. "You know I've always loved a man with a visor full of pinpoint holes."

He laughs. "The crown of branches is definitely way more attractive."

My hand migrates down his chest, feeling the hard, sculpted muscles underneath his t-shirt. "You have been working out."

"Yeah, it was very important that I get into shape . . . to play a *teleporter*. Why does Farpoint walk *anywhere*? They should have made me put on fifty pounds for all the exercise he probably gets."

I laugh, and I think it's probably the most pure, honestly happy laugh I've had in years. I'm giddy with the miracle of being in Blake's arms again, of hearing that he loves me and always has, of the possibilities ahead.

The fear is still there, that he'll eventually realize he was right to leave in the first place, that being with me and all my issues is worse than he remembers. Fear that this will all go badly and I'll be devastated all over again. But I push that fear down the same way I would shove away those flickers of hope, and I focus on right here and now.

Because right here and now I'm with Blake, and he wants to be with me—he still loves me!—and my whole world makes sense in a way I never thought it would again.

ELEVEN

Blake

I'm lying in Kim's hotel room, running my hand lazily down her bare back as she presses against me in bed, my whole body satisfied in this soul-deep way it hasn't been for years, and I'm sifting through memories I'd tried to forget.

"Do you remember when we used to do this?" I ask. "Back before we had the kids. Every once in a while, when we'd have the same days off, we'd just be naked in bed like this for hours and hours. Getting up only to get the delivery food and let the dogs and pig out."

Kim smiles. "Mmm, I do. It was a day like that when I decided that if you asked me to marry you, I was going to say yes."

I groan. "And then it took me almost two more *years* to ask you, because I had no idea you'd already decided that."

She shrugs. "I wanted you to ask when you were ready."

I was ready a long time before I asked—which I did in the bathroom of the Chinese Theater with security outside to keep away the paparazzi who had just witnessed Kim vomit right in the center of the red carpet. We were sitting there, waiting for the results of a pregnancy test brought to us by my agent, because we had to know right then and couldn't wait. That's when I'd realized that this might be my very last chance to ask

Kim to marry me before she'd think it was just because she was pregnant. And nothing could have been further from the truth.

She's heard this before, but I'm about to tell her all over again, when a loud thump sounds through the adjoining door, and I hear Luke shouting, "Mom! We're hooooooooome!"

"Shit." Kim sits upright in bed and draws the covers up around her breasts as if the kids might burst through the door at any moment. From the sounds of pounding, it seems the kids have every intention of doing just that, but the door is locked from this side.

"Okay!" I hear Marguerite say. "Sounds like they're not back from the set yet. You can practice your door drumming when they get back."

There's a loud groan from both of the kids and the squeak of springs as one or both of them flop on the couch.

"Party's over," I say to Kim, reaching over the side of the bed and retrieving my t-shirt. "Are you ready for this?"

Kim clutches the blanket with white knuckles. "Are you sure we should tell them?"

My throat constricts. I know I want this—I've always wanted to be with Kim, and if I'd known what she needed was for me to fight for her, I would have done it a long time ago.

But it's been six years, and there's all this hurt between us now. More than a decade's worth.

"We don't have to if you aren't sure," I say. "You can have time to think about it."

She looks afraid. "Do you want to think about it?"

I reach over and tuck her hair back behind her ear, and this one motion calms me. "There's nothing to think about for me. I want you. I've always wanted you. I wish I could turn back time, but if I can't, then what I want is to not lose one more second of the time we still have."

Kim's blue eyes shine, and she loosens her grip on the blanket. "Really?"

"Really. So let's do this." I find my pants and my boxers and

99

finish getting dressed while Kim fishes new clothes out of her suitcase and tosses the last set into a laundry bag hanging from the closet door. I use a comb and some product from Kim's counter to tame my obvious sex-hair, and Kim does the same. I put on my socks and shoes for good measure, and Kim makes the bed. We do one final sweep for evidence—during which Kim has the forethought to throw away the condom sitting on the nightstand beside the phone. Then she walks to the hall door, cringes, and opens and closes it loudly, like she just walked in.

The knocking is back two seconds later. "Mom?" Luke yells through the door.

Kim wipes her hands on her pants, gives me one last concerned look and unlocks the door.

It flies open before she can get to the handle.

"Mom!" Luke shouts. "You'll never believe what we saw at Legoland! They had a Death Star just like my Death Star but this one was the size of the *real* Death Star!" Luke sees me standing in the room with his mother, but he doesn't even pause, just begins bouncing back and forth between the two of us.

"There is no *real* Death Star!" Ivy shouts from the other room. "Even if there was, this one wasn't the size of a *real* Death Star because the *real* Death Star was the size of a planet—" She breaks off abruptly as she swings around the corner and sees me standing there with my hands in my pockets and probably looking guilty as hell. "What are you doing here?"

"And a dragon, Dad!" Luke yells. "A real life dragon!"

Ivy doesn't even bother to tell Lukas that there's no such thing as a real dragon, and that if there were, it would probably be larger than the Legoland statue. Instead, she's looking between her mom and me, eyes narrowed.

Kim sighs. "Have a seat, Ivy. We'd like to talk to you about something."

"I knew it," Ivy says. "This is about my computer, isn't it? Can I have it back yet?"

"Nope," I say. "Not about your computer."

"And a Lego car that was the size of a really real car and looked like you could really drive it, and I think maybe you could because it had a Lego steering wheel and a Lego gas pedal and maybe one of those really real Lego engines that let you make robots like the one I want for my birthday!"

"Awesome," Kim says. I can tell she's trying, but it still comes out half-hearted.

"My phone?" Ivy says with the last trace of hope in her voice.

"Not your phone, either," I tell her. "Seriously. Sit."

Ivy groans like she's passing a really dramatic kidney stone and flops down on Kim's bed. I grab the two chairs from the table and I sit down in one and Kim takes the other, while Lukas continues to run back and forth yelling something about a steam engine that may or may not have been made out of Legos.

"Hey, buddy," I say. "Have a seat. We need to tell you something."

Luke bounces onto the bed with enough force to jostle his sister, who now both looks and sounds like she's on her deathbed. I give Kim half a smile. She closes her eyes briefly. "Your father and I have decided to date again," she says.

This is enough to make Ivy stop mid-groan and look up in surprise. Even Luke mostly stops bouncing and stares at us.

"Who are you dating?" he asks. "Is it Roger and Simone?"

I can't help but laugh a little at that, though from the look on her face, Kim does not find this as funny.

"Each other," she clarifies.

I reach out and take her hand.

"Oh," Luke says. "Can you both take us to Legoland?"

That was easy. Ivy's eyes narrow again, and I take it we're not going to be so lucky twice. "What do you mean, each other?" she says. "You can't do that. You hate each other."

"We do not," I say. "I love your mother. I've told you that a hundred times."

Ivy rolls her eyes. "Yeah, like, you love her because she's our mom."

"No," I say. "That's what you thought I meant, but it wasn't."

Kim squeezes my hand, and Ivy glares at both of us. "So, what? You guys are going to go out on dates sometimes and leave us with Marguerite? And that's it?"

I glance at Kim. I'm not sure how to answer that. I mean, I pretty much never want to be away from her again, but—

"Honey," Kim says, "the intention is that your dad and I want to be together. So we're going to spend a lot of time together. And with you guys, as a family."

I smile at that, but Ivy's face contorts in horror. "What about the condo?" she asks.

Oops. More things we haven't discussed. "I'll keep the condo for now. But if everything goes well—"

I glance at Kim, and she has that nervous look in her eyes. My impulse is to think that I'm overstepping, that she's not sure she wants any of this.

But she said that she does. She wants me to fight for her, and this time, I'm going to.

"If everything goes well, I'll stay with you guys at the ranch."

Ivy jumps up off the bed. "But I have friends at the condo! Why don't you guys just have sex sometimes and leave everything else the same?"

"*Ivy*," Kim says.

Luke is staring between the three of us like he's not entirely sure what's happening, and I can't really blame him.

"First of all, our sex lives are none of your business," I say to Ivy. "And second, that's not what we want."

"But what about what I want?" Ivy wails. "You're just being selfish. You're not even thinking about us."

Kim is clearly fighting hard to keep her voice even. "Ivy, what is so horrible about your father and I having a relationship?"

"Because you hate each other!" Ivy says again, glaring. "What happens the *next* time you get divorced?"

"*Ivy*," Kim snaps.

"What?" Ivy snaps right back. "Are you saying you won't?"

My stomach ties in knots. I look back and forth between Kim, who looks thoroughly miserable, and Ivy, who is possibly more upset about this than she was about her phone and computer. Lukas has backed up against the headboard of the bed like he just wants to get out of the middle.

I've done this to them. When I walked out on Kim, I hurt every single one of them, and it doesn't matter that it isn't what I intended.

All three of them deserve better than me.

"Ivy," I say. "I think you need to calm down, and then we can discuss this."

"I'm not going to calm down!" Ivy shrieks. "You're ruining my life. Isn't that right, Luke?"

Luke looks alarmed, like he was hoping to just blend into the headboard like a chameleon.

"I don't think Luke is upset about this," Kim says.

"He is!" Ivy insists. "Tell them how upset you are, Luke."

"I'm upset," Luke says. "Very upset."

I believe he is, because Ivy is a force of nature when she's angry.

"Why are you upset, Luke?" I ask.

Luke's eyes widen like I've just asked him to make Sophie's Choice, and he flattens himself even more against the headboard. Ivy glares daggers at him.

"Is it because Ivy's upset?" Kim asks.

Ivy lets out another guttural groan. "You don't even know how bad this is!" she shouts at Luke.

"Okay," Kim says. "Tell us how bad this is."

Ivy crosses her arms and emotes angrily at us. She's always been good at that, ever since she was little. It was cuter when she was two.

I take a deep breath before I speak. "All right. You're obviously too upset to articulate this right now. So I want you to make a list of your specific concerns, and then we will all sit down and address them."

Luke brightens at this. "I want to make a list!"

Of course he does. "Excellent. Let us know when you have those lists made, okay?"

Ivy glowers at us. "It doesn't matter. You're just going to do whatever you want, anyway."

"We're adults, Ivy," Kim says. "But if we can do this in a way that's easier for you, we will."

Ivy huffs and storms out of the room. The three of us physically deflate.

"Sorry about that, Luke," I tell him.

Luke looks at me with wide eyes. "Can I go play with my Legos now?"

"Yes," Kim tells him. "That's a great idea."

Luke flees the room and slams the door behind him. Or maybe Ivy was waiting to slam the door. I can't be sure.

Kim lets out a groan that is a close approximation of Ivy's and slides down in her chair. "That went well. Are you regretting this yet?"

After all these years of missing her, I could never. "No. You?"

She shakes her head.

I only hope that we can get everything under control before she realizes that this is all my fault and decides I'm the one who's not worth fighting for, after all.

TWELVE

Kim

Waking up next to Blake is surreal; there's this moment where I feel like I've been pulled back in time. I expect to be in our old bed in our old house and to roll over and check the baby monitor to see if Luke is rustling around in his crib.

My brain catches up soon enough, and I just lie there in the dark. We're still in the pre-dawn hours, my alarm minutes away from chiming. I breathe in the scent of Blake right up next to me, enjoying the warm weight of his arm draped over my waist. Both of these help with the fears gnawing at the edges of my thoughts, trying to fight their way into the bliss of being back together.

Telling the kids about us was a disaster that I probably should have anticipated. Lukas is an easy-going kid, but Ivy has always been resistant to change. And having her parents back together will be a big change in her life. But I know that's not the whole problem. She's scared, which I understand—I am, too.

After that, we called our publicists and agents, who told us that yes, the news of our grope-fest had indeed spread far and wide. Everyone seemed supportive of our plan to just announce that we're getting back together, via both Blake's Twitter idea and press releases our publicists drafted on the spot. I appreciated the support—not that I wouldn't have told either Josh or my publicist, Tara, to do it anyway if they disapproved, but it made me feel like maybe Blake and I really aren't making some huge crazy mistake.

We're not making a mistake, I tell myself. *The mistake was getting divorced. The mistake was letting things get so bad.*

I let out a slow breath, thinking about the dinner Blake and I had in this very room, just the two of us. Our phones put on sleep mode so no one could disturb us, the reactions of the rest of the world—and even our kids—pushed aside for the night so we could eat and talk and laugh and cry (that last bit only me, because, well, I'm Kim.) So we could just be us.

In part, it was like getting to know each other all over again, learning some of the ways in which the last six years have changed us. But mostly it was just confirming that the man I've loved for so long is, in everything that truly matters, still the same Blake—my best friend and the love of my life.

I only hope he feels the same about me. Based on the glorious, desperate way the night ended, I'm pretty sure he does. I smile with the giddy thrill of it all.

I shift so I can cuddle closer, and my alarm starts braying.

Blake makes a sleepy sound partway between a groan and a laugh. "Oh my god. Is there a donkey in our bedroom?"

I hit the button to shut off the alarm and stretch out against him. "That's a recording of Kramer the burro. I got him a few months ago. He's pretty chatty."

"Right, Kramer. Missing a leg and partially deaf?"

"Yeah," I say, impressed he knows this.

"The kids always fill me in on the latest animals at the ranch," he says, his lips tugging up on one side. "And I may have a really good memory for anything that felt like a connection to you and your life."

I can hear the unspoken words—that the ranch was part of the life that was supposed to be *ours*. Something I always felt, too. The thought that now it can be makes me so incredibly happy.

"Well, that good memory will come in handy, because you have lots of animals to meet, with lots of conditions to remember. Costanza alone—"

Costanza.

I gasp, sitting up so quickly I get a head rush.

"What's wrong?" Blake asks, but I'm already scrambling for my phone.

"Oh my god, I totally forgot about Costanza!" I frantically enter the password and see dozens of texts, which I expected after last night's major bomb-dropping on the press and Twitterverse. I scroll through, looking for Aaron's name. "How could I do that? How could I totally forget my *dog*?"

"Hey, he's going to be fine," Blake says, sitting up and stroking my back, which has gone all kinds of tense. "Your assistant had him, right? We'll make sure he gets compensated for the extra hours and—"

"It's not just that. Costanza has really bad separation anxiety, and he needs meds for his vertigo, and I can't believe I completely forgot about him."

Sure enough, there are a few texts from Aaron. *Hi Ms. Watterson, I heard you weren't planning on coming back to set today. Do you want me to bring Costanza to your hotel?*

Hi again. Just checking in on whether you want me to bring Costanza to you.

Since I didn't hear back from you, I just brought him to my hotel with me. Hope that's okay.

I groan. I have some idea of how Costanza might have handled a night in a strange hotel with a person who is not me, and it's not good.

Blake squeezes my arm, but I'm glad he doesn't try to tell me that it's okay, I had a lot going on yesterday, yada yada yada (in the most *Seinfeld* sense). Because yeah, that's true, but none of that will make me feel better, at least until I know my dog is okay. I text Aaron and apologize, asking about Costanza, and get a text back immediately, despite the pre-dawn hour:

He's good. I gave him his meds and will bring him to the set with me.

I let out a breath of relief.

"Is he okay?" Blake asks.

"Yeah. Aaron's a great assistant. I just feel awful about it."

Blake pulls me in and kisses the side of my head. "We'll make it up to Costanza. And Aaron. Lots of treats for one, lots of fantastic networking contacts for the other. You can decide who gets what."

I smile. Blake has always been good at making me feel better no matter how stressed out I get—at least when I'm not in the throes of a postpartum OCD meltdown.

"The real trick is going to be dealing with all the rest of this," he says, waggling his phone at me, which is bursting with its own share of texts and urgent voice mails from seemingly everyone connected to us or this movie.

"I don't know about you, but I'm divvying most of it up between Tara and Josh. Which I will do in the car on the way to set."

"Good call." Then he leans in, running his hand up my bare thigh. "Though does this mean I don't get to make out with my girlfriend in the backseat of the car?"

I grin, my body flushing with heat. "It means the quicker we get these calls taken care of, the better. But for now, we need to put clothes on."

He groans, but in a good-natured way. Despite how much we both want to stay in bed, the professional part of me is already too embarrassed by costing Troy and the others a full day of shooting yesterday. I'll be damned if I don't show up on time and ready to do my job today, and I know Blake feels the same.

So we get up and shower—this we do individually, because we both know how distracted we'll get taking a shower together. Then we meet back in the kids' room, where Luke is already up and happily playing with Legos. Ivy is buried under a mound of blankets, her hair poofing up over the pillow. She's either asleep or pretending to be, so she can avoid us all.

My heart twists, thinking of her reaction yesterday. She was six when we got divorced; no doubt she remembers the nonstop fighting and tension toward the end.

What happens the next time you get divorced?

I look over at Blake, crouched down to examine Luke's latest creation. The thoughts start bubbling to the surface like water beginning to boil.

What if we can't do this? What if we fail again?
What will be the cost to our kids?

I push the thoughts down and breathe deeply to suppress the rising panic. I'm able to, for now. I try not to worry about the inevitable times when I can't, when the meds and the cognitive techniques won't be enough. Will Blake really want to deal with that all over again?

We give Luke a hug goodbye, and I slip a note onto Ivy's pillow, with a quick drawing of a monkey holding a heart. I'm not a great artist, but she used to love it when I'd put little drawings of animals in her backpack for her to find at school. Granted, that ended a year ago when she deemed herself too old for bad drawings of cute animals from her mother, but I hope she'll still feel the love that's meant by it, especially when it's not at risk of being discovered by anyone her age.

Blake sees it and smiles a little sadly. I'm not sure if he's remembering when I started doing that when Ivy first went to kindergarten, or if he's worried, like I am, about how long it will take Ivy to come around on this huge change we've sprung on her.

Both my security guards and Blake's are waiting out in the hallway for us. They're professionals and have clearly been prepped. They don't even blink at Blake and me holding hands, and they don't ask questions.

Outside the hotel, though, the paparazzi are another thing

entirely. There's a much larger crowd than even on the first day of shooting, spilling out past the hotel valet area and requiring wrangling from police to not totally block the street. I swear every Miami-based paparazzo must be here, as well as however many took the red-eye straight from LA the minute our press release hit the internet. Cameras and microphones are everywhere, voices screaming questions the minute we emerge from the hotel.

"Blake, Kim, are you really back together?"

"Is this reconciliation just a publicity stunt?"

"Kim, Blake, over here, look over here!"

"What do you think Roger will say about this, Kim? Did he have any warning it's over between you two?"

I grit my teeth at the implication that I'm cheating on the guy I broke up with over a year ago. And the publicity stunt thing—I should have expected that, but really?

People try to shove through the barricade of well-muscled security guys the security firm has waiting for just this moment. One woman manages to slip through, and she shoves a microphone so forcefully toward Blake's face that she nearly hits him in the jaw. She's yanked back by security, and we're able to make it through and into the waiting car.

As soon as the doors shut, closing us away from the now-muffled chaos outside, I'm able to breathe again. Blake slumps into the leather seat.

"God, I haven't seen them that riled up since . . ." He trails off, and I squeeze his hand.

"Since the day the news of our divorce broke," I finish for him, and he nods.

"Well, if I'm going to risk getting clocked in the face by a reporter with bad depth perception, I definitely prefer these circumstances." He smiles and the tension eases. I smile back at him.

"Me too."

We make our calls and send our texts and emails. And we do

manage to get a few minutes of making out before we arrive; I'm eternally grateful for tinted windows and discreet drivers who pretend not to know or care what's going on in their backseat.

There's a much smaller crowd of paparazzi waiting when we reach the set, but still sizable enough that it's obvious someone— or probably several someones—let slip today's filming location. There's a security perimeter set up so we don't have to get out of the car until we're well past the screaming crowd, which is clamoring over every car in the hopes that Watterpless is within.

I'm not sure if it was Josh or Camilla or maybe even Sarah or Troy who had the foresight to bulk up security, both here and at the hotel, but I'm glad they did.

Things are better once we're actually in the cordoned-off areas on set, though I notice how many eyes follow us, how many phones are pointed in our direction. Blake and I keep holding hands, and I'm glad all this renewed attention isn't freaking him out. But the truth is, we're Watterpless. We've had years and years to get used to this sort of thing, even if today is on the extreme side.

We're Watterpless, I repeat to myself, that phrase sending a thrill through me.

We're Watterpless again.

That thrill has me smiling, even as pictures are taken of Blake and me giving each other a kiss as we head off to our respective trailers. As I walk into my trailer and—

My smile drops. My trailer reeks of urine, and there, kneeling on the floor and trying to sop it up, is Aaron. And huddled into a quivering ball of boxer nerves over by the couch is Constanza.

"Oh my god, I'm so sorry," I say to both of them.

Costanza hears me and whimpers, and I rush over to kneel by his side. He trembles against me, frantically licking at my face and hair and anything in the remote vicinity of his tongue.

"I'm sorry," Aaron says, though his voice is heavy with exhaustion. "I walked him before bringing him in, but he still pis—um, relieved himself."

I cringe. "Let me guess. On your pants again?"

There's a pause before Aaron replies. "Yep," he says, with a bit more of an edge than usual.

I groan. Costanza hasn't stopped peeing on Aaron's leg since the first day, and I've heard from Sarah's assistant, Gary, that he has to bring all his pants to set with him and get them laundered daily.

"How much damage did he do to your hotel room? I'll obviously pay for it, I just—"

Aaron sits back on his heels, gripping the urine-soaked towel. There are dark circles under his eyes. "It's fine. I mean, I can wash the clothes he peed on. Mainly he just howled all night. I tried petting him, taking him on walks in the middle of the night, everything. The only thing that worked to get him to stop was letting him crawl into bed with me." He stops, but I can tell there's more, and I raise an eyebrow. "I had to cuddle up against him to get any sleep," he finally blurts out. "Like full-body contact. And he kept farting, and I couldn't move away an inch or—" Aaron cuts off, his face getting red, and he presses his lips together tightly, breathing in through his nose. "I'm sorry, Ms. Watterson. I didn't mean to complain, I shouldn't—"

"God, no, Aaron, I'm sorry. You have every right to complain." Though I'm valiantly trying to hold in a giggle at the image of Aaron spooning a huge, gassy, anxiety-ridden dog through the night. "This is totally my fault. You should never have had to take him overnight. But I'm so grateful you did. I owe you, big time."

He makes a gesture like he's trying to dismiss this, but we both know it's true.

"No, really," I say. "I'll make sure you get all new pants when this shoot is done. And any introductions or connections I can help you with—or Blake, too, he'd be glad to help—really, feel free to ask."

Aaron's expression is still tense, but he gives a little smile. "Thanks, Ms. Watterson. I really appreciate that." He stands up. "I got your call sheet and coffee ready." He gestures to the vanity where he always has them set when I get here. "And I'm happy for you and Mr. Pless."

I thank him again and he takes off. Then I sit and hold my trembling dog a little longer, until his nervous shaking turns into loud snores of sleep. "I owe you big time, too," I whisper, kissing his sweet head. "Everything's going to be okay. I'll make sure of it. Me and Blake, the movie, the kids. You. Everything. I'm not going to mess up this time, I promise."

I'm trying to assure myself most of all.

THIRTEEN

Blake

It's hard for me not to grin as I head to my trailer. My hand feels empty without Kim's in it, and I wish we were sharing a trailer so we could spend time together while we get ready for today's shoot, but I'm just so glad to be with her again—and publicly, even—that it softens the sting.

Troy is talking with some of the set people outside my trailer, probably because he wants to catch me as soon as I arrive. They all eye me as I approach, and I'm glad that, if nothing else, it's me he's going to chew out about our stunt yesterday and not Kim.

"Ready to work today?" Troy asks.

"Ready," I say. "I'm sorry about yesterday, and I appreciate your patience with us."

Troy gives me a look that says that patience had nothing to do with it, which is fair. "Pull a move like that again on my set, and you're gone. I don't care who you are. I will replace you."

I meet his eyes. I doubt he really could, but he can sure make our lives on set miserable, and I can't let him put that kind of pressure on Kim. "We're professionals, but we're also people. You knew when you signed on to make this movie that there was likely going to be some drama between us. It's a hard situation for everyone, and we're going to need you to cut us some slack."

"I cut you a whole day of filming," Troy says. "Are there going to be any further interruptions?"

The truth is, I don't know. "We're going to do everything we can to be there when you need us. I can't speak for acts of god, but—"

Troy folds his arms. "I just don't want to hear about any more acts of god destroying my costumes and interrupting my shoots. Keep your acts of god to your off times, all right? I've got my hands full trying to keep the press out, and we've got a movie to make."

I want to punch Troy in the face for trivializing what's happening and for suggesting that the paparazzi is our fault, though I'm realizing now that Troy is probably pissed we didn't consult him before making our announcement. And probably for not waiting until a time deemed appropriate by the marketing department.

"We're all on the same team," I tell him. "We won't let personal stuff interfere with doing our jobs again."

"Good. I'm counting on you to be part of the team." He stalks off, and the beleaguered set people who had skirted away to give us a wide berth trail after him.

I hope Kim isn't going to get that same speech. Pressure from directors tends to get in her head a lot faster than mine, and even I'm feeling the heat.

Kelsey is waiting for me with some new additions to my costume—which has either been thoroughly cleaned or is an entirely new set. She raises her eyebrows at me like she expects a story, and I break into a grin. Even Troy's anger can't ruin today, because I'm back with Kim, and everyone knows it.

"Someone's happy this morning," Kelsey says.

My idiot-grin widens. "Hell yes, I am."

"I read your announcement. When you guys left set yesterday, I assumed it was just exes hooking up, but I know you really wanted this. Congratulations."

"Thanks," I say, then grimace. "I'm so sorry about what I did

115

to the costume."

"It's not the worst thing I've ever seen an actor do to their costume. But if you guys are going to hook up on set, could you please gently remove your costume pieces first? You guys got fake blood in the weirdest places."

I suppose I should be embarrassed about that, but I'm too happy to do anything but laugh. "Noted."

"Okay, so I've made some alterations to your sleeves, hoping to make them easier to get on and off without letting them move around too much on camera. Put these on and let me know what you think. And while you do that, tell me everything. I definitely need to hear the Watterpless dirt."

Kelsey perches on a stool and looks at me expectantly. I take off my shirt and slip into the piece that goes under Farpoint's sleeveless vest. She's right. It is a lot easier to put on.

"There's not a lot of dirt that isn't public," I say. "At least that I can talk about." I'm now one of two people in Kim's life aside from medical professionals who know about her OCD. I'm not about to share that with anyone else. "Oh, here's something. Actually I could use your advice." We've already established Kelsey is closer to my daughter's age than mine, so maybe she'll have some perspective.

"Shoot," Kelsey says.

"This isn't public, but when we told our kids, my daughter kind of flipped out."

"Really? Not happy to have Mom and Dad getting along?"

That's an understatement. "No. She was already pretty mad at us before, and now, apparently, we're ruining her life."

Kelsey smirks. "I bet she's a daddy's girl, huh?"

"Yeah, we've always been close. And I get that it's sudden for her. Hell, it's sudden for us too. Ivy's never been big on change."

"She probably doesn't want to share you," Kelsey says with a shrug.

"That's not really the part I need advice with. You're much closer to the rebellious teenage years than I am."

116

"Okaaaay." Kelsey gets up and comes over, checking the fit of the costume piece around my wrists.

"So Ivy's started talking with this boy online. And he's fifteen."

"How old is she?"

"Twelve," I say. "And so we took away her phone and her computer, mostly because she lied to Kim about him, but also because she's talking to a fifteen-year-old boy online."

Kelsey wrinkles her nose. "Yeah, you're screwed. I can already tell you're screwed."

"So I think some of her being upset about us is more that she's upset *at* us, you know? But no matter how many times we explain it, she doesn't seem to get that we're trying to protect her."

"No, and she never will. You're SOL, dude. Because the worst thing you can do is tell her not to see him, but it's also the only thing you *can* do, because she's twelve years old. Good luck with that." She picks up the leather vest. "Okay, put on the rest of your costume and let me see how it fits underneath."

I groan. "We really are screwed, aren't we?"

She shrugs. "At least you and Kim are in this together? That is seriously bad timing, though."

It is. "I feel like I messed everything up years ago, when we got divorced. If I had just stuck around and tried harder, none of us would be in this mess. What if I screw it up again? That would be even worse for them."

Kelsey helps me into the outer vest. Makeup will apply the visor later, which I notice is also back, shiny and clean. "Then don't fuck it up, right?"

"Ha," I say. "If only it were so easy."

"Maybe it is. Maybe I should get you one of those little plastic bracelets printed with it. Don't fuck it up, Blake. DFIU. I wonder if there's a market for those."

I smile. "Good to know my problems are profitable to someone. It sure isn't my family."

Kelsey stands back and looks at my costume, then scrunches up her face. I'm not sure if this is a comment on my appearance

117

or my life. "Okay, maybe if you hadn't messed up, you'd still be married. But I don't think that you still being married would have any effect on your daughter and this boy. That was caused by you having a girl. And you have, like, six more years before she's not legally your responsibility anymore! I don't envy you."

I close my eyes. "She's always been such a good, responsible kid."

"Ooooh, those are the worst. When a good girl goes bad, watch out."

I shake my head. Ivy's only twelve years old, and all she's done is talk to an older boy online. I shouldn't overreact. Just because she's whining for her phone back and mad at me and Kim for changing her life doesn't mean that she's going to make any big mistakes.

She's Ivy, and we've always been able to talk. "Maybe I just need to talk to her more. Or give her space." Those two things are opposites, and either one could be the right answer. "I've been a parent for twelve years, so you'd think I'd have figured it out by now."

"If it were me, I'd go with the space option," Kelsey says. "But I'm not a parent. And given what I put my parents through, I have a whole truckload of karma waiting to drop on my head if I ever do decide to have a kid."

When I'm all zipped into Farpoint's overcoat, Kelsey hands me his shoe inserts. "Put these on, and I'll be back to make sure they fit okay today. We're trying to get them so they don't rub your heels, but the foam is giving me fits." She peers out of the trailer. "Meanwhile, I see Aaron giving that dog a walk, and I'm going to go flirt with him. Give me a couple minutes."

"How's that going? You and Aaron, I mean?"

Kelsey frowns. "He seems oddly immune to my advances. I'm starting to wonder if my gaydar is faulty. He doesn't give off the vibe, but maybe."

"Look, I owe you for the costume trouble. I'll talk to Kim and see what we can find out."

"Totally!" she says with a grin. "I will absolutely collect payment in information."

"And maybe we'll be able to set you up." I realize I'm turning into one of those happy relationship people who feels the need to get everyone else into a relationship, too, but whatever. Kelsey wants to date this guy, and he's Kim's assistant. We should be able to facilitate something or at least find out if he's available.

In fact, that sounds like it could be fun.

FOURTEEN

Kim

The next couple days become a strange blur—a nice rosy-tinged, happy one, mostly, due to the thrill of being with Blake again. Filming this movie with Blake is now an entirely different experience than it had been previous to our hookup in my trailer. It's almost like it was back at the beginning, back when we fell in love on *Over It*. We're being professional, showing up on time—which means several minutes early—for each shoot, doing our jobs, but we can barely keep our hands off each other in between.

I'd feel significantly better if the situation with Ivy were resolved, but she's spent the last few evenings avoiding both of us, saying she's working on her list. She's enough my daughter that I imagine she really has been working on it—and that said list will end up being several pages long, with concerns ranked in order of importance.

But whereas before being on set was something to endure, with all the pain acting with Blake again caused, now I'm back to feeling the excitement of what I get to do for a living—I'm a frigging action hero. And I get to make a movie with the man I love, who loves me. Who is also a frigging action hero. It's awesome, and we are so lucky in so many ways.

Being with Blake has always been good for giving me that perspective.

Today's shoot is on a downtown Miami street, closed off by police and bustling with extras filling in for pedestrian traffic. I'm not in this particular scene, but even though it's roughly a million degrees out, and I could be cooling off in my trailer, I love to watch Blake work.

I also love to tease him about having to wear his costume when I've got another hour I can spend in jean shorts and a tank top.

Troy yells out for everyone to get back to their marks. The extras shuffle around, and Blake and Bertram find their taped Xs on the sidewalk to run through it again—a scene in which Farpoint is newly arrived on Earth and looking wide-eyed at the dubious wonders of downtown Miami. He's walking with Naked Mole Rat (wearing a regular business suit, but still looking like a hairless man who recently emerged from a flour explosion), who is trying to convince Farpoint to join forces with him against a "lawless enemy" (me), but Farpoint can't stop staring at the weird people and clothes and yippy purse dogs.

The scene itself—choreographed with pinpoint precision for the long, continuous shot that is one of Troy's directorial trademarks—is fairly funny as is, but Blake's expressions and comic timing elevate it. Even though I've seen it run several times through the monitor set up where I'm hanging out behind Troy, I still laugh at all the right spots. So does Sarah Paltrow, who isn't as humorless as I assumed from that first day, and the handful of PAs who are also watching. Even Troy chuckles when Farpoint passes the little boy wearing the Batman costume, and they both give each other wary looks.

"Aaaand cut," Troy calls out. "That's gold, everyone. Good job."

The extras mill about, and the little kid in the Batman costume runs over to Blake and starts engaging him in an animated conversation, judging by the big hand motions the kid is making. His mom jogs over to him from across the street, concern on her face—the extras and bit players are under instruction not to mob Blake (or me or Bertram) between scenes—but Blake crouches down by the kid and is happily chatting with him, even though I'm sure he's dying to get out of the sun (not to mention that leather costume).

I can't stop smiling.

"Glad to see *someone's* enjoying themselves in this heat," Bertram says, approaching me while dramatically patting the sweat from his face with a handkerchief.

"Well, I have been in the shade for the last two hours." I take a nice long sip from my iced latte. "And I'm not suffocating under a layer of white body powder. You should try *that*."

"Very funny, Kimberly. Remind me to show the same sympathy when you're back in your fishnets and stripper heels." He slumps into the chair Sarah just evacuated next to me, then follows my gaze to where Blake is letting the kid try on his golden pinpoint visor. "I'm always skeptical about getting back together with exes, you know."

"I do know," I say. He's told me a variation of this a half-dozen times over the last couple days, usually followed by some story involving yet another failed—but racy—reconciliation with Marcus. I twist the straw in the plastic cup, and it makes a low squeaky sound.

Bertram looks over at me. "I must say, though, these last few days you've been much more like the Kim Watterson I remember from our first Hemlock movie." He pauses. "Unguardedly happy."

I smile over at him. I found out I was pregnant with Luke during the filming of *Hemlock*. The OCD was at a low ebb, and Blake and I were in a really good place again. I was so happy. Unguardedly so, even.

It breaks my heart to think of how little happiness I've had in the last six years that could be described that way. I've always been a guarded person, a careful one—Blake is the only man who's ever made me feel like I could let my guard down. Before a couple days ago, I would have said that only made it all hurt more, but I'm no longer so sure.

Maybe it would have hurt just as much, anyway. And those walls I put back up toward the end of the marriage were the very things that cost me everything.

What scares me is that I'm not sure I know how to keep them from coming back.

"So you approve, then," I say.

Bertram gives me a wry smile. "Like you've ever needed my approval, Kimberly." He shrugs. "I am happy if you're happy. And that face of his would certainly be a nice thing to wake up to in the morning."

"His *face*, huh?" I tease. "That's the part you'd like to wake up to?"

Bertram snickers. "Well, I wouldn't say no to—"

"Bertram!" booms out a voice, like he's trying to be heard from the cheap seats, even though he's only steps behind us. We both jump, and Bertram audibly groans.

I don't need to turn around to see that it's Peter Dryden, Farpoint's on-screen nemesis and quickly becoming Bertram's off-screen one.

"There you are, you son of a gun," Peter says, clapping Bertram on the shoulder. Bertram glares down at Peter's hand. "I'm beginning to feel like you're avoiding me," Peter continues, with a chuckle that implies he couldn't imagine anything of the sort. Then, before Bertram can reply, Peter grips my shoulder as well. His hands are clammy on my skin, and I have to stifle a grimace. "And hello to you, Kim. You are looking positively radiant today, as always." He gives me a long look. "It's a shame my hit show, *Cuffs*, was a little before your day. You would have made an incredible Sergeant Delana."

From the way he says that—and the way his gaze dips briefly down to my breasts—I can only assume Sergeant Delana was his romantic lead. Probably off-screen, as well. Peter Dryden, while pretentious and skeezy, was probably fairly attractive in those days, though he's been botoxed all to hell since.

123

"I was probably filming diaper commercials back then." I'm not actually sure about this, since I have no idea when *Cuffs* was on, but I figure a reminder of our large age gap isn't a bad idea.

Peter frowns, but unfortunately doesn't take his hand off my shoulder. Or Bertram's.

"You know, Bertram," Peter intones, "our next scene is an important one. Perhaps we should try again that technique I taught you the other day. Have you told Kim about it?" Seemingly without hearing Bertram's muttered "Good god, not this," Peter looks back at me.

"It's a spectacular technique for bonding two actors before a scene," Peter says. "For connecting on a deep level."

"Really? Sounds fascinating." I raise an eyebrow at Bertram, who slumps deeper in his chair.

"I'm always seeking new ways to improve my craft, as we all are, of course. To truly find the soul in the art . . ." Peter continues to drone on, but my attention is back to Blake, who, after giving the kid a high five, is walking toward us, smiling at me with that gorgeous, heart-melting grin of his.

His assistant, Cassie, hands him a bottle of chilled water—Bertram glowers, probably wondering why in the hell *his* assistant isn't here with water—and Blake walks up beside us just as Peter dives into describing the actual technique.

" . . . And the true beauty of this technique—as I explained to Sir O'Dell here, when I was teaching it to him—is in its simplicity. It's called the Hug Connection, and it is just that. Two professionals, spending two full minutes doing nothing more than hugging one another. Staring into each other's eyes. Connecting."

My eyes widen, imagining Peter and Bertram hugging and staring into each other's eyes for two minutes. Bertram squirms miserably under Peter's grasp.

"I gave him twenty seconds," Bertram says flatly, turning his glare to me as if daring me to say anything.

"And even that made our scene tenfold better!" Peter squeezes both our shoulders, and I can see Blake trying to hold in a laugh. "Which is why we should do the full two minutes before our next scene. Really utilize the full capabilities—"

"Sorry, chap," Bertram says, jumping up from his seat. "I've got my acupuncturist waiting for me. I'm terribly late. I will see you later, Kimberly, Blake."

"Perfect, I'm headed that way myself," Peter says, lighting up. He turns to Blake, conveniently not seeing how Bertram looks like he's considering whether acupuncture needles can be used as murder weapons. "Blake, why don't you tell Kim about how well that technique worked for us? And Bertram, I have more thoughts on how we can really find the spirit of the dialogue in the—Bertram, you scoundrel, wait up!"

Peter scrambles to catch up with Bertram, who is all but fleeing to his trailer. I look back at Blake, whose cheeks are red. That's confirmation enough, but I'm still going to ask.

"Please," I say, "tell me you and Peter Dryden had a 'Hug Connection.'"

Blake groans. "Before our first scene together. He called it 'profound.' I called it the most awkward two minutes of my entire life."

I laugh so hard that tears spring to my eyes.

Blake's smile turns soft, incredulous. "Totally was worth it, though, just to hear you laugh like that. God, I've missed that." He sits next to me and links his fingers through mine.

I smile back at him. "Yeah, me too."

"So my publicist is breathing down my neck about getting interviews set up," Blake says. "You have any thoughts on that?"

I chew on the inside of my cheek. Tara's been doing the same to me, and I get it—other than our much re-tweeted reconciliation and our official press releases, we've both gone radio silent about the future of Watterpless, and the press is going nuts for more. I've been avoiding it as much as possible, mainly because I have no desire right now to deal with the public reaction any more than absolutely necessary. Like doing so will somehow pop our happy little bubble.

We're Watterpless, and this is part of the price we pay for the careers we have. But thinking about all the interviews and endless questions, all the attention on what caused our divorce in the first place, which will mean more half-truths, because I'm not even remotely ready for the world to know about my diagnosis . . .

I can feel worries starting to churn in my mind like I've hit some mental spin cycle button. I look down at my latte, swirling the melting ice cubes around.

"I've already got an on set interview tomorrow with *Entertainment Weekly*," I say. "It was scheduled weeks ago." That reporter is probably shitting themselves at their good fortune— the opportunity to get the first real scoop since the news broke. "I was thinking of just keeping to the press release party line, you know? We're dating again, we're spending as much time with each other and our kids as we can—that sort of thing. Mostly keep the focus on the movie."

Blake nods. "Troy will be happy with that."

There's something about the way he looks out at the crowd of extras being herded into place for the next scene, rather than looking at me, that makes me feel the need to ask, "But you aren't?"

His eyes cut back to me, and he frowns a little. "No, it's not that. I think that sounds like a good strategy."

I can't tell if he's being totally honest about this; we've had so many years apart, pretending to feel okay when we really weren't.

"Cassie thinks she's found us a good therapist," Blake says suddenly, studying his recently-trimmed fingernails.

"That's good," I say, but the spin cycle speeds up. Is he worried about what the therapist will say about us? What if the therapist convinces him how hard it is to live with someone with my condition?

I squeeze the arm of the chair with my free hand. The

what-ifs can pull me under like a riptide if I let them, but I can't. Nothing will pop the bubble faster than an OCD panic disaster.

Distraction doesn't always work, but I give it a try anyway.

"Check it out," I say, gesturing to the part of the sidewalk that's been turned into a craft services station. Behind the tables spread with food, and in front of a video game store that's closed down for the afternoon, Aaron is standing with Costanza on a leash, talking to Kelsey.

Blake looks over there. "Go, Kelsey. He looks pretty happy, too. Maybe she doesn't need our help, after all."

Aaron *is* smiling widely at something she's saying, so I think for a moment he's right. But then Aaron hands the leash over, and Kelsey starts walking Costanza down the street, her curls bouncing with each step.

"Or maybe he was just happy to get a break from Costanza duty." I love my dog like crazy, but I can't blame the kid for this—I get that not everyone is an animal person to begin with, and getting pissed on daily certainly wouldn't help. Nor did the whole spooning situation.

Kelsey looks over her shoulder, as if to see if Aaron is checking her out as she walks away, but he isn't. He's tapping furiously on his phone.

"Huh," Blake says. "Yeah, that's not good."

"He could be really busy. He does have other duties as my assistant beyond walking Costanza."

"Or he's gay."

I can tell by the mischievous gleam in his eye that Blake has got a plan here, and I'm pretty sure I know what it is, but I can't resist playing along. And focusing on Aaron and Kelsey does make for a nice distraction.

"Or he's got a girlfriend," I say.

"I suppose there's no way to know." Blake sighs dramatically.

"You want me to go find out, don't you? Because you think it'll be funny to watch me try to get this information without giving away our plan to hook him up with Kelsey."

Blake shrugs. "I mean, Kelsey really likes him, and you and I do think it would be fun to set them up, and it would be a shame if we were all just wasting our efforts—"

"Fine. I'll do it. If only to prove I can."

Blake holds up his hands. "I never doubt what Kim Watterson can do when she puts her mind to it. Never have, never will."

I glare at him, but it's totally fake, and he knows it. This, too, reminds me of the old days on set, when we'd dare each other to do stupid things, like refilling a co-star's water bottle with vodka or sneaking one of the fake corpse heads into the director's bathroom. Nothing that would cause anyone real trouble or get us a rep as being hard to work with—Blake knows how much that would bother me, and honestly, he wouldn't love it either.

Finding out whether my assistant is gay or has a girlfriend isn't exactly sneaking movie props around. But I'm not about to back down from a challenge, especially an easy one.

Except . . .

The minute I reach my assistant, and say, all too brightly, "Hey, Aaron!" I realize this may not be as easy as I thought.

Aaron looks up from his phone, surprised. And with a bit of a guilty expression. "Ms. Watterson," he says. He stuffs his phone in his pocket. "Kelsey from wardrobe offered to take Costanza on his walk. I hope that's okay."

This would be the perfect segue to bring up Kelsey, but I'm not supposed to let him know we want to set them up.

"Oh, yeah, totally," I say, sounding like a far more casual person than I actually am. And maybe a little bit like I've taken up smoking weed.

This would have been easier if I'd created a character to play beforehand. A character who understands the art of subtlety. But it's too late now.

"I've taken care of the schedule for your interview tomorrow and emailed that to you. And I moved your appointment with your trainer back an hour, like you asked."

"Great. All great." I pause. "So, I realized the other day that I don't feel like I've taken the time to get to know you. You know, where you grew up, what kind of movies you like, if you have a girlfriend."

Uh-oh. I put too much emphasis on that last one. His eyebrows rise, and I feel myself flush.

Shit. I'm his boss. Does he think I'm hitting on him? That could be sexual harassment. Could he accuse me of sexual harassment just for *asking* if he has a girlfriend? What would that do to my career?

"I'm not—" I start, shaking my head. "I mean, I'm with Blake now. Like, we're together. Romantically."

"Um, yeah. I'm aware." Aaron looks at me like I've lost my mind. Which I apparently have, along with all powers of normal human interaction.

I resist the urge to glare back at Blake, who must have known this would happen. He knows how easily I get flustered when I have to talk around things.

But I also can't fail in the challenge. I never do.

"Right," I say. "So I'm not hitting on you."

"I got that." Aaron looks a little insulted now.

"I just like to know about my assistants' lives, you know? Get to know who they really are. And their girlfriend—or boyfriend, or spouse, whatever—is part of that."

"Okay," Aaron says slowly. "I don't have any of those right now."

Well, that's one question answered. No current relationship.

"Right now," I say. "But you did?"

"Um, yeah. I've had girlfriends." He blinks. "Are you wanting to find someone to talk to about Blake? Because I'm not really a relationship expert or anything, and I'm not sure I—"

"No," I say quickly. "No, nothing like that." God, I need to be done with this conversation. And pray Aaron doesn't report to some tabloid what a nutcase Kim Watterson is. From now on, I will be the picture of professionalism as far as my assistant is concerned. "Never mind. Thanks for the work on my schedule. And with Costanza. I'd like him to get some extra time at that dog park this afternoon, if possible."

"Yeah, sure," Aaron says. "Of course."

I turn and walk back to Blake, shaking my head at the wide grin he's giving me.

"How'd it go?" he asks, all too casually.

I punch him in the shoulder, and he winces. "That good, huh?" he asks.

"I, being me, managed to accidentally hit on him, then reject him, then—I *think*—imply that maybe he's never been in a relationship."

Blake fights valiantly to hold in a laugh and fails. The sound of it makes my embarrassment worth it—pretty much exactly like he said about his Hug Connection.

"But," I say with a smile, "I found out that he is not gay, and he doesn't have a girlfriend or wife. So I got the information, anyway."

Blake slings his arm around my waist and pulls me up against him. "That's my Kim."

I could hear him say those words forever.

FIFTEEN

Blake

My assistant Cassie spent most of a day finding us a therapist in the Miami area who is trustworthy enough to handle celebrity clients, doesn't balk at the idea of handling paparazzi, and can see us on short notice. I gather we're paying through the nose for all the hassle this is creating for the therapist, but she still found a highly recommended marriage counselor who's willing to meet with us the next evening in his basement office at his home in a gated community. It sounds like an excellent setup—private, secluded, and most importantly, immediate.

All the way there, Kim jitters her leg up and down, looking nervously out the window. I stretch an arm around her and pull her closer—at least as far as the seatbelts will allow. "What's wrong?" I ask.

She shrugs, then sighs. "I'm afraid the therapist will say we're all wrong for each other. That we shouldn't be getting back together at all, let alone this quickly."

"If he says that, then we find another therapist."

Kim seems to shrink beneath my arm. "But what if he's right?"

I know it's mostly fear talking, but it still stings to hear that she thinks this is possible. "Do you want to be with me?"

Kim nods. "So much."

I never get tired of hearing her say that. "Then I don't care if we're right for each other. I want to be with you, and I'm going to do everything I can to make it work."

Kim still doesn't seem sure, and it terrifies me.

The driver enters the code to the gated community and pulls through, and the gate swings closed behind us. I can see a couple of cars parking on the street behind us—paparazzi who followed us from the hotel. Another benefit of meeting in a residential neighborhood is that it'll take longer for them to figure out that we're seeing a therapist, if they figure it out at all. I'm not concerned about news of this being public—getting help is a good thing, and I wish we'd done it a long time ago—but I know it'll bother Kim if it hits the gossip sites.

We pull up in front of a house, and Kim puts on her sunglasses before we leave the car. Our therapist must be waiting for us, because he steps out before we even reach the door and introduces himself, then directs us around to the business entrance.

Dr. Welsley is an older guy, probably in his late fifties or early sixties, but he's in good shape—the kind of guy who uses a calorie counting fitness app and juices his own organic smoothies. The grounds of his house are carefully manicured. He walks us around to a glass door with slotted blinds encased in the window and lets us into a spacious den that's been turned into an office. There's a spotless desk with a computer, a huge bookcase covered in psychology books and a wide selection of travel books from all over the world.

Kim's gripping my hand tightly, and I squeeze reassuringly. The truth is, I'm nervous. If anyone's about to be told that they aren't right for this relationship, it's going to be me. Besides, Kim's done this whole therapy thing before, and I'm realizing I should have asked her more questions about what it's like.

Dr. Welsley sits in a big, leather armchair and offers us a love seat across from him. I always pictured therapy happening in a tiny office, and in this large space, I feel exposed.

"So," Dr. Welsley says. "Tell me why you're here."

"We're divorced," I say. "That was a huge mistake, and we want to be together again. But since we messed things up so badly last time, we need help."

Dr. Welsley smiles and picks up a notepad from the coffee table between us. "Why don't you start at the beginning, so I can get some perspective on your relationship."

We tell him the entire story, beginning with how we met. Kim and I go back and forth, swapping stories of how things used to be and how they started to go wrong. I talk about always feeling helpless, unable to make her happy, and she says that she always felt like she was making me miserable, that someday I was going to realize she wasn't worth it. And then, from her perspective, I did.

"That's not what happened, though," I say. "I felt like I was hurting her, and for her sake, I needed to stop."

We tell him briefly about getting back together, and I realize that most of our session has gone by, just telling him our history. A lump forms in my throat.

It isn't enough. Not that I expect one therapy session to solve everything, but we need help *now*.

"All right," Dr. Welsley says. "Blake, I want you to tell me about Kim."

"What?" I ask.

"Tell me about Kim," Dr. Welsley says. "Pretend she's not here. How would you describe her to me?"

"We're almost out of time," I tell him. "Don't you have any advice for us?"

Dr. Welsley laughs. "You're paying me by the hour, Blake. We can stay here all night if you need to. Trust me on this."

I take a deep breath. "Kim is my favorite person in the entire world," I say. "She's smart and driven and wonderful. She's a fantastic mom, and I can't imagine wanting to share kids with anyone else." I look over at her. There are tears in her eyes, and I feel some starting to burn behind mine, too. "I love her more

133

than anything," I say, and Kim reaches over and takes my other hand.

"And does she have any faults?" Dr. Welsley asks.

I shrug. "Sure. Mostly that she's too hard on herself, and she worries too much about letting other people down."

Kim looks like she wants to argue, but she doesn't.

Dr. Welsley smiles. "Thank you. Kim, would you tell me about Blake?"

I'm suddenly embarrassed—I don't want Kim to feel like she has to say nice things about me just because I did about her. I was only being honest. "You can tell him the truth," I say.

Kim hesitates, and I brace myself. I've hurt her so badly; she can't help but have some negative things to say. "Blake is incredible," she says. "He's a deeply good person, patient and kind. He's an excellent actor—he has a gift that, with all my years of experience, I had to struggle to keep up with. He's a committed father, and he's great with the kids. He's fun to be around, and I know he hates it when I say that, because sometimes he feels like that's all he is. But he makes me laugh, and I don't think he understands what a gift that is to someone like me who takes life too seriously."

I close my eyes. I want to argue with her. A person who's patient doesn't abandon their spouse when things get hard. I don't know how she can speak so highly of me. Those things weren't true when we were together, and they certainly aren't—

"Blake," Dr. Welsley says. "It seems like that's hard for you to hear."

I open my eyes. The tears are very close now, and I don't want to cry in front of Kim. "I guess I don't think that's true."

"Which part?" Dr. Welsley asks.

"All of it. I mean, yeah, I make her laugh, but it's nothing compared to what she gives me."

"It's not nothing," Kim says. "And that wasn't an exhaustive list of everything I love about you."

"Shouldn't she have to talk about my faults?" I'm suddenly desperate to hear them, like I'm more comfortable with those than the good things.

Dr. Welsley is right. This is all hard for me to hear.

"Blake underestimates himself," Kim says. "He thinks that because he fell into his career without really trying, he doesn't deserve it. I don't know about the last six years, but when we were married, he felt like he was pretending, and someday people were going to realize that he couldn't really act, that he didn't belong."

"Imposter syndrome," Dr. Welsley adds. Kim nods.

"It's not a syndrome if it's true," I say. I'm not sure how this conversation became all about me, but I guess I'm the reason we got divorced, so it's relevant. "You know how I got into acting? I had a friend who was a casting assistant on a beach movie, and she thought I was the right type for a part they needed to cast. So she asked me to come in, and I was like, sure, whatever. Then I showed up to the audition and acted like a person, and they fell all over themselves and hired me for this side part. My friend helped me figure out how to get an agent, which was easy because I already had a part, and she just kept getting me roles."

"So you credit your friend and your agent with your success," Dr. Welsley says.

"Yeah, in the beginning." I don't see why this is such a bad thing. It is, in fact, what happened, and just because I'm a movie star and people want to treat me like I'm special doesn't make it true. "Then I met Kim, and she's the reason I really made it. I've always credited her with my success, even when we were divorced."

"You are divorced," Dr. Welsley says.

"Right." I cringe. I've been thinking of her like she's my wife again, even though we aren't remarried. It seems strange for her to go back to being my girlfriend. She hasn't been that in over twelve years. We have kids together now, and so much history. "But the point is that she's the one who taught me how to build a career. Without her, I would have wandered from part to part, taking whatever romantic comedies got thrown at me until I stopped being relevant. But Kim talked me into auditioning for lots of things. She convinced me that if I wanted to have a long-term career, I needed to branch out, try different roles, intentionally evolve my image. She's the reason I did indie films. I wanted to see if I could play a bad person, so I did a film where I played a hit man, and then I played an addict and a serial killer. It was fun, and I liked it, so I kept looking for roles like that, which is why I am where I am. I never would have done that if it wasn't for Kim."

"Is that true, Kim?"

Kim shakes her head, and I want to argue before she even speaks, but I hold my tongue. I don't want the therapist to think I won't listen to her.

Do I not listen to her?

"Blake had so much natural talent," she says. "But he didn't know the business. So yeah, he learned some things from me, just like I learned some things from him."

I roll my eyes. "What could you possibly—"

"I learned how to enjoy my job," she cuts back in. "And I know Blake is going to say that's not important, but as someone who worked this job since I was a kid, it was everything. I took it so seriously that it became just like any other job. But seeing it all through Blake's eyes—he made it magical. The way it ought to be. He helped me remember how fantastically lucky I am to be able to act for a living, and when I was with him, it all felt like a fairytale."

My throat closes. "I felt that way, too."

"But he gives me too much credit. I didn't talk him into taking those roles. I just suggested that he could. He did all the work himself."

I open my mouth to disagree, but she keeps talking. "And Blake will tell you it wasn't work, but he worked his ass off for those roles."

I rub my forehead. "I did some work. But I wouldn't have if it weren't for—"

Dr. Welsley sits forward in the chair. "Blake, why do you

think you have such a hard time taking credit for your success?"

"Because I don't deserve credit for it."

"You're a very successful actor, who by all accounts is a wonderful father and such a good person that even his ex-wife has only good things to say about him. Yet you don't think you deserve credit for any of it. Why is that?"

I shake my head. I'm starting to get angry, and while I know that is irrational, I can't help it. "What Kim has to say about me says more about her than it does about me."

Kim sighs. "That's not true." She looks like she's not quite done, and I lean back on the love seat.

"Go ahead," I tell her. "Say whatever you want to."

But I'm not prepared for what she says.

"It's because of his childhood," Kim says. "Blake's dad is kind of a hard-ass, and Blake's always been a fun-loving person. His dad used to call him a screwup for goofing off. He told him he was a baby every time he cried, until finally Blake just stopped."

The tears are all too close right now, and I look out the window instead of at her, fighting them back. I'd forgotten I told her about that. I told her a lot of things, but I didn't realize she remembered.

"And he was always told in school that he was stupid," Kim continues. "He wasn't diagnosed with dyslexia until he was almost fourteen. He still has a hard time reading. It was one of the first things he told me about himself when I met him, because he was sitting on set spending time with the script. He always needs extra time, and he hates last-minute changes, but he works so hard to make up for it, so it never affects his performance. I remember being so impressed that he didn't hide it, but the truth is that he still believes he's not smart. Not being able to read, it affects everything. Blake is so intelligent, but he doesn't feel like he fits the stereotype of a smart person, because smart people read. Our daughter Ivy learned to read early, and I think a lot of that was the praise that she got from her dad for it. He was so proud of her for not being like him, when really

137

she is, in so many ways."

The corners of my eyes are burning. That's true, about Ivy, and I know Luke has picked up on it. I hate myself for it, because if he's inherited my problems—and the genetic odds and early indicators suggest that he has—

I'm going to make him feel exactly the same way I do.

"I'm sorry," I say.

"For what?" Dr. Welsley asks.

Kim's brows draw together, like she doesn't know what I'm apologizing for either.

Even I'm not sure. I find myself picking at the beads on the decorative pillow I'm smooshed up against and manage to stop before I pull one off. "For being messed up, I guess. It affects our family, and I'm sorry."

Kim laughs, and I turn to stare at her.

"Blake," she says. "I'm the one with crazy obsessions that drive us both insane. I'm the one who's messed up and hurts our family."

"Maybe," Dr. Welsley says, in a way that indicates he doesn't think there's much "maybe" about it, "you both have things to work on that have negatively affected your family and your relationship, and that's okay, because it's part of being human."

Both Kim and I glare at him. She doesn't like this prospect any more than I do.

"I guess," Kim says, "that my main worry is that I'm too broken. That Blake won't be able to be happy with me, because I'm too difficult to live with."

My heart aches. "I'm so sorry I made you feel that way."

"I'd like you to consider," Dr. Welsley says, "that perhaps she feels that way, but you didn't make her."

That would be nice, but it isn't true. "I left her for having a mental illness."

"No," Kim says. "You didn't know about it."

"It doesn't matter if I knew," I argue. "I did it all the same."

"Would you have left if you knew?" Dr. Welsley asks.

It's not really a question. I've already told him that I wouldn't have. "No."

"Then I'd say it mattered quite a bit."

Kim sucks her lips inward. "I should have been more honest with you. If I hadn't been so afraid that you'd leave if you knew how crazy I was, then—"

"See?" I say. "I made you feel like I'd leave you for having problems, and then I *did*. How can you say it wasn't my fault?"

She sighs in frustration, and my chest tightens. I recognize that sigh. It was the beginning of a lot of fights we had, and the last thing I want is to fight with her now. I'm feeling the same fears now that she felt in the car. Does this mean that I'm not good enough for her? Have they both just realized that we can't do this?

"It sounds to me," Dr. Welsley says, "like you both need to work on forgiving yourselves."

I don't like the sound of that at all. "I don't deserve forgiveness for what I did to my family."

"Kim," Dr. Welsley says. "Have you forgiven Blake for what he did to your family?"

Kim hesitates. "I don't think Blake did anything wrong. I drove him away."

"I left you," I say, and it comes out sharper than I mean it to.

"That's true," Dr. Welsley says. "Kim, can you forgive Blake for that?"

Kim thinks about that for a long moment, and I'm afraid she's going to say no. "I was angry about it for a long time," she says. "That he didn't fight for me, that he didn't want to stay. But now that I know what really happened, yes. I think I forgave him immediately, because I don't think it was really his fault."

Dr. Welsley nods. "And Blake, do you forgive Kim for pushing you away?"

"She was sick. It wasn't her fault. It was never her fault she was so miserable with me."

"I wasn't miserable with you," Kim says. "I was miserable

because I was sick."

"Did the divorce hurt you?" Dr. Welsley asks me.

"Yeah," I say. "It hurt like hell, but I'm the one who did that to Kim, and to our kids, and to myself."

"And Kim was a helpless victim."

I pause. Kim is a lot of things, but never helpless. "I wouldn't say that."

"So can you admit that maybe Kim had a part in the dissolution of your relationship, the way most relationships that dissolve have fault on both sides?"

When he puts it that way, it does seem more reasonable. I still want to insist it was all on me, but I can see that I'm being stubborn. "Yeah, okay," I say. "That makes sense."

"And can you forgive her for it?"

"Of course. Absolutely."

Kim looks at me like this is a revelation, when really, I feel like her part in it was so small that I don't know how I could help but forgive her.

"So if you've forgiven each other, then it only makes sense that you should forgive yourselves, doesn't it? If even your ex-spouse isn't bitter, then it seems unreasonable to hold on to that pain."

"It does," I say. "But I can't help it."

Kim nods, and it breaks my heart that she feels the same way.

"It's really not your fault," I tell her.

"Well, it's really not yours, either," she says.

Dr. Welsley smiles.

"What?" I ask him. "You're *happy* about this?"

"Oh, I'm thrilled," Dr. Welsley says. "Most divorced people have some level of contempt for each other, but you two very clearly love each other, not just in theory, but in practice."

He's right that I love Kim more than anything. And by some miracle, she still loves me. That has to mean something.

"So," Kim says in a small voice, "do you think we have a chance?"

"I think you have better than that," Dr. Welsley says. "I think if you're both willing to work at it, you're going to be fine. But you do have real problems, so it'll take work."

I nod. This is what I thought we were here for. "So what do we do?"

"I have two suggestions. One is that you both work on forgiving yourselves for the past. There's nothing you can do about your divorce now. You need to work forward and heal."

I'm pretty sure he's right about that. I just wish I knew how.

"And second, I've observed that you both take far too much responsibility for each other's happiness."

We both stare at him in stunned silence.

"It seems to me," Kim says slowly, "that people in a relationship should take responsibility for each other's happiness."

"I'm not sure how we wouldn't," I add.

Dr. Welsley sits back again in his chair. "What if I told you you're not responsible for making each other happy? And you never were."

"I don't think I believe that," I say.

"I know," he says. "And because of that, every time Kim feels a negative emotion, you feel like you've failed her."

"Because I have failed her," I tell him. "A lot."

"You made some mistakes. But mistakes aren't the same as failure, and not every negative emotion Kim has is because of your mistakes. The majority are probably because she's a person, and people are unhappy sometimes."

"And because of my OCD," Kim says.

"That can certainly make things more complicated, yes." He taps his pen lightly on his notepad as he waits for our reaction.

We both look at each other. I'm not sure that Dr. Welsley is right, but I guess we're here to hear what he has to say. And since he thinks we can make it, I don't want to argue with him too much.

When he sees we're done protesting, he continues. "So what I'd like you to do, along with trying to forgive yourselves, is to work on letting go of responsibility for each other's emotions, and work on loving each other instead."

"I'm not sure how that's different," Kim says. "Being with Blake makes me happy." She looks back at me like she's desperate for me to understand this.

"Were you happy in the throes of your postpartum disorder?" he asks her.

"No," she says. "But—"

"You were with Blake then. Did he make you happy?"

"No," I say, that familiar anger at myself still there, always there. "I did the opposite."

"But it wasn't his *fault*," Kim says. She sounds close to tears again, and we're both squeezing each other's hands for dear life.

"No, it wasn't," Dr. Welsley says. "You were unhappy, and it wasn't his fault, because he's not responsible for your happiness. And you aren't responsible for his, either. Blake, were you happy right before your divorce?"

"No," I say. "But I wasn't as miserable as I was after."

"Why is that?"

"Because being with Kim makes me happy." I know this is the wrong answer, given the direction he's leading us, but I'm still not sure why.

"I want you to consider," Dr. Welsley says, "that perhaps being together is your best environment for happiness, but that this doesn't mean that you can or should make each other happy. No human being can be happy all the time. It's not a fair burden for your relationship to bear."

Oh. I guess I see his point.

Kim's tugging her lower lip between her teeth. "I think I'm having a hard time wrapping my head around what that looks like in practice. Like, am I not supposed to do things that I know will make Blake happy?"

"You should absolutely do those things," Dr. Welsley says. "But do them because you love him, not because you want to make him happy. Do you see the difference there? In one case, you've placed a burden upon yourself that if he's not happy, you failed. And in the other, if there are circumstances that make Blake unhappy regardless of your actions, you're still loving him. You've set for yourself parameters in which you can succeed."

That sounds more complicated than it probably should. Kim looks at me wearily, and I feel the same.

But then I realize she's looking to me for an answer, to know whether I'm willing to do this for her, even if it's hard, even if I'm not sure I completely understand. She's waiting to know if she's worth it to me.

This time, I'm going to choose to fight for her—if not to make her happy, then because I'm in love with her.

"Okay," I say. "I can try that."

"Me too," Kim says.

"Good." Dr. Welsley sets the notepad and pen down on the coffee table. "I'd like you to take some time to process that and give it a try. Then come back in a few days, and we'll talk about how it went."

I take a deep breath. I'm terrified that I'll fail at this, too, and from the tension in every inch of Kim's frame, I'm pretty sure she feels the same.

"Okay," I say. "We'll try." I let go of Kim's hand and wrap my arms around her, kissing her on the top of her head.

I want this to work. It *has* to work.

Because above all else, I cannot lose her again.

SIXTEEN

Kim

As soon as we get back to the hotel and enter the kids' room, we are accosted by a large wiggly mass of fur and slobber—well, after Costanza walks into the doorframe first and then manages to find my legs. Aaron dropped him off while Blake and I were at our therapy appointment, undoubtedly hoping to avoid another night with a gassy boxer in his bed.

Blake and I both crouch down to pet a happily whimpering Costanza. "Hey, you," Blake says, scratching behind Costanza's pointed ears like he and the dog have been pals for years.

Blake never grew up with animals or any real desire to have them—with the exception of a pig, which dream was fulfilled when I surprised him with Ugly Naked Pig—but he's always been a natural with them. Playing with them, even cleaning up messes or administering meds in the most awkward of animal orifices, he never complained. For a while I'd attributed it to him knowing what he was getting into by choosing to be with me, but I soon became convinced he actually loved taking care of the animals.

He's always said I'm the one with the good heart, but the truth is, he's always had such a good heart himself. He never could see how incredible he is, and that therapy session showed how much he still struggles with that.

I wish I knew how to help him see himself the way I see him. I've always wished that.

The door to Blake's old room is cracked open. We let Marguerite have it, so she has her own space, and we've got security in the hall all night anyway, so we don't have to worry about anyone coming or going unnoticed through the kids' hallway door. Marguerite peeks out and gives us a wave, then shuts the door to give us some family privacy.

"Mom! Dad!" Luke squeals, after a belated moment in which he rights a toppled Lego tower—probably knocked over by Costanza in his run over to us. "I tried a new food today! It had cheese and it was so good, and it was called . . . something." His little brow furrows adorably.

"Arepas," Ivy's voice sounds from the floor between her bed and the wall. "Marguerite says they're Columbian."

"Sounds awesome," Blake says, and I smile. I'm doubtful there was a single vegetable in there, but any time Lukas is willing to put a new food in his mouth, it's worth a celebration.

"Are you hiding back there, Ivy?" I ask.

"I dropped my favorite purple marker," she says sourly. Then her head pops up, and she climbs up on the bed and marks a paper in her hand with the purple marker. She clears her throat dramatically. "I just finished my list." She stares both Blake and me down, her lips pressed together tightly.

I feel a knot in my gut. When was the last time I saw my little girl really smile? Certainly not in the last several days. Well before Blake and I got back together, really, but this isn't helping.

"Okay, good," Blake says. He looks over at me, and I can see he's not any more enthused to have this conversation than I am, especially so soon after the therapy session we haven't had time to really process. But being a parent generally means having the conversations you least want to have at the times that are most inconvenient to have them.

145

I want to take his hand and hold it, but I'm not sure we should rub our togetherness in Ivy's face at this exact moment. So I sit down in the nearest armchair and press my hands to my knees. "Do you want to go over it now? And Luke, do you have your list?"

Ivy nods curtly, and Luke springs up. "I do! A whole list!" He bounds across his bed to the nightstand, and pulls a paper out of the drawer. From what I can tell, there's only a few short words scattered randomly on the page and a bunch of Star Wars stickers.

Ivy's, on the other hand, is printed in her meticulously neat handwriting, and, as I suspected, color-coded.

I hold in a sigh. "Okay, let's hear it."

Blake takes the chair next to mine. Costanza, surprisingly, goes over to him and sits on his feet. This would make me all the happy, except I'm dreading hearing what Ivy will have to say.

Her voice still rings in my head. *What happens the next time you get divorced?*

"Fine." She sits primly on the edge of the bed. "First problem: I have friends at Dad's condo, and I only see them when I'm over there."

That seems an easy enough obstacle to overcome. Apparently Blake agrees, because he nods and says, "The condo and the ranch aren't that far from each other. We can still bring you over to see your friends there anytime you want."

Ivy's chin juts out. "But I also want to keep my bedroom at the condo and my bedroom at the ranch, because I like both my beds and—"

"This sounds like a separate problem," I say. "I think it's Luke's turn now."

Ivy's mouth snaps shut, but she stays silent.

Luke brightens and looks down at his paper. Then he squints as he tries to remember any worries he had. "Oh, yeah! I don't want to lose my Legos. I have Legos at both houses."

Another easy one. "You won't lose any Legos, honey," I say.

"When Dad moves into the ranch, you can bring all the Legos and all your other toys over from the condo, and you'll have them all at the ranch."

Luke opens his mouth, but Ivy cuts him off.

"My turn," she says. "I want to keep both my bedrooms." She says this like a challenge; she knows we're not about to give her a second bedroom in the same house—not that the ranch doesn't have the space for it, but we've never been the type of parents to indulge our kids' every whim.

Blake glances over at me again, then back to Ivy. "We'll probably keep the condo for a bit, so you won't lose your bedroom there immediately," he says, and I feel that same nervous chest tightening I felt the first time he told the kids he was planning on keeping the condo until we made sure this worked between us.

It makes sense, I know it does. It's smart. He shouldn't give up his home until he has some proof we can do this—that he can really put up with my issues. I'm a cautious person, so having a practical plan in case of our failure should make me feel better.

It doesn't, though. It just scares me more.

"But," Blake continues, "when I move into the ranch, you won't have two bedrooms anymore. So you'll have to decide which furniture set you like better. Most of your non-furniture stuff you can probably keep and—"

"But I like both my beds!"

"Then maybe you can get rid of enough furniture that you can fit both beds in one room," Blake says. "That'll be your choice. But you get one bedroom."

I admit, I'm surprised by the firmness in his voice. I always thought Ivy was able to wheedle more out of her dad than me—she always did when she was younger, though I suppose that was more along the lines of a second cookie, not a second bedroom.

Ivy glares and folds her arms.

"Luke?" I say, already wearied.

Luke looks up from where he's drawing a path from one

sticker on his paper to the next, and he takes on a very serious expression. "I have hobbit Legos at the condo and my orcs at the ranch. If I put them in the same bedroom, the orcs might carry off the hobbits."

Blake and I exchange a look—he's trying not to laugh, just like me. Thank god for seven-year-old problems.

"You have a playroom at the ranch," I say. "Can you keep the hobbits in your bedroom and the orcs in the playroom?"

He considers, then nods. "Okay," he says happily. His feet swing as they dangle off the bed.

"Ivy?" Blake says.

Ivy consults her list, no doubt trying to pick a tough one. "I'm going to have to watch you kiss and be all gross like that. And neither Luke or I should have to see that."

"Your parents will kiss," Blake says flatly. "That's your big concern? Yeah, we're going to kiss. Kids see their parents kiss sometimes. Plus, you can always, you know, not look."

The dry way he says it almost gets another laugh out of me. But I wonder what her worry really is. I didn't bring Roger around the kids all that often—the fact that I never felt comfortable with him spending the night when my kids were home, even after years together, should have been a sign to both of us—but it's not like she never saw us kiss before, and she never had a problem with that. I'm guessing she's seen Blake kiss Simone and his other girlfriends and similarly not cared.

It's more than that; it's a deeper fear. It's Blake and me specifically, and I'm about to ask why, but she jumps in again.

"And you're going to have sex! Which is even grosser!"

"And which you will *not* be seeing," I say quickly.

Luke gasps. "You're going to have a baby!" He actually seems excited about this prospect.

Blake makes a little strangled noise, and I shake my head. "That's not always what happens when two people have sex," I say.

"But are you?" Ivy demands, her eyes wide. It's clear this didn't occur to her.

148

To be fair, the thought of Blake and me having another child someday hadn't occurred to me, either. I'd thought many times over the years that I'd love to have one more—even with the risk of another postpartum OCD flare-up—but I couldn't see myself having a child with anyone but Blake.

Would Blake want that someday?

There are so many things we haven't talked about, things I'm afraid to bring up. Being together again is such an unexpected gift—one I'm so afraid to have taken away, I've been scared to think beyond the immediate future.

Neither of us has spoken for several shocked seconds, and Blake has an expression I can't read. "We don't have any plans for that right now," he says carefully.

"You got pregnant with me by accident." Ivy's cheeks are bright red. "So maybe you don't need to plan for it to happen."

"Getting pregnant with you was a *wonderful surprise*," I say. "But yeah, we can't predict everything in the future." I hope even that much doesn't feel like too much pressure on Blake. I can feel the pulse in my wrist against my knee, faster than usual. "Right now we're focusing on us and you two, on the family we have now."

Blake doesn't say anything, but he nods.

Her eyes narrow. "You're not saying no, though. Neither of you!"

"Ive—" Blake starts, but Ivy cuts him off.

"I'm adding this To. The. List." She dramatically writes THEY WILL HAVE A BABY on her paper in bright purple marker. "Because it's not fair. Luke, tell them it's not fair."

Luke has that trapped look again. "But babies are cute. People babies and animal babies—"

"Luke, stop *being* a baby!"

"Ivy!" both Blake and I warn at the same time. Ivy rolls her eyes and mutters an apology.

Luke wrinkles his nose at her. "My list says 'Ivy is mean.'"

I have a hard time arguing with that.

149

"Ivy is having a difficult time adjusting," Blake says. "But we're doing our best to address all the concerns, and we'd appreciate it if she would do her best to lose the attitude."

Ivy tugs at the ends of her long auburn hair, wrapping it around her finger. It reminds me of how she used to do that as a little girl when she would sleep. It was adorable, and I used to love watching her do it, even though in the morning she'd end up with tangles.

Until one day, I had the thought of her long hair wrapping itself around her neck, strangling her. That thought caught in my brain, until I could picture nothing else every time I put my daughter to bed. I would wake up over and over to check on her, and drove Blake crazy asking over and over if we should cut her hair—without, of course, telling him what I was really afraid of, because I knew how insane it sounded, knew there was no way he could understand.

I finally called a stylist one day when I couldn't take it anymore, and he cut her hair chin-length. Ivy cried, because she missed her "princess hair." I cried, later and by myself, because I was so afraid of my own mind.

The fear is starting to claw at me, and I force myself to take deep breaths again—in slowly, out slowly. I'm not sure if I look paler all of a sudden, or if my breathing exercises are more noticeable than I'd thought, because Blake gives me a concerned look and reaches over to take my hand.

It helps. I give him a small smile.

"My turn," Ivy says, with a little less attitude—I can tell she's still just as upset, but she's trying to be calm about it. "The paparazzi are worse now. They're everywhere and they won't leave us alone, even with all the security, and it's really annoying."

Blake sighs. "Yeah. It is annoying, huh. But that's kind of our lives, you know? The paparazzi always get worse when anything new happens with us. And this is a big one. But it will die down and go back to the way it was before."

Marguerite's kept us updated every day, and it sounds like the security is definitely keeping the kids safe from getting swarmed, but there's not much they can do about the shouted questions every time they go outside or to some place that can't easily be cordoned off.

He's right that it will die down eventually, but until then, our kids are getting asked how they feel about us getting back together, whether they miss Roger and Simone (I think even Portia got thrown in there), if there's a wedding date yet . . . all big emotional stuff they should be able to process in private and not have strangers try to exploit. It makes me furious and guilt-ridden, all at once.

It's not like they've never had to deal with paparazzi intrusion, but I already felt bad enough about that. This is a whole other level, and I feel so selfish doing this to them.

I bite my lower lip. "Maybe we could do an interview somewhere big like *People*. Give them the information they really want, and they'll back off a bit."

Blake looks sharply at me, and I don't blame him—I literally just hours ago said we were going to keep things vague with the press. But if it's what our kids need . . .

Ivy's angry expression smoothes out so suddenly, I can practically see the lightbulb going on in her head. A devious lightbulb. "*Yes*," she says adamantly. "Let's do that."

I remember as a kid wondering how my parents always seemed to know what I was thinking, especially if I was planning to do something I shouldn't. When I became a parent, I realized it's not that there's some psychic ability gifted along with the baby. Kids are just never as sneaky as they think they are.

"No, Ivy," I say. "You're not going to do an interview about how we're ruining your life."

"Absolutely not," Blake agrees.

Ivy's twelve-year-old death glare at having her brilliant plan crushed could be weaponized. "Even if you are ruining my life, and the world should know."

I feel a headache beginning to form right between my eyes. "I've seriously had enough with this sassy tone."

"This is my voice now," Ivy says. Luke's eyes widen, and he begins scribbling on his paper.

"Ivy—" Blake starts, but Ivy cuts him off. Again.

"Neither of you care about us anymore. All you care about is yourselves."

"That's not true." Blake's lips press into a firm line. "We're your parents, always. And if this was going to put you in some kind of actual danger, we wouldn't do it."

"But—"

Luke cuts her off now. "It's my turn!" Then he holds up his list and points at Ivy. "This is Ivy's voice now!"

"Yeah, that's a concern for all of us, buddy," Blake mutters under his breath, raking his hand through his hair.

I squeeze his other hand, but there's a drip of ice going down my spine.

Actual danger.

Is something that's clearly so emotionally difficult for our daughter an actual danger?

I've been afraid of so many dangers to my children that weren't real threats, been driven crazy with those fears. It's been better since I've been on the meds, but I still can't be sure sometimes if my fears are valid or not.

I'm glad the others are all talking because my throat is so dry, I'm not sure I can.

"This isn't fair," Ivy yells, jumping to her feet, and stomping them for good measure. "You're all ganging up on me! You said this is a family, but it's not. It's Team Anti-Ivy!"

"We're not Team Anti-Ivy," Blake says with no small amount of exhaustion. "We're Team Cooperation, and you're being Team Sassy Tone."

I can only imagine how many interviewers would kill to hear Blake Pless using the words "sassy tone" in such an unironic way. Normally this would make me laugh, but I'm a long way from laughing at the moment.

"And," Blake continues, "you can join our team at any time. We really want you to."

Ivy shakes her head. "You don't want to cooperate. You just want to say you're the parents and you can do whatever you want, and I can't even talk to a really nice boy just because he's a little older than me, and it's not fair!"

She folds her paper crisply down the center, and then again into quarters, and drops it on the floor—which is basically the Ivy version of crumpling it up (neither she nor I can stand crumpled papers.) Costanza gets up to snuffle at the paper and starts trying to eat it.

She grabs Costanza's collar and tugs it. "Come on, Costanza. They don't care about us."

Costanza spits out the paper and follows her with his now purple-stained tongue lolling out and stump tail wagging happily as she stomps off to the bathroom—the only room she can close herself into—and slams the door.

"She's really mad," Luke whispers, wide-eyed.

"I know, buddy." Blake rubs at his forehead like my headache is catching.

On that note, we end our second, equally unsuccessful family meeting. Blake plays Legos with Luke on the floor while I return some phone calls. I check in with Tara about the *EW* interview tomorrow, and then with Helene, my CAO, about how Urkel's neutering went (great, until he somehow got his post-op Cone of Shame stuck in a doggie gate) and the various options the contractor quoted on the little house I want to build for my feline leukemia patients, who can't be kept with non-infected cats because of the contagious nature of the disease.

All of this makes me miss my animals and the ranch, and wish we were all back there right now. We will be soon, at least for a few days, as Blake and I—along with Troy and the others—have a break in shooting to be on a couple panels at San Diego Comic-Con.

More than anything, I want to be with Blake on the ranch, want him to feel at home there like he always should have been.

Will he still want that, now that the realities of our situation are starting to intrude on the bubble?

Will it make things worse for Ivy?

These questions are circling around my mind when Blake takes his turn making his business calls and Luke and I play Connect Four. Ivy eventually gets bored enough sulking in the bathroom with Costanza that they come out and join us for dinner, which we ordered from room service. She refuses to let herself be pulled into any actual dinner conversation, though, even when Blake brings up some great nearby surfing locations he's been checking out online. There's a moment when her eyes light up with excitement—he mentions a beach where one of the famous surfers they're both obsessed with regularly goes—but she shuts even that down.

She's a stubborn one, our Ivy.

Finally, bedtime rolls around—eight o'clock, though Ivy's allowed to stay up reading until nine-thirty—and we get them tucked in and are able to retreat to our room. Costanza finds his dog bed and collapses into it, snoring almost as soon as he drops.

My exhausted body wants to do the same and just sleep for days, but my spinning mind isn't about to let that happen. Blake looks over at me like he's about to say something, but then looks away. He obviously has things on his mind, too.

I'm scared to find out what exactly it is he's afraid to say.

While Blake brushes his teeth, I strip down to my underwear and a comfy cotton shirt I like to sleep in. He emerges from the bathroom wearing just his boxers, and it's an incredible sight. I want to pull him into bed and press myself against the muscles of his chest, wrap myself in his strong arms. My body wants to do more than sleep right now—it aches all over.

But fear makes my heart ache even more.

I sit on the very edge of the bed. "What if this really isn't good for Ivy? What if we're actually hurting her somehow?

Emotionally, I mean."

Blake freezes. Then he blinks, his hand tightening around the t-shirt balled up in it. "Are you having second thoughts about whether we should be together?"

He didn't deny that it might be bad for Ivy. He must be worried about it too. And the speed to which he jumped to us not being together—

The icy drip down my spine is steady now, faster. I'm not sure I can breathe, but I do somehow, anyway. "Are you?"

There's a pause, where he stares down at the t-shirt in his hand; it's the one he wore today, a plain navy cotton shirt that hugs him perfectly and probably smells like sunshine and the ocean, like him. I half want to jump up and take it from his hands and hug it to me, like even if he leaves, I can still keep this one tiny piece of him.

I pull my legs up to my chest and wrap my arms around them instead.

He clears his throat. "Maybe we rushed into this," he says, and I'm pretty sure I can actually hear my heart begin to crack apart.

Oh god. Is this happening?

Again?

My whole body is ice now. "Maybe." I'm not sure what else I can say. If this is what he was afraid to tell me, if this is all already too much for him . . .

He sets the t-shirt down on the dresser and leans against its polished surface with both hands like it's holding him upright. Because he's afraid to say more, to hurt me all over again?

I pull my legs tighter against me. I'm sitting in a fetal position.

"If you don't think this is a good idea anymore," I start, my throat already feeling thick with the tears I'm afraid to start crying, "If you don't think it's worth it, I under—"

"What?" He looks back at me with wide eyes, then straightens. "Wait, wait," he repeats, even though I haven't moved or spoken. "What is this conversation about?"

"What do you mean?"

He sits right next to me on the edge of the bed. We're not touching, but he's only inches away; I can feel the heat from his skin. "I *mean*, I think we've had a lot of conversations over the years where we weren't talking about the same thing. And it led to the worst mistake of my life. So I need to know"—here he swallows, his Adam's apple bobbing up and down—"is this conversation about you not wanting to be with me because of Ivy?"

Me not wanting to be with him? "No! I thought maybe you—" I squeeze my eyes shut, trying to sort through the chaos of fears pinging around my brain, and I realize I'm not really afraid we're causing Ivy any actual danger. Stress, yes. Emotional difficulty, yes. But nothing that can't be worked through, nothing that isn't just a human thing to feel when life changes in ways you don't like or expect.

"You said to her we wouldn't do this if it caused her to be in danger," I continue, and my voice sounds small. "And you were right. We're good parents. We would never deliberately harm our children. But if she continues to struggle with this—" I shake my head. "I thought maybe you'd want to give up on us, that the cost would be too high. And maybe you'd be right to, but I don't know if I could, not without trying everything possible—" My voice breaks, and the tears start to leak out.

"Oh my god," Blake breathes, and it's not some admonition, it's like relief. Then his arms are around me, and he pulls me against him. "Oh my god," he repeats. "Okay. Shit. Okay." I'm not sure what to make of this, but he's holding me, which feels so good I can't bring myself to ask.

"We're doing that thing again," he says. "It's like the painting with the bunny or the duck, you know? Because when you seemed so scared, I thought *you* wanted to leave *me* because of how tough this is on Ivy. That it wasn't worth it to *you* for us to figure this out."

My breath catches. "So you aren't having second thoughts? When you said that maybe we rushed into things—"

"No." He puts his hands on my cheeks, turning me so I'm

156

looking right into his bottle-green eyes. "No. I want to be with you, Kim. I *need* to be with you. But I was so afraid that you were having second thoughts, and so I was trying to say what I thought you wanted to hear, and *oh my god* we need to stop doing this." He cringes, then presses his lips to my forehead.

The ice inside is melting away. I'm so relieved I'm nearly dizzy with it. Even as I'm struck with the truth of his words.

I groan. "I did it to you again, the same thing I did before. I brought up the thing about Ivy because deep down I wanted you to tell me it would all be okay. That you weren't going to leave me. But I didn't just ask you about it. I expected you to read my mind, and I didn't even know that's what I was doing, and—"

"It's okay." He hugs me. "Hey, it's okay. We're both learning. I let my fears take me to the worst possible conclusion and then did the same thing *I* did before. I tried to make you happy, which, according to our therapist, I shouldn't be taking responsibility for anyway, let alone when I'm wrong about what you actually want . . ."

He trails off and rubs his forehead again, and I let out a little chuckle. "We suck at this," I say.

"Yeah, we do." He smiles at me. "But I want to figure it out, whatever it takes."

The ice has melted entirely. I'm a pool of warmth, encircled by him. "Me too. Whatever it takes."

We just hold each other for a few moments, and I listen to the sound of his heart, steady and comforting.

"As for Ivy," he says. "She may not like this now. She may even be miserable. But that's not putting her in any real danger, physically or even emotionally. We can make this work. We will."

I nod, and something else occurs to me. "Maybe we aren't responsible for making Ivy happy. We should try to provide the best environment possible for her to be happy. And she has two parents who love her and want what's best for her—that's got to be the best environment for a kid, right?"

"Right," Blake agrees. "And maybe she doesn't want those two parents to be in such close contact, but that's not her call. Maybe, if we're worried about how much she's struggling, we can do some kind of family therapy or therapy for just her. We'll do what we need to do." He nudges me gently with his nose against my temple. "Together."

God, how I like the sound of that. I tilt my face up, and he leans down and we kiss and kiss and kiss, our hands wandering and our breath joining and our hearts pounding.

Together.

SEVENTEEN

Blake

Waking up with Kim is something I'm not sure I'm ever going to get used to. In my first moments of consciousness, I'm alone again, waking up without her, trying to ignore the ache that never really goes away. Then I become aware of her scent, like sunshine and lemons, of her hair tangled on my pillow, the touch of her ankle resting against mine.

I stretch my arms around her, and Kim all but purrs and stretches out along my body. On the floor, I can hear Costanza stirring. The dog doesn't seem to hate me, but I think he senses that I'm his competition for Kim's affection, because he tends to get extra needy whenever she and I are together.

At least he hasn't taken to peeing on my pant leg.

Lukas bangs on the door with a series of sharp blows. "Mooooooooooooom!" he shouts. "Wake uuuuuuuuuuuup!"

I groan and pull on my boxers. Kim's wearing a night shirt already, like she always does, and I wave toward the shower. "You can go first, if you want."

She grabs me by the hand and pulls me down for a kiss, which makes me want to ignore Luke and our call time and the rest of this crazy world and just fall back into bed with her for the next few hours, at least.

159

But instead I go to the door and unlock it, while Kim ducks into the bathroom.

"Hey, buddy," I say to Luke as I open the door.

He comes bounding into the room. "Dad! Dad Dad Dad!"

"Yeah, that's me." I wish I had Lukas's enthusiasm for anything this early in the morning.

Anything, I suppose, but staying in bed with Kim.

"Ivy was texting Christopher *all night*!" Luke announces.

"Lukas!" Ivy shouts and comes flying in from their room even faster than Luke did. "Shut your mouth!"

I fold my arms. "How could Ivy have been texting Christopher," I ask Luke, "when she doesn't have a phone?"

Ivy grabs Luke with one arm around his waist and lifts him off the ground, pulling him backward while clamping her other hand over his mouth. She immediately shrieks and drops him onto his hands and knees, then backs away, wiping her palm on her pants. "Ew! Gross! Don't *lick* me!"

"Well done, Luke," I say. "Answer my question."

Ivy looks at me like I'm a traitor to her nation, which I suppose at this moment I am. Behind me, I hear the door to the bathroom opening again. I hate that Kim doesn't think I can handle this alone, but to be fair, it's not going great so far.

"She stole Marguerite's phone!" Luke says. "She put it back just now, but I saw her texting under a blanket."

Shit. I turn to Ivy and give her the parental stare of truth. Ivy wilts under it, which tells me everything I need to know.

"Ivy," I say. "We told you you're not allowed to contact that boy. You want us to give your electronics back, but how are we going to be able to do that when you deliberately disobey us?"

Ivy draws herself up to her full height. "What are you going to do to me? There's nothing else you can take away from me. You were never going to trust me again, anyway."

I close my eyes and take a deep breath to refrain from joining in her hysterics. The more Ivy ignores our decisions about Christopher, the more I think there's really something

160

wrong with this whole situation. I know that kids make terrible decisions when their hormones kick into overdrive, but—

"It's true, isn't it?" Ivy shouts at me. "I hate you, and I hate Mom, and I hate this family!"

She storms back into their room and slams the door. I hear it lock from the other side, and Lukas looks up at me plaintively.

"It's okay, buddy," I tell him, even though I don't feel it myself. I'm not sure how much of Ivy's problems are because she's a young girl infatuated with an older boy and how much because she wants to get back at Kim and me for, as she puts it, ruining her life. "Want to play games on my phone?"

"Ooooh, yes!" Luke says. That trick works every time, and it's possible I'm abusing it, but all I really want to do right now is talk to Kim. The bathroom door is cracked but not all the way open—I guess she did feel like I could handle the situation, but wanted to hear the whole thing, and I can hardly blame her for that. I open the door and find her leaning against the marble counter, still in her night shirt. She looks at me with wide eyes.

"Another successful encounter with our daughter," I say.

Kim's face scrunches sympathetically, and she puts her arms around me. "I'm sorry. I wanted to help, but I also . . . didn't."

"It's fine. It's not like I'm not used to dealing with our kids on my own." I cringe. That sounded accusatory, and I'm about to apologize, but Kim speaks first.

"Did you . . . does she talk to you like that a lot?"

Shit. I've spent so long not wanting her to know how often Ivy throws fits at my house. I know she and Kim must butt heads, being so alike, but to hear Ivy tell it, her mother always does everything right. "Not like *that*," I say. "I mean, it's far from the first time she's yelled that she hates me, but usually she cools off after fifteen minutes or so and we talk about it."

Kim is staring at me like she can't believe this, which makes me feel even worse about the state of my parenting. "Our Ivy. Yells that she hates *you*."

"Yeah," I say.

Kim laughs. "I always thought that she only said that to me. She's always telling me how you never make her clean her room. Or take out the trash."

"Ha. Well, from what I hear, you never leave dishes in the sink, or use paper plates, or forget to do the laundry until she runs out of underwear."

"I did all those things when we were married."

I smile. "I know. But maybe when Ivy was yelling that she'd rather be with you, it hurt enough that I was more inclined to believe her."

Kim rolls her eyes up at the ceiling. "She's been playing us against each other. I thought we were really good at keeping that from happening."

"I don't think we can totally blame ourselves. Our daughter is obnoxiously clever." I groan. "And we need to make her apologize to Marguerite about the phone, and then see if the data is still there so we know exactly what happened."

"What are we going to do about her?" Kim burrows deeper into my chest.

I really don't know. "She's right and she's wrong. Technically there are more things we could take away from her—going to the beach while we're here, for example. But I'm worried it would just make it worse."

She nods. "But we can't reward this behavior, either."

"We should make sure Marguerite locks her phone, to start with."

"That's the thing," Kim says. "I'm pretty sure she does."

"Great. I do not want to know how Ivy figured out the password. It's like parenting Ethan Hunt."

"And when Luke grows up, it'll be like parenting MacGyver."

I laugh and squeeze her tighter. Our family might be a mess, but it feels good to *be* a family again.

I only wish I had the confidence that this time, I'd be able to do it right.

EIGHTEEN

Kim

Ivy's mood doesn't improve over the next several days. For that matter, neither does Troy's. We're behind schedule, the paparazzi continue to mob our shooting locations, and Troy pulls me aside at one point to ask why we couldn't wait to "do this until we're ramping up publicity, when it would actually be useful," as if Blake and I should be timing our family decisions based on what's best for the film. One of the stunt men broke his ankle, a sound tech guy showed up to work wasted and dropped a boom mic on one of the extras, and all the press surrounding the filming is becoming increasingly negative—and solely focused on Blake and me. Film sets always have their own mood, just like people, and this one is in desperate need of a Xanax.

I'm hoping the break for Comic-Con—and especially the couple days back home—is just what we all need.

Ivy, at least, does seem in slightly better spirits as we fly back to LA in the private plane the film provides for us due to my rider about accommodations for Costanza (thank you, Josh). She sits in the big leather seat, her long legs drawn up under her, chatting with Luke about all the costumes they hope to see at the con. Well, Luke does most of the chatting, but Ivy isn't rolling her eyes or letting out any aggrieved sighs, so I count that as progress.

When Costanza, who's sleeping stretched out on the floor between us, starts kicking his legs and making happy little dream noises, she even looks over at me and smiles—until she remembers she's mad at me and looks away again.

Blake dozes in the seat next to me, the kids chat, Costanza chases dream squirrels, Marguerite studies, and I allow myself to bask in the contented feeling of the whole scene.

Before I'm ready for that quiet calm to end, the plane lands. Helene meets us at the airfield to take Costanza to the ranch, and there's a car to take the rest of us straight to the convention.

I've been to Comic-Con a few times for my previous Hemlock movies, and yet I still stare at the huge, colorfully costumed crowd at the convention center, people spilling out around the edges like the time Ivy added bubble bath soap to our dishwasher.

Blake squeezes my hand. "Game face time," he says, as much to himself as to me. The press stuff for big films like this can be exhausting, especially at major events like Comic-Con.

Luke is pressed up against the window, wide-eyed, and even Ivy bounces in her seat with excitement.

"Time to Dash!" Luke announces. He's dressing up as Dash from *The Incredibles,* and he digs his mask out of the duffel bag we brought containing costumes for both the kids and Marguerite. Not only is dressing up fun, having costumes with masks will keep the kids anonymous in the crowd—a luxury they don't get all that often.

A large part of me wishes Blake and I could do the same.

"Okay, remember to stay close to Marguerite the whole time," I say with a pointed look at Luke, who has an unfortunate habit of wandering.

Luke nods, though I have a feeling the excitement is chasing my words out of his head before they have a chance to stick. My chest tightens, picturing him disappearing into the massive crowd, the people shifting and churning around him like a riptide, leaving no trace of my little boy behind.

My breath grows shallow. Not just at the horrible image but at the kind of heft it has. The kind I've learned to identify as a thought that will play over and over, insisting that if I don't text Marguerite every five minutes or think about my son enough, something terrible will happen to him.

The meds don't prevent these thoughts completely, though they're much rarer now. *It's not real*, I tell myself. *Just OCD.* Then I lean down and give Luke a huge hug, which he quickly wriggles out of. Still, cuddling my son even for a brief moment is enough to give my brain the little dopamine boost it needs to kick itself out of its rut.

"Don't worry," Marguerite says. "I told Luke if he doesn't hold my hand, I'm going to tie our hands together with a big red ribbon. One with mushy hearts all over it."

Luke wrinkles his nose but giggles as Marguerite tickles his side.

I let out a breath. Marguerite's got this; she always does.

The thought subsides with my quick mental trick—another benefit of the meds and loads of practice. It may yet come back, though.

I'm glad I'm going to have Blake with me if it does. I look up and notice he's watching me carefully. Is he starting to be able to tell when an OCD thought hits? When I have to coax my brain back to sanity?

If so, is that a good thing?

Ivy pulls out her own mask—she's in a matching *Incredibles* costume as Violet—as the car pulls around to the VIP area cordoned off for celebs, and Marguerite puts on the mask to become Elastigirl. Then convention liaisons meet us and escort Blake and me to the celebrity green room, while Marguerite and the kids head out to the main convention halls.

The first panel Blake and I are on goes well. It's set in a huge room with thousands of attendees, but the room itself is so dark we can't really see more than a general mass out there, like we're on stage at a rock concert. We're on the panel with Troy and Bertram (whose flight arrived late, leaving him rushing up onto the stage, looking flushed and annoyed), as well as Hannah Verhoeven, the girl whose webcomic was the genesis of this movie. She's young, in her mid-twenties at most, and looks perpetually startled—though maybe that's just the look she gets when put on a stage in front of so many people, along with the A-list stars of the movie that only exists because of her.

Feeling the comforting weight of Blake's hand on my knee under the table, I remind myself to thank her. Profusely.

Despite the massive crowd, the panel goes well. The questions were pre-screened and all asked by the moderator, a slight, charismatic Indian-American guy named Jai who does some big comics podcast. He asks one question about Blake's and my relationship, but it's pretty softball as far as these things go, and Blake quips about how grateful he is for my very specific attraction to guys wearing shiny gold visors. The crowd laughs and cheers, and then we're back to movie-specific questions.

Which makes all of us—especially Troy—very happy, something I needed after days and days of growing stress on set, a good portion of which I can't help but feel responsible for.

We're escorted off for a few hours of VIP photos and autographs. Then one more panel, and our Comic-Con obligations will be fulfilled, and we can actually spend a night at home. As a family. With Blake.

I can't wait.

It's this thought that carries me through until that last panel, which I can tell right away is going to be different than the previous one. This room is much smaller, well lit, and the crowd seated in front of us is limited to one hundred people—the mega-fans and reporters willing to pay a hefty amount for tickets to this event where they're allowed to ask the questions themselves.

Normally I prefer smaller group interactions with my fans, but with all the issues surrounding Blake and me, this crowd scares me far more than the stadium-level masses.

Like at the other panel, we're set up at a long table, with water bottles for each of us and a placard with our names in front of our designated seat. I've got Blake on one side of me and Bertram on the other.

Troy's down at the end, talking with Sarah, who isn't going to be on the panel but has a reserved seat in the front row, with a little brown-haired boy wearing glasses who looks about four or five. She rarely talks about her son—she doesn't ever seem inclined to engage in personal conversations in general—but I've seen the pictures she keeps on her daily schedule clipboard.

Bertram groans when he sees the placard on the other side of him, labeled *Peter Dryden*. "Not again," he mutters. "I was stuck next to the man on the flight here, and I swear, Kimberly, there isn't enough wine in all the first class cabins in the world to make that trip palatable."

Blake leans over, making sure to cover his mic. "Why don't you take the jet with us back? We've got room. And a fully stocked bar."

Bertram wilts in dramatic relief. "Bless you, Blake."

I grin at Blake, and he winks at me. If he's been hoping to get my old friend's favor, he's definitely on the right track.

Peter Dryden himself takes his seat moments later. "My apologies to all of you for running late," he says in his deep, self-important tone. "I had a reunion shoot with all the other *Cuffs* stars, and you know how fans of such a long-running, popular series can be, they just—"

Fortunately, the moderator starts before Peter can drone on about his mob of ancient cop show fans. It's the same moderator as our last panel, Jai the podcaster, and he seems just as peppy and upbeat. Of course, he didn't spend the last few hours smiling for photos or getting hand-cramps from hundreds of signatures.

"I could give you all an intro of these people sitting right here next to me," Jai says with a big grin, "but you guys wouldn't have paid three hundred bucks a seat if you didn't already know.

So lets go straight to what you really want—and I don't mean a date with Blake Pless, ladies."

The crowd laughs, and Blake gives a nice self-aware wave. I feel a little more relaxed. Jai's good at this; I can see why his podcast is so big.

"What you really want," he continues, "is to ask these fine folks all your burning questions about the upcoming Hemlock/ Farpoint movie. So let's not waste any of that expensive time, yeah? Ask away!"

I'm a little worried about questions being shouted at us en masse like so often happens with the paparazzi, but this crowd's been prepped beforehand to raise their hands and wait for the convention workers standing at the edges to pass them the wireless mic.

A big guy with a kind, bearded face and a Hemlock t-shirt gets the mic first. "So any chance we get a date with Kim?" he asks. The crowd laughs, and several guys whistle.

I laugh as well, especially when Blake leans into his microphone and says in this perfectly droll tone, "No."

More laughs and cheers.

"Worth a try," the big guy says with a grin. "Honestly, I don't have a question. I just want to say that I've always been a major Hemlock fan—and Kim, you just kill it in this role. I'm a fan of Hannah's work, and I can't wait to see this movie."

"Aww, thanks so much," I say, grinning back at him. "I can't wait for you all to see it, too. We're having such a great time." This isn't entirely true—being back with Blake aside—but in this moment I can almost believe it. This is going well.

The next person stands up, a tall, lanky guy wearing bulky foam armor and with a matching sword strapped across his back. "I disagree," he says, with no other preamble. "This movie concept makes no sense whatsoever. Farpoint and Hemlock don't belong in the same universe. This whole thing is a mockery to the fans of both comics."

My eyes widen. Damn, nothing like going straight for the

jugular. Did this guy really pay three hundred bucks just to say that to us?

"Well, a lot of fans of Hannah's brilliant webcomic would disagree," Troy says smoothly, but I can almost hear his teeth grinding. "And while we all realize this is a unique departure from the stories in the traditional comics, I think when you watch the finished film, you'll see that mockery of fans is the furthest thing from any of our minds. We're bringing the best of both comics' worlds together in a really fantastic story."

"I agree," a teenage girl on the other side of the room dressed in a Sailor Moon costume says, and Troy starts to thank her before she shakes her head. "With the guy with the sword, I mean. Guidepost is the one sending Farpoint to Earth? Hannah Verhoeven isn't a *real* fan. If she was, she'd know from *Farpoint* Issue Three-Nineteen that Guidepost can't send people to other dimensions without the Helm of Engolos, which was destroyed by Farpoint himself. Did he somehow reforge the helm? From what—a *new cosmic ore?*" Her voice drips with sarcasm, and several people clap.

I have no idea what she's talking about, but I'm glad for poor startled Hannah's sake that she isn't on this panel.

Troy opens his mouth, but Bertram leans in. "If I may," he says, and Troy nods.

"When it comes to adaptations such as this," Bertram says, "there is a certain amount of allowance for artistry that must be given—"

"Artistry, indeed," Peter jumps in, clapping Bertram on the back with a loud smack. "And let me tell you, I can't speak to Guidepost's powers or whatever headwear is required, but I can tell you all about the art of making a film such as this. My dear friend Bertram and I, we have a saying about the art, and—"

"Wait," the guy with the sword interrupts, which is probably a good thing. Bertram is squeezing his water bottle like he's about to bludgeon Peter Dryden with it. "Are you saying that you—the actor playing Guidepost—don't know about his powers? See?" He gestures to the audience, many of whom are looking increasingly angry themselves, and there's a low sound of muttering around the room. The tides are turning against us quickly. "None of you care about the actual source material!"

Peter's mouth is working soundlessly, seemingly shocked at how little these people care about his supposed dear friendship with Bertram or his views on the art of filmmaking.

Troy glares at him, then tries to smooth out that glare for the audience. "As I said before, I think you'll find when you see the film that all of us involved care deeply about these characters and—"

"What about Laserpoint?" A girl wearing a giant robot suit—is she one of the Transformers?—has somehow gotten the mic from Sailor Moon without it first going through the convention volunteers, the closest of which is trying to wedge himself into the aisle to regain the mic and thus control. "She's way better for Farpoint, and she's actually in his universe. She should be the one Farpoint is with, not Hemlock."

"I should be the one Blake Pless is with!" another girl with long purple hair from the second row shouts, sans mic. She stands up so we—and I'm guessing especially Blake—can see the ample amount of cleavage formed by her tight corset. And the word BLAKE written across the top of said cleavage in sparkly glitter.

Blake chuckles self-consciously—he always gets a little uncomfortable around the more, well, *overt* fans.

I lean into my mic and do a spot-on imitation of Blake from before. "No."

This gets some laughter, but it's obvious that many of them are now too worked up with their issues about the movie.

Corset Girl pouts and glares at me, apparently not getting that I was just playing around—I've never felt overly threatened by random girls gushing over Blake, and I certainly can't blame them—and I try to think of something to say to soften my joke, but Transformers girl jumps back in.

"Laserpoint! Laserpoint! Laser—" Her chants get cut off as the convention worker tugs the mic away from her. No one else joins in the chants—I don't know who Laserpoint is, but this girl appears to be her only die-hard fan.

"Okay," Jai says, standing up at the table and trying to re-establish order. "I know you are all excited to share your opinions—and cleavage-writing—with our stars here, but let's stick to the rules we all know from grade school, yeah? Raise our hands, wait our turn, don't be dicks?"

A few more laughs and lots of applause.

"How about letting this gentleman toward the front speak," Jai says. "He's had his hand up for awhile." A convention worker hands a guy wearing nice jeans and nondescript polo shirt the mic.

Polo Shirt smiles. "Thank you. So I think what we all really want to hear about is Blake and Kim."

Oh no. This guy has reporter written all over him.

"So my question is for Kim," he says, and I have to fight not to cringe. "How could you forgive Blake for his infidelity?"

My stomach drops, and I'm pretty sure my mouth along with it, but no words come out for a moment. Blake shoots me a concerned look, but he can't exactly cut in on this one.

We've never directly addressed the cheating rumors, either of us. And we've kept ignoring the question since getting back together, waiting for me to be ready to make more than a surface statement about the causes of our divorce.

But the truth is, I've been letting him take the fall too long for problems in our marriage that I'm mostly responsible for. Because it was easier for me. I feel sick with the thought.

"There was no infidelity," I say.

Blake's eyes widen in surprise at my sudden candor—I'm not one for PR revelations that haven't been planned and rehearsed in advance. I hear some scoffs among the surprised murmurs in the audience.

"It's true," I continue, growing unreasonably mad at these people for failing to believe me now, even though by not addressing it before, we all but confirmed the rumor. "We had problems in our marriage, but our divorce wasn't due to anyone cheating. And it was never because we didn't love each other."

I don't know why I felt the need to add that last part, but Blake's surprised look softens, and he squeezes my knee. "Definitely not," he adds.

"So you confirm the story your previous nanny Claire just released?" The mic has been passed to a woman I assume is another reporter, though she's at least attempted to blend into the crowd by wearing a Farpoint t-shirt and replica gold visor.

Blake and I both look at her, confused. "What story?" I ask. If it's a big story, it really must have *just* been released—like, within the last couple hours—or I no doubt would have heard about it already from Tara or Josh.

The woman smiles, and I see the press badge when she shifts to adjust her visor. "Claire did an interview with our team at *Stars Today*, in which she talks about how she never slept with Blake, and yet she's been harassed and bullied for years, both online and off, for being the woman who broke up Watterpless. She says you both threw her under the bus by never denying the rumors."

My stomach feels like it just took a flying leap off the Grand Canyon.

Oh god, Claire. I was going through so much pain, so much darkness in those days, I honestly didn't even think about what that rumor would do to her. Not then and not since. She hadn't been our nanny long, pretty much only a few months by the time the divorce was announced, but she was nice and good with the kids, and—

And *oh shit*, how could we do that to her?

I look at Blake and Blake looks at me, and I can tell he's thinking the exact same thing I am. He recovers quicker than me, though, at least enough to say, "Um. We hadn't heard that. But clearly we owe Claire an apology." I can tell he's trying to figure out the most diplomatic way to go on, but another guy from the audience stands up and is handed a microphone. This guy is beefy and bald and dressed like Naked Mole Rat, shaved eyebrows and all.

"Let's bring this back to the comics," he says, and I don't know whether to be relieved or cry.

Judging by the look of world-weary resignation on Troy's face, he can't decide either.

"The real problem here," Naked Mole Rat fan says, "is that everyone keeps forgetting that Hemlock can't really be with Farpoint. Not without killing him."

Oh god, not this again.

I can't keep myself from letting out an audible groan, even as the crowd erupts in chatter. They know where he's going with this, and in my experience from previous Comic-Cons, they all have an impassioned opinion.

"That's right," he says, pleased with himself. "The poison pussy. Hemlock will kill Farpoint as soon as they—"

"That's not canon!" Sailor Moon shouts. "Hemlock having a poison pussy is only a factor in the first Doctor Supernova arc—"

"Which everyone knows is the best Hemlock continuity," Naked Mole Rat shoots back.

"Disagree! The Doctor Supernova arc was only good in the most recent reboot," my bearded fan from the beginning of the panel shouts. "And there was no mention of Kim—I mean, Hemlock—having a poison pussy."

I can feel my cheeks burning bright red, and I want to beg them to stop talking about my character's theoretical death vagina. Which, for the record, is not a thing in any of my movies. My Hemlock poisons people the good old-fashioned way—with needles and poison-tipped assassin blades.

Blake looks like he might be about to step in, but Jai beats him to it. "Microphone etiquette, people! And remember that you paid money to talk to the stars of the film, not argue with each other, yeah? Save that shit for my podcast."

But the crowd doesn't seem to be calming down, and corset girl shoves forward, practically climbing over the people in the front row. "You want a pussy that's not poison, Blake?" she shouts.

I gape. "Whoa, seriously?" I manage at the same time that Blake frowns and says, "Hey, that's not okay—"

"How could you take Kim back?" she says, dodging the hands of convention security finally stepping in. "She's such an uptight bitch."

Blake half-stands up, grabbing the mic in front of him. "Don't say that about my wife," he snaps, and the room goes suddenly still, with the exception of the corset girl struggling as security pulls her from the room.

My pulse pounds in my neck.

To hear him call me that again . . . it's surreal and incredible and makes me flush all over.

But for him to say that right now, in front of all these people . . .

"Your *wife?*" the reporter in the polo shirt asks, eager as a lion spotting a limping gazelle at the back of the herd. "Are you saying the two of you got re-married?"

Blake sits back down, his face pale. "No, I—It was a slip of the tongue. We were married for so long, and I—I just . . ." He's clearly distressed, and I get it—the press will run with this for weeks, pestering our families, our kids, and our friends to find out if we got re-married.

"Was it just a slip? Or was there some secret wedding ceremony you don't want your fans to know about?" The reporter leans forward, and I swear half the room does too.

"No," I say firmly, jumping in to try to help out. "There was no secret ceremony. We aren't re-married. *Just dating.*"

I think I see Blake blanch, but it's such an imperceptible thing, there and gone, and then he's nodding, agreeing with me.

Should I not have said that? But it's true, and if we go back to not denying false rumors . . .

I remember what Claire said—or supposedly said—and now

I really do want to cry. How could it not have occurred to me what the public might do to her?

The microphone ends up in the hands of another guy, one who hasn't spoken yet, wearing fishnet pantyhose and platform stripper boots on bottom and a camo military jacket and buzzcut on top. I'm not sure if this is a character or a political statement or both. "This question is actually for Sarah Paltrow, the AD."

Sarah turns in surprise from her seat in the front row, though her little boy—long since abandoning interest in the panel to play games on her phone—doesn't seem to notice.

"Are you still with soap opera star Ryan Lansing?" the soldier/stripper asks.

There's a moment where the convention employee nearest her shoots a questioning look at Jai, as if asking whether she should hand Sarah the mic or not. Jai shrugs, and I get the feeling he's about as ready for a stiff drink as the rest of us.

Sarah is handed the microphone. "Um, no. I haven't seen him in seven years."

"So he isn't the father of your lovechild?"

"No," she growls.

Jai sighs and jumps back in the fray. "Let's save the questions for the people on the panel, yeah? God. How about a movie-related question? And by that, I mean a question related to *this movie?*"

The crowd is buzzing again, and Blake still looks profoundly uncomfortable, and my head is spinning with all the guilt and accusations and talk about my pussy—

Then I see Marguerite at the back of the room, with Luke's hand clutched tightly in hers. A couple of uniformed security are beside her, and she looks panicked.

My insides freeze.

"Blake," I say quietly, not paying attention to the possibly movie-related question another audience member is asking. But he has already seen them.

"Excuse us a minute," he says, and both he and I walk down

from the raised platform and hurry to meet Marguerite and the security at the side of the room. Panic is building in my chest.

Bertram is answering whatever question was asked, but most of the people in the room are watching—and filming—us.

I forget about all of the eyes and phones on us a second later as Marguerite whispers frantically, "It's Ivy. She's missing."

NINETEEN

Blake

If I were to make a list of the top ten worst places to lose one of my kids, San Diego Comic-Con would be number one. There are other places with potentially more people, sure—football stadiums and concerts and maybe even amusement parks—but nowhere else are the attendees so laser-focused on spotting celebrities in crowds as dense and impenetrable as a jungle. A deep, colorful, cosplay-filled jungle where an angry twelve-year-old girl could easily disappear.

I don't apologize to Troy—which we're all going to pay for later—when I tell one of the con staff that we're having a family emergency and step out of the panel room. The hall is full of people waiting for the next panel, and several of them make a move toward me with various things in their hands that they no doubt want me to sign.

The security guard thankfully does his job, stepping between me and the fans and ushering Kim and Marguerite and a beleaguered-looking Luke behind him. "Private party," he says to the fans, and herds us into a smallish room nearby that isn't currently in use.

"Oh my god," Kim says to Marguerite. "What happened?"

"She took my phone again," Marguerite says. "And she texted that boy."

Marguerite holds out the phone for us to see, and sure enough, there are a few text messages, in which Ivy and presumably Chris arrange to meet outside the convention hall.

I want to shake Ivy. There were a lot of reasons we didn't want her talking to him, reasons I didn't go into detail about because I didn't want to scare her, because somehow I guess I thought I still had some kind of sway over her just because I'm her father. But clearly I should have recognized the moment that I lost all control, should have scared her much more than I did, because then maybe she wouldn't be running around San Diego with an older boy that I still know next to nothing about.

"We've already been to their meeting place," Marguerite says. She looks close to tears, and Luke and Kim look the same. "It's the first place I went, but they were long gone. Security is looking for her. She just—one minute she was there, and the next she was gone, and I—"

"It's okay," I tell her. "If Ivy wanted to give us the slip, she would have, no matter who was with her. It's not your fault." I put a hand on Luke's shoulder. "Maybe you and Luke should go get a soda or something."

Marguerite doesn't look convinced that this wasn't her fault, and I'm sure in her position I'd feel the same way. But if she's already told everything she knows to security, there's not much more she can do.

"Thank you," I say, and she herds Luke out. As he shuffles past us, he reaches for Kim's hand.

"What about Ivy?" he asks. "Is she gone forever?"

Kim freezes, like she doesn't know what to say, and I know all the horrible things that must be going through her head, because they're also going through mine.

"No, buddy," I tell him. "She just ran off to meet a friend. She wasn't supposed to do that, so we're upset, but she'll be back, okay?"

"But we bothered you while you were working," Luke says. "We're never supposed to bother you while you're working."

I hate that my kid thinks this, but Kim and I are generally unreachable while we're filming, so it's not unjustified. "It's okay," I tell him. "You guys did the right thing."

He nods. Kim wraps him in a tight hug, and then Marguerite ushers him off.

It's going to take more than a soda to calm them both down.

Kim grips my hand and turns to the security guard. "Do you need a description of her? Any ideas where we could look?"

The guard squirms a bit, like he doesn't want to tell her what he's about to say. "We've got the entire security team on the lookout for her. Your nanny gave us a description of what she's wearing, but if she met up with a friend outside the convention center, she might have left the premises. At that point, there's nothing we can do."

"We need to get out there and look," I say. But even as the words leave my mouth, I know this is impossible. We'll be recognized instantly and will have to shoulder through mobs of fans who want to get pictures and autographs.

"Except that we're about the last people who could be doing that," Kim says.

I close my eyes. I hate to say this, but we don't really have any other options. "We need to report this to the police."

Kim nods, as does the security guard. "I'll get one of our on-site officers to come talk to you."

Then he disappears.

Kim's knees seem to give out from underneath her, and she sinks into a chair. This room looks like it's used for small conferences, and I hope that we aren't about to be invaded by attendees of some scheduled event.

I sit beside Kim, still holding her hand. "I don't know whether to be angry or scared or both."

"I'm going with both."

"I talked to him, and he's really a fifteen-year-old boy, not a forty-year-old man or something. So he's probably not trying to kidnap her."

"Probably not, right?" Kim puts her head in her hands.

I wrap my arm around her. "This is hell on your OCD, yeah?"

She stiffens slightly, then nods. "I'm not totally sure what's real, you know? Is Ivy in mortal peril? Is it possible we'll never find her? Because my mind thinks these are really likely outcomes, but logically, probably not, right?"

I kneel down in front of Kim. "No," I tell her. "Probably not. Probably Ivy is off somewhere kissing this boy, and that's it. Then she's going to come back, and we're going to have to figure out what to do with her."

Kim wraps her arms around my neck, holding on tight. "That's true, isn't it?"

"Yes." I don't love this prospect, but it's certainly better than other options. "And I have no idea what we're going to do or say to get through to her. I really don't." I halfway want to kill her myself for being so reckless, for defying us so openly.

But god, if anything happens to her . . .

The door opens, and the security guard brings in a police officer. For the next hour, we give reports to the police, and then are ushered into the security office alongside a man dressed like the clown from *IT* and a girl only a bit older than Ivy who looks like she's been crying. We're given a private waiting room at the back and are left on our own again, unable to do anything but worry.

We check our phones again and again, in case she finds some way to text us, but there's nothing—just the numerous texts from our agents and publicists about Claire's interview. Which is definitely something we're going to need to address, but neither of us can focus on it now.

My daughter has been gone for almost two hours now, somewhere in or around the convention center. I don't think this kid is going to kidnap her, but god, I don't *know*, do I? He could be working with someone else who has darker intentions. Or Ivy herself might have decided to run away, thinking that'll be all fun and games and kisses with cute boys and not realizing she's making herself vulnerable for people who want to—

"We shouldn't have brought her to the convention," Kim says. "We should have sent her home to the ranch with Helene."

I shake my head. "We decided taking everything away from her would just make it worse."

"Look at what's happened!" Kim says. "Can it get worse than this?"

Yes, unfortunately. And I really don't want it to. "You're probably right."

I collapse onto an uncomfortable couch while Kim paces the length of the small waiting room, back and forth, back and forth. I wish I knew what to say to make her feel better, but the truth is, I'm not even sure what to say to myself. I haven't felt so out of control since the divorce, like I have no idea what to do as a husband, as a father.

Oh, god. And I'm not even Kim's husband. I'm not, and I have to figure out how to stop thinking like I am, because, as she insisted, we're just *dating*. After what I did to her, I don't know if she'll ever be able to trust me like that again.

She probably shouldn't, and—

The waiting room door opens, and the officer who took our report stands there, a radio in his hand. "Two officers found your daughter at an ice cream place a few blocks away," he tells us. "They're bringing her back now."

My heart just about falls out of my chest. Kim sinks onto the couch next to me, hugging her arms around herself, and I reach up to rub her shoulders.

"Thank you," I say to him.

The officer nods. "Wait here. It'll only be a few minutes."

He closes the door again, and I wrap my arms around Kim from behind. "She's okay."

"She is, right? If she was having ice cream, then nothing terrible happened to her."

"Sound logic," I say. "But it means we have to figure out how we're going to handle this."

I'm hoping Kim is going to have some lengthy and well thought-out Kim-plan about exactly what we should do to turn Ivy back into our daughter who cares what we think and respects rules.

But instead we just stare at each other in silence.

"We have to punish her," Kim says finally. "Because this behavior has to stop."

"I'd say we leave her at the ranch with a full-time nanny when we go back to film, but that's closer to this boy and therefore more dangerous."

"Plus," Kim adds, "I'm never letting her out of my sight again."

I nod. "She's going to need to be supervised. And not allowed to leave the hotel. That means we'll need someone else with her, because it's not fair to punish Luke, too."

"Maybe we could have somebody watch her on set. It would feel less like a punishment, and I'd be able to know where she is all the time."

I'm quiet for a long moment. If Kim's OCD fills her with fear of what could happen to the kids when she isn't watching, is it better for her to let them go and see that it doesn't happen, or better to keep them near, so she doesn't have to worry?

"Do you think that's what you need?" I ask.

Kim throws up her hands. "I need our lives to not be falling apart around us, but that's not happening, is it?"

I'm quiet for a moment, and Kim squeezes her eyes shut. "I'm sorry," she says. "God, I'm sorry. I suck at this."

She sucks at this? "I think we established that we both suck at this. And we're working on it."

"We are, right?" She keeps asking that question, needing me to confirm to her over and over that things will be okay. And that's where I went wrong before. I didn't step up. I didn't fight for us. I let the building burn down around us.

"Yes," I say. "Yes, we're working on it, and we're going to be okay and so is Ivy."

Kim looks at once like she doubts this and like it's the thing she needed to hear most in the world.

So at least I'm doing half of this right.

The door opens again, and Ivy is standing there with an officer behind her. "We'll give you a few minutes," the officer says. "Take your time."

Ivy stares right at Kim and me with a scowl on her face, I presume because her ice cream date got interrupted by the police. If she thinks we're going to apologize for that, she's wrong.

"Oh, my god, Ivy," Kim says, standing up and grabbing Ivy by the shoulders. This serves both as a hug and to pull her into the room so that the officer can close the door behind her. Kim finishes hugging Ivy—who isn't hugging her back—and then grabs Ivy by both her shoulders and looks her in the eye. "Are you okay?"

"*Yeah*," Ivy says. "I was just getting ice cream. I left the text messages on Marguerite's phone so you'd know I didn't get, like, kidnapped or anything. You didn't have to call the police."

Kim's face hardens. "We absolutely did have to call the police when you ran off in a big city filled with people you don't know. How were we supposed to know you were okay?"

Ivy shrugs and shoulders Kim off. Kim retreats to the couch beside me, while Ivy sinks into a swiveling office chair. "You don't even think I can be gone for an hour. Other kids my age get to babysit, and I'm not even allowed to go down the block with someone my age."

My throat tightens. "Ivy," I say in a warning tone, "this isn't about you not getting the freedom you want. It's about you running off at a crowded event to see someone we've specifically told you not to see. We were worried sick about you." I don't mention the interrupted panel. I'm afraid that, like Luke, Ivy will feel more guilty about that than she does about worrying us, and I hate that my kids don't think they can reach their parents when they need them.

"Besides," Kim says, "you do get to babysit Luke."

Ivy rolls her eyes. "Yeah. At the *ranch*. It's not even that what I did was so dangerous. It's just because I'm *Ivy Pless*."

She says her name with disdain, and I once again want to shake her. "No. It's because you're a twelve-year-old who ran away from her parents. It might be more dangerous because of who you are, but in this case, the consequences could have been the same either way."

Ivy looks down at her shoes, and I realize she's no longer wearing her Violet costume. She must have changed before meeting Christopher, and is now in shorts and a plain lavender t-shirt.

I can't exactly blame her for that, but it also means she wasn't wearing her mask.

"Whatever," she says. "I'm not going to see him anymore, okay? Doesn't that make you happy?"

Nothing about this situation makes me happy, but I'm also suspicious that she's willing to give up now. "Why is that?" I ask.

Ivy stares at me, clearly startled. "Why is what?"

"Why aren't you going to see him again?"

"Because you won't let me. Duh."

"I wouldn't let you today, either," I say. "Didn't seem to stop you."

Ivy glares down at her shoes again. "Because I think he peed himself when the cops showed up."

I hold in a laugh at that. I *bet* he did. I must not hold in my happiness well enough, because Ivy turns her glare back to me.

"So you got your way," she says. "Can we just forget about it now?"

"Absolutely not," Kim says.

Ivy lets out a whine, and at that exact moment, I know for sure that my sweet, responsible little girl has morphed into a hormonal teenager right before my eyes. I didn't realize how fully until now. "It's not like I did anything all that bad!" she says. "I just wanted to kiss a boy."

"And how did that go?" I ask.

Ivy looks surprised that I asked. Her mouth settles into a sullen line. "Meh."

Kim leans forward with her hands on her knees. "You may not have meant to do anything all that bad. But what you did was put yourself in a lot of danger."

Ivy shakes her head. "Christopher isn't—"

Kim talks right over her. "You still could have been kidnapped. You could have been raped, Ivy."

Ivy's whole body tenses, as does Kim's. I reach for Kim's hand. This is good. It needed to be said.

"Christopher isn't dangerous," Ivy says quietly. "He bought me ice cream."

I want to deconstruct the fallacy in that statement, but instead I nod. "I'm glad he wasn't dangerous. But you couldn't have known that for sure, and even if you could, we're your parents. There are some decisions we let you make for yourself, but not this one. We've told you over and over again that we don't want you talking to this boy, and you keep breaking the rules over and over again to do so."

"Right," Ivy says bitterly. "But you get to do whatever you want because you're the grown-ups, so you're allowed to ruin my life."

"What do you want us to do, Ivy?" I ask. "What do you think we should do in this situation?"

Ivy looks dubious that I've asked this, and I take that as a win. The more unpredictable we are, the less she seems to hunker down and whine that her life isn't fair. "I want you to break up and for things to go back to the way they were."

"Why?" Kim asks.

I'm pretty sure it was because we were easier to manipulate when we were both miserable and apart, but I don't think throwing that in Ivy's face at this moment is going to help.

Ivy bites her lip. "Because I don't want anything to change."

"You weren't upset like this when I was dating Simone," I

185

point out. "Or when your mother was dating Roger. And if we'd married other people, things still would have changed. So why is this such a problem for you?"

Ivy wraps her arms around her waist and says softly, "You were never going to marry those people. You didn't really like them."

I'm at once impressed and surprised that she knows this. "That's true," I say. "Your mother and I were never really happy with other people. That's part of why we're back together now, because we want to be happy in the way we only are when we're together."

"That's not true," Ivy says. "You were happy. You'd be fine."

"No, I wasn't." I'm not sure if I ought to be disclosing things like this to my rebellious twelve-year-old, but nothing else I've done has worked, so I figure I can't make the situation worse. "I was miserable without your mother. You think I was happy because I was happy to have you, happy to be with you and Luke, but apart from that, I was lonely and I missed your mother more than you'll ever know."

Ivy stares at me like I'm betraying her, and I can't help but feel the same. "You asked what I want, but it doesn't matter, does it?" she snaps.

My throat tightens. I shouldn't have told Ivy the truth, because it only makes me more angry when she throws it back in my face. "I am so disappointed in you," I say to her. "I can't believe you're so selfish that you can't be slightly inconvenienced for other people's happiness."

"I'm disappointed in you, too!" Ivy yells at me. "You don't care about us at all!"

"Yes, we do," Kim says. Her voice is tired, and I'm sure Ivy can hear that as well as I do. "What we don't understand is what you're losing that is so important to you. Is this really about having two bedrooms?"

Ivy is quiet for a moment, drawing in on herself. "Lukas and I were always the most important thing to both of you."

186

I let out a slow breath. That sounds like the first real thing she's said in this conversation, and it makes sense. She feels a rivalry with me and with Kim, for occupying the other parent's attention.

"Ivy," I tell her, "you're still one of the most important people in my life. You always will be."

"For me, too," Kim says. "You and Luke will always be our priority."

Ivy looks doubtful, and it breaks my heart.

"However," Kim says, sounding resigned, "this isn't about our choices or about Christopher. This is about your deceitful and reckless behavior. It needs to change, Ivy. And until it does, we're going to have to have you supervised at all times, because we can't trust that you won't do this again."

Ivy sinks in her chair like a stone, and I nod. "Your mom's right."

"Fine," Ivy says.

But it isn't. Not even a little bit. And I don't know what we can do to make it be again.

TWENTY

Kim

After all that happened with Ivy, it takes until the next morning—when Blake and I are sitting at the back patio table having brunch—before I feel like my body is no longer a tight knot of exposed nerves.

Being back at the ranch helps. Being surrounded by the familiar chaos and the vast space of acres of land—space to breathe, space to think. And especially knowing that Ivy's safe, even if she has refused to emerge from her room since we got home last night, despite efforts by both Blake and me.

I look at Blake, who has stopped eating his veggie omelet to laugh at the antics of Daphne the goat, who has somehow gotten herself up onto the roof of the feed shed and is taunting one of the ranch hands who is trying to coax her down with a broom.

I smile, warmth spreading through me at the sound of that laugh.

We're all safe and we're all home. My whole family.

"I feel like I should go help him," Blake says. "Maybe if someone got up on a ladder from the other side—"

"Then Daphne gets really excited about the game and starts bleating in a way that somehow summons all the other goats to converge on the shed and join in until the shed roof collapses," I say. "Trust me. It's better to leave it to George and his broom."

Blake considers this. "I believe you. I also believe I need to see this goatpocalypse in person."

"You're welcome to. Just be prepared for George to turn his broom on you. He's fierce with that thing."

Blake laughs again. God, it's so good to be with him here. To wake up in my bedroom with him, to take a tour of the ranch just after sunrise, to introduce him to all my employee friends as well as my animal friends. Some of the human friends were a little starstruck to finally meet the Pless part of Watterpless, having long since gotten over being starstruck by me, but the animals, in true form, only cared about getting breakfast, not so much about how famous the hands were that dished it out. Luke joined us partway through and eagerly showed off his favorite animals and demonstrated how to properly feed Susan, the chicken with the broken beak.

Blake took it all in, warmly greeting each person and animal, nodding at my (or Luke's) description of each canine health issue or feline dietary need, helping to clean up when the roving pack of dogs managed to rip into a big bag of dog food that Amber accidentally left sitting out on one of the golf carts.

He seemed to enjoy it all, but I got the sense that he was a bit overwhelmed. I don't blame him—it's a lot, and hearing about ranch life from the kids isn't the same as the day-to-day living of it.

I try not to worry that he'll be too overwhelmed. That the reality of this ranch, of our life together on it, won't match up to the dream.

I take another bite of my own veggie omelet, a sip of fresh-squeezed orange juice. One of our phones resting on the table buzzes—his this time. Mine went off just a few minutes ago and ten minutes before that.

Blake grimaces but doesn't reach for it. Honestly, we probably should have left the phones inside rather than letting them stress us out with every call or text, but I know myself well enough to know I'd be just as stressed with it out of sight. "One of these times we're going to have to actually answer these things," he says. "I really don't want to see the SWAT team Camilla will send out if she thinks I've disappeared."

I laugh, but there's not much humor in it. "Any chance anyone will believe Costanza ate our phones?"

Costanza, who is lying on the patio by my feet, licking at some spot on the concrete, lifts his head when he hears his name, and I scratch him behind the ears.

"Probably several people in wardrobe would, after that incident with my leather bracers."

Now I'm the one grimacing. We weren't really paying attention one day in my trailer between scenes—busy with, um, other things—and Costanza chowed down on those bracers like they were steaks. He was shitting buckles for the next three days.

Kelsey thought this was hilarious, but many of the other wardrobe assistants—and Sarah—were less amused.

"Camilla, on the other hand, would probably be onto us," Blake says.

I sigh. "I know we're going to have to deal with the fallout from how badly that panel went in general, but I think first we need to figure out how we want to handle the issue with Claire." Our agents and publicists have some really good suggestions for dealing with the public angle. But that's not enough. I twist my lips, poking my omelet around with my fork. "However we do the public apology, I'd like to apologize in person to Claire, if she's willing to see us. I feel terrible, and I don't want her to think we're just worried about PR."

"Though I'd hardly fault her for thinking that." He lets out a breath, his forehead creased. The revelation about Claire is hitting him hard, too. "But yeah, I agree. I don't know that we have time, though, for an in-person meet-up until after we get back from Miami again."

He's right. We've got a private flight back tonight for another

190

month of filming.

"Maybe we can at least get her on the phone. Then, if she's up for it, schedule something for when we're back." I rub the tension knot forming right between my eyes. "Send her about a hundred apology fruit baskets in the meantime." I haven't been able to bring myself to read the interview, but from the texts I've gotten from both Josh and Tara, it sounds pretty bad. She's mad at us, and I don't blame her. Not that I think the harassment wouldn't have happened at all if we had set things straight from the beginning—some people were bound to believe the rumors, no matter what we said—but our silence made things worse. It made us complicit in it.

Blake chuckles sadly. "Yeah, nothing says, 'Sorry we implicated you in a nonexistent affair' like a hundred fruit baskets." But he gives my knee a squeeze, and I put my hand on his and see him relax a little.

I pause, not wanting to bring up more stressful issues. But lately it seems like there's no avoiding them.

"What do we want to do about Ivy?" I finally ask, as we both watch the ducks drifting lazily on the sun-dappled pond.

Blake looks over at me. "Do you really think it's best to keep her on set with us? For you, I mean?"

I don't necessarily think what's best for me matters if it's best for Ivy, but I appreciate his concern. "I think it'll help, knowing we can keep a closer eye on her. And I really liked the idea you had last night about having her walk Costanza instead of having Aaron do it. She could use some responsibility."

"I'm sure Aaron could use a break from his role as Costanza's personal fire hydrant."

"She'll still have to be under constant supervision," I say. "Which she'll hate. But what else can we do?"

Blake shakes his head. "Nothing. We're doing everything we can." He laces his fingers through mine. "Maybe this sounds terrible, but as much as I hate how stressful all this is for us and the kids, it's so nice to be making these kinds of decisions together again."

I smile. "Yeah, that part's really nice."

He looks back out at the ranch. George has managed to wrangle Daphne down from the feed shed, and she's chewing on his pants leg while he scratches her head. The dog pack goes charging by, barking, and Daphne bleats angrily at them. Costanza lifts his head again. He's curious about the dog pack. Friendly with them individually, but still too afraid to leave my side and join the group.

He'll get there, but not until we get a chance to really settle in after filming's done.

Blake tosses him a small piece of butter toast, which bounces off Costanza's nose before he eagerly gobbles it up and paws at Blake's leg for more. Blake smiles, but there's something hesitant in his expression.

"Do you think," he says, and then pauses. "Do you think there's really a place for me here on the ranch?"

My heart constricts. Does he think there isn't? Does he hope there isn't, because it's all too much for him? Does he—

"It's just," he says, "this place is so incredible. And you and the kids and Helene and George and—" he frowns, probably because he can't remember the names of the other ranch workers he met. "You have this all worked out, the routine and structure. You know all the animals and every single thing they need, and it's this well-oiled machine. And if I had been here from the beginning, I'd be part of it. You know? But . . ." He trails off.

My fears dissolve, because I get it now. He wants there to be a place for him, desperately.

I'm not the only one who needs to be assured that it's going to be okay.

I hold his hand tight in mine. "Yes, there's a place for you. There always has been."

He looks over at me, his expression a mixture of doubt and hope.

"I needed this place after our divorce," I continue, "because it felt like maybe it would give me this fresh start. Finally achieving this dream I'd always had. But it stopped being just my dream a long time ago. It was our dream, and it was like every piece of it was still a piece of you and me." I can feel tears pricking at the corners of my eyes. "I loved making this happen, but there's always been something missing without you."

His own eyes are shining, and a single tear slips out.

Is Blake crying? *Blake*?

"Really?" he asks.

"Really."

Blake wipes away the tear, but then there's another tracking down his cheek, and he swears and covers his face with his hands.

I can't believe what I'm seeing. I reach over and grab his hands, pulling them away from his face. "You never cry," I say quietly.

"I never used to," Blake says. "Until my pig died."

I swallow, hard. That used to bother me, knowing he could spare emotion for his beloved pet—not that I'm going to criticize anyone for being attached to an animal—but not for me. Now, though, I wonder if that's what happened at all. "Ivy told me you cried about that," I admit. "I was jealous that you could be so upset over that but not over the divorce."

"It was about the divorce," he says. "It was like I held it together all that time, and then I lost the last thing you gave me. The last piece of our life I had besides the kids. Suddenly all the emotion I pushed aside when I lost you came flooding back, and I cried for days. I couldn't stop. I thought maybe I never would."

I grip both his hands, and he squeezes his eyes shut as more tears leak out.

"I'm sorry," I say. "You never should have had to go through that."

Blake sniffles and takes a deep breath, getting ahold of himself again. I almost wish he wouldn't—not that I want him to hurt, but I want him to feel like he can let me see this side of him, let me in on his pain.

This, though, is a start.

"I'm excited you want to be part of the ranch," I tell him. "If you think this place is such a well-oiled machine, it's only because you've caught us on a good day. Just wait until the next big thunderstorm hits and we've got a spooked horse kicking his stall apart and several cats that need to be kept from scratching each other's eyes out and a herd of terrified dogs all trying to sleep in bed with us. We *always* need help."

He chuckles. "Yeah, okay. It's just a lot to keep track of. I hope I can keep up."

"I'm not worried. You caught up pretty quick when we first moved in together. There wasn't a ranch then, but there was Chandler Bing, and he was like a ranchful of problems all by himself."

Chandler Bing was my adorable, senior, three-legged Jack Russell terrier. A little dog with an outsized personality and a list of medical requirements bigger than he was. All of which Blake took on without a second thought—though not without a snarky comment or two about how he'd never thought that moving in with a girlfriend would involve so many applications of dog ass-medicine.

He grins. "God, he totally was. I miss that dog. And Ugly Naked Pig."

"Me too. But you'll love the rest of these guys. And I have binders with all the info—color-coded, of course—in case you need it."

He rolls his eyes good-naturedly. "Why am I not surprised." But he seems happier. Less afraid.

I've hurt him in so many ways, hurt *us*, but it's nice to see that I can get this right sometimes.

He raises an eyebrow. "Speaking of dogs climbing into bed . . ."

Oh no.

"That *bed*," he says. "I require an explanation for *that bed*."

I groan. I knew this was coming, even before late last night when we entered my bedroom, exhausted and emotionally drained. Blake took one look at my massive canopied oak bed—carved to look like bamboo shoots and covered with script that might be Chinese but I'm not actually sure—and said, "You're telling me *all about this* tomorrow," and crawled into said bed and fell asleep.

"Yeah, so there's a story," I say.

"It seems like there would have to be."

I wrinkle my nose. Do I really want to tell him this story? Then again, he'll probably find it hilarious.

Maybe.

"So about six months after our divorce, I was talking to my friend Deena, remember her?"

Now he's the one who groans, but with a laugh. "Yes. And somehow I'm not surprised that she's involved in this."

Deena was one of my co-stars way back on *Spy High*. I don't see her very often, not since the show ended when I was nineteen, but I can trace many of my more regrettable life decisions back to the times I do see her, a fact Blake knows all too well.

But she's definitely fun to hang out with.

"So Deena was giving me grief about still being hung up on you after all that time—"

"Yeah, that whole six months. God, Kim, get past that eight-year relationship already, right?" Blake tickles my side and I laugh.

It feels so good to be able to laugh about stuff like this. I've spent so many years crying about it. Or trying to pretend I'm okay when I'm not.

"And she and Kate took me out drinking, and at some point after a few too many White Russians—"

"Uh-oh. Your Achilles cocktail."

"—Deena convinced me that I couldn't keep sleeping in the same bed we had when we were married. Too many memories of too much great sex."

"I'm not going to argue with that." He grins.

"So we got home and decided that the best, most cleansing way to rid myself of said memories was to burn it. The bed." I pause. "I set fire to our bed."

His mouth drops open. "Shit, are you serious? I don't know whether to be impressed or horrified."

I cringe. "Well, it turns out our mattress was semi-flame resistant. So Deena suggested we pour lighter fluid on it—"

"Okay, I'm going with horrified. Were you all right?"

"Um, yeah. I mean, it scared the shit out of all of us, how big the fire got. And while Kate called the fire department, Deena and I tried to put it out with the fire extinguisher, but we were really drunk, and by the time the firemen showed up, half of my bedroom was gone and Deena and I looked like we'd been wrestling in whipped cream on *Girls Gone Wild*."

"Oh my god," Blake says, his eyes wide. "You set fire to our bed while it was still *in your bedroom*? How on earth did I not hear about this? How on earth did the whole world not hear about this?"

This is a question I have wondered many times over the years. "Well, you had the kids that night. And I guess we got lucky by getting the world's most discreet firemen." I pause, and then sigh. This is part I really don't want to share, but it's kind of important for the full story, so I blurt the rest out. "And then after the fire was put out, I may have really openly hit on one of the firemen and invited him to stay over and everyone else left and then we, um . . . yeah."

Blake chuckles, but it's strained. "Wow. A firefighter, huh?"

I get how he's feeling. I hate thinking about all the girls—all the gorgeous, gorgeous women—he's slept with in those years we were apart. Before, it was because of how much it hurt knowing he'd gotten over me so fast. Now it's this sense of sorrow—that it should never have happened, because we should never have been apart to begin with.

"I hardly remember anything about him, really," I say,

though I'm not sure that helps much. "But the point is, he must have had some kind of furniture-sales gig on the side, because he referred me to this website where I could get these 'really classy, upscale bedroom sets,' I think he called them. And so after he left, while still drunk, I must have ordered the monstrosity that currently dominates my bedroom. Because it arrived a week later—the 'Luxury of the Orient' it is named." I shake my head in deep regret.

"Wow," Blake says again, and I'm not sure if he's referring to the story itself, or if his brain is still caught on my drunken firefighter sex. "Um, so—"

"Why is it still there five and half years later?" I ask, and he nods. "Because this thing is huge and weighs a thousand pounds, and requires multiple burly men to move anywhere. And I figured that somehow I'd been fortunate enough to avoid the tabloids finding out about the whole bed-pyre, let alone the incident with the firefighter, and I didn't need any more potential witnesses willing to sell a story about Kim Watterson's giant racially-insensitive bed."

"Yeah, that makes sense." He takes a sip of orange juice. "What culture is it even supposed to be? Is it, like, some harem bed? Because it's definitely big enough. And tacky enough."

I laugh. "Roger used to joke that if we ever had a flood we could load the animals into it two by two."

Blake's smile slips a little.

"God, I'm sorry. I shouldn't have mentioned Roger."

"No, it's not that, not really." Blake shrugs with one shoulder. "I mean, you were with him for three years. He was a big part of your life. I don't think it's fair—or even right—that you never talk about him."

I chew on the inside of my cheek. He's right, of course. And I'm definitely well over Roger—the main problem with Roger being that I was never actually in love with him to begin with.

But it still feels kind of shitty to bring up that part of my life to Blake. To make him picture me with someone else, all those pieces of a shared life that he wasn't part of. A shared life that, had we both not been idiots, never would have been with anyone but him.

"It's just . . ." Blake starts, then squints up at the sky. "This is stupid. But I hate thinking of him having a sense of humor. Or making you laugh like I did." He gives me a side-eye look. "Honestly, I like thinking of him as this super-boring, balding guy with a flabby stomach."

I've just taken a sip of my orange juice and nearly choke on it in an attempt to keep from spitting it all over our brunch. "Have you ever actually *seen* a picture of Roger?" I can't help but say, when I can speak again. Because, yeah, he's no Blake Pless, but he's a pretty far cry from the Hunchback of Notre Dame.

Blake wrinkles his nose. "A few hundred, maybe."

I know what he means. I couldn't avoid seeing pics of him and Portia, or him and Simone, or even him and that bimbo he was seen with about a year after the divorce—even though according to her outspoken (and admittedly kind of hilarious) comments on a survival reality show, they only went on two dates and he never slept with her. She claimed she wasn't sure if he was gay, still sad about the divorce, or bloated from eating too much dairy at dinner.

I'd felt pretty certain it wasn't any of those things—um, particularly the first—but I believed the rest of it. Even before I knew that Blake's type was actually *me*, I could tell that his type, in addition to being hot and blond, was also women who can carry on a conversation that isn't about hair care products or Tori Spelling.

He gives me a self-conscious smile. "But yeah, I might have imagined Roger with a few extra flaws—and pounds—on him for my own sanity. And it really kills me to think he might have actually been"—here he winces—"funny."

"I get it," I say. "And yeah, he had a sense of humor. But no one *ever* makes me laugh like you do."

He smiles, and I slide my hand up his shirt, feeling the tight muscles underneath.

"And he definitely didn't have these abs," I add.

"Well, he should take up teleporting. Apparently it's good for the core."

That gets a laugh out of me, and I'm about to suggest I inspect these abs a bit closer, perhaps in a giant bed of vaguely Asian cultural appropriation, when his expression turns serious again.

"You were with Roger for a really long time," he says, toying with the fork in his hand. "What made you stay so long if you knew you weren't in love with him?"

This feels like a loaded question, and yet it's a fair one. Three years is a long time for a relationship in our world, let alone a relationship I knew, deep down, wasn't going anywhere.

I want to be totally honest with Blake, but I don't want to hurt him. I'm pretty sure these things are mutually exclusive when it comes to this.

"Roger was great, you know? A really good guy, who really cared about me."

Blake nods, and I can tell he doesn't want to hear a laundry list of my ex-boyfriend's finer qualities, so I move along.

"I convinced myself that the reason I was staying with him was because maybe someday I would love him back the way he loved me." I swallow around the thick lump forming in my throat. "But I—I don't think that was true. I think I always knew I wouldn't."

Blake runs his thumb over the tops of my knuckles, but doesn't say anything.

"I think I stayed with him because it was comfortable. And—" I draw in a deep breath. "I knew he'd never leave me."

Blake flinches, then looks away, blinking too fast. And I know, he blames himself so much for that, and I shouldn't have told him, shouldn't have made him feel worse about something that wasn't really his fault, not when I was pushing him away so hard—

"God, I'm sorry, Kim." His voice is bleak with six years of regret.

I scoot my chair closer to his, so our knees are touching, and lean into him, resting my head against his shoulder. "Me too," I say softly. I wonder how long before we stop feeling the need to apologize to each other for this. We're definitely not there yet, either of us.

"But that . . . it still wasn't enough," I continue. "Because Roger wasn't you, and he was never going to be you. And *you* were what I really needed." He puts his arm around me and hugs me tight, and it feels so good, even though the small metal armrest between us cuts into my waist. "You were with Simone awhile, too," I say. "Not three years, but still. Was there something you had with her that I'll never be able to give you? Something you might regret having lost—with her, or with Portia, or Colleen, or any of them?"

He takes a moment to consider, and while I appreciate him wanting to give me the same honesty I gave him, I hate how panicky I start to feel.

"No two people are exactly the same," he says slowly. "And yeah, I got different things out of each relationship. And it wasn't like dating you, but that was the problem. I was with them to fill the void of losing you, and none of them could ever fill that. So no, there's nothing I'll regret having lost by not being with them. Because I'm with you, and you are everything I want." He presses his forehead against mine. "And I'm not leaving you again, I promise."

"I know." I'm getting closer and closer to really being able to believe it, even though my nerves constantly want to barge in and tell me otherwise.

"In fact," he says, and there's that hesitance in his tone again. "I know we said we'd wait until our family is ready, and Ivy's not exactly there yet, but I'd be up for getting married again soon. Making it work, like we should have." His lips quirk up at the sides. "Clearly I can't keep from calling you my wife in public settings."

"Clearly," I say, but it's barely more than a breath. My brain and heart are pulling me all over the place.

I want to be his wife again, so badly. But right now all I can picture is us at the altar—maybe in a church this time, or maybe outdoors like our first wedding—with Ivy standing next to us, miserable, hating us both. Planning her next big escape from the hell we've somehow made of her life. And the sound of choppers overhead as the paparazzi wait to get the perfect pic of the wedding everyone will be calling a publicity stunt to prop up a film increasingly plagued with bad press. And my parents—god, my parents, I've avoided their calls for weeks because I really don't want to hear their opinions on my being back with Blake—sitting there in disapproval of the man I love, a man they've never given a fair shot.

All that stress will be hell for my OCD, maybe enough to turn me back into the woman that made us both miserable, and maybe, even if it's just for a moment, he'll regret wanting to marry me again *on our wedding day*—

I'm stiff with tension again, my muscles bunched up, and I know he can feel it, though hopefully he can't feel the way my heart is pounding hard enough to break through my ribcage.

His lips part; his hand slips away from my shoulder. "Yeah, no, it's a bad idea."

"No, it's—I just don't think I'm ready for that yet," I say. "With everything going on with Ivy, and I just—"

"It's okay." He squeezes me close again, but he's looking back at the duck pond. "It's okay."

But I don't think it is, not really, and I wish I knew how to make it so.

"I love you," I say, because I need him to know that. Like maybe that will make putting up with all my fears and crazy brain worth it.

"I know." He lifts my hand to kiss the back of my knuckles. "I love you too."

My phone buzzes again, and we both groan.

"You should probably deal with that, and I can go try yet

again to talk to our daughter—holy shit, that is a big turtle."

I follow his gaze to where there is, in fact, a big turtle slowly making his way across the patio in front of us. "That's Newman. He's a tortoise. He's got a chunk of his shell missing, and his skin gets easily irritated by dirt and stuff, and he shouldn't be out of the house. I must have left the sliding door open."

"Right," Blake says. "Newman. The house tortoise. I'll get it all figured out."

Now I'm kissing the backs of his knuckles. "I know you will."

We both will, I think to myself as I go to lug Newman back into the house, Costanza padding along beside me, and start returning phone calls.

TWENTY-ONE

Blake

When Ivy doesn't emerge from her bedroom by noon, I knock once, and then invade her space. I was half worried she was on some sort of hunger strike, but she looks up at me from her bed, guiltily holding an Oreo out of a half-empty package.

I guess she has been out of her room at some point. Either way, I'm not going to pick a fight about that today. "Hey," I say. "I still need to hear about how your first kiss went." I sit down on her bed, like this is totally natural. A month ago, it probably would have been.

Now Ivy wrinkles her nose at me. "You can't ask about my first kiss. You're my *dad.*"

My heart squeezes. I'd always hoped that Ivy and I had a close enough relationship that she would feel comfortable talking to me about stuff, even if I am her dad. "Sure I can. You don't have to tell me. But I'd love to hear about it."

I lean back against the headboard and wait, and Ivy sighs. "You are so weird."

Weird is a step up from ruining her life, so I'll take it. "Just because you're mad at me doesn't mean I don't care about what's going on in your life. How was it?"

"It was kind of gross, actually," she says reluctantly.

There is no part of me that is sad to hear this. "Yeah?"

Ivy nods. "I mean, at first it was okay, I guess. But then he put his tongue in my mouth, and he tasted like Cheetos, and he wiggled it up and down like a worm." Ivy makes a gagging sound, and I laugh.

"Yeah, okay," I say. "The tongue thing is good when you both know what you're doing, but it takes some getting used to."

Ivy looks sideways at me, like she expects that I have some agenda here. And I do. I want to connect with my daughter.

"You're not supposed to be okay with this," she says. "You're mad at me."

Sometimes she's so much like her mother that it takes my breath away. "Yeah, okay. But that doesn't mean I can't hear about what's happening." I pause. "So, not in a hurry to kiss anyone else, I'm guessing?"

"I'm grounded for the rest of my life, anyway."

"Because that stopped you before."

When she sees that I'm smiling, one corner of her mouth turns up before she turns it back down again.

Good. This is progress.

"I know you're upset about your mom and me," I say. "But you have to know that this doesn't change anything between us, right? You're my daughter. Nothing can ever change how much I love you."

Ivy shrugs, but she looks a little sheepish, so I think maybe she believes me.

"I know you don't want to give up the condo," I say. "And I get that. We've had good times there."

"*I* have. *You* were unhappy."

I get why this feels like a betrayal to her, and I'm sorry about it, but I still want to be honest. "I was unhappy there," I say. "But there were two bright spots that made me happy in the middle of it all."

Ivy wrinkles her nose at me again. "Me and Lukas?"

"Yep. You guys are everything to me."

"We *were*," Ivy says.

I shake my head. I want her to understand what I'm saying, but it's not something I understood myself before I was a father. "You know, when your mom was pregnant with Luke, I worried that I wouldn't be able to love him as much as I loved you."

Ivy looks surprised. "Really?"

"Yeah," I say. "Because I loved you so much, I couldn't imagine ever loving another little person the same way."

"But you did." She doesn't sound jealous or annoyed—more concerned on her brother's behalf. Which I take as a good sign.

I nod. "Then Luke was born, and he was my kid, and I loved him just as much. But I didn't love you any less, you know? And that's when I understood that love isn't finite. It isn't some pie that gets divided between the people in your life, so that everyone gets less when someone else is added. Love is like a bright light. Everyone can sit under it equally."

Ivy looks suspicious. "So it's supposed to be okay for you and Mom to get back together, because you don't love us any less."

There's a part of me that feels like an idiot saying all this, when I'm not even sure how things are going to work out with Kim and me. It's so strange, being here in her world, a world she built without me, where I'm not sure how I fit, even if she promises that I will. I'm in this all the way, but she's understandably reticent to dive into anything permanent. And I get that. It's fine. It should be fine.

But it doesn't take away the ache, and I can't help but feel like I'm standing with my toes hanging over a steep cliff, one that goes down and down and down forever.

"You don't agree," I say.

Ivy sighs, but at least she's not screaming at me. "Maybe it's okay if you love each other. But that didn't stop you from fighting all the time before."

It's true. Ivy clearly remembers more about the time before the divorce than I thought she did. Maybe even more than I thought she knew at the time. She was sharp, even as a six-year-old.

"I know you don't have any reason to trust me on this," I tell her. "But things are different now."

"Different how?"

It's an honest question, and she's asking it almost without attitude, which makes me want to tell her the truth.

But the truth isn't entirely mine to tell.

"I'm going to do my best to explain it to you," I say, "because I think that you're mature enough to handle it."

Ivy shifts nervously. "Okay."

I take a deep breath. "I left and filed for divorce because I thought I was making your mother miserable. She was so unhappy, and I thought that by leaving, I was giving her the opportunity to find something better."

Ivy looks confused. "But if you made her unhappy before—"

"That's the thing. I thought that's what was happening, but it wasn't true. Your mom was unhappy for reasons that had nothing to do with me."

"Why was she unhappy?"

"That's not mine to share with you. That's something you need to hear from your mom, when she's ready. But it didn't have anything to do with me or you or Lukas."

Ivy glares at her bright-colored comforter, and I can feel her shutting down again.

"But the difference," I continue, "is that now I understand what was actually going on. And your mom understands that I never wanted to leave her, that if I'd known what was happening, I would have stayed."

"So the divorce was Mom's fault," Ivy says.

"No," I say quickly. "It wasn't her fault at all."

"But if she was unhappy, and she didn't tell you why—"

"She didn't know, either." I'm worried that I'm getting dangerously close to betraying Kim's trust, or maybe I already have. But Ivy clearly needs me to be open with her, so I have to strike some kind of balance. "Sometimes when you're going through something, it's not always totally clear what's happening, even to you."

Ivy shakes her head. "Adults are so stupid."

I laugh. "Yeah, okay. Maybe we are. But you don't seem to be able to explain exactly what's going on with you all the time. So maybe you're crossing over into stupid adulthood faster than I'd like."

Ivy crosses her arms. "I still don't like it."

"I know. But we're still your parents, even when you don't like our choices. We're still responsible for keeping you safe, and you still need to follow our rules. You understand that, right?" She glares at me, and I smile back at her. "Hey, all I ask is that you understand. You don't have to like it."

"What are you guys going to do to me?" she asks.

Oh, boy. This could backfire on me. Hard. And I don't want to give up what little progress we've just made.

"No more outings with Marguerite," I say. "Instead, you'll stay on set with us and help us take care of Costanza."

She eyes me suspiciously. "My punishment is I have to play with Costanza?"

I smile. "I know. We're such monsters."

Ivy continues to stare at me like she's waiting for the other shoe to drop.

"You know we're not looking to punish you, right? We're trying to make sure you're safe."

"Okay. But school will be starting in a month."

"Yeah," I say. "And we'll be done with location shooting by then, and working at the studio. So that won't be a problem."

"But I have summer homework for advanced reading," she says. "I've read all the books, but I have to write a bunch of reports on them, and I don't have my computer, so I can't do it."

She has a point. I'm pretty sure she's been furiously reading the books for her summer assignment because she wanted to make this particular argument. "I'll talk to your mom. We'll figure out some kind of supervised computer time schedule."

That sort of thing is definitely Kim's department.

"But I'm going to have all that time on set," she says.

"And I wish we could trust you to follow our rules without us watching." I elbow her. "But you understand why we can't, right?"

Ivy grumbles something that might be a grudging yes or a disgruntled no. Either way, I've made my point.

I put a hand on her shoulder. "I'll talk to your mother. We'll work something out."

Ivy rolls over away from me and scarfs down another Oreo. She looks up at me guiltily, like she expects me to take the package with me, but I don't.

I meant what I said. I just want her to be safe. And if I allow her this little rebellion, well.

We can fight that battle when we're standing on more stable ground.

TWENTY-TWO

Kim

We're back on set in Miami, ready to film another scene on a blocked-off downtown street, although this time I'm the one acting. And we have a new co-star on set—an eighteen-year-old newly-minted heartthrob named Tanner Berg, who is on some CW show about an angel who hunts werewolves. Or maybe a werewolf who hunts angels? Either way, he's a relatively minor role in this movie, playing Hemlock's nephew (and the sole remaining family member she has left after Naked Mole Rat killed her sister in the first movie), so Troy was able to put all his scenes together in these last few weeks to accommodate his TV shooting schedule.

"It's really cool getting to work with you," Tanner says in between takes, as a stylist carefully re-shapes the blond hair that is supposed to look haphazardly flopped over one of his blue eyes. "Like, you're totally legit."

I'm not exactly sure what he means by that—a reference to my acting cred?—but it sounds like a sincere compliment. "Thanks. It sounds like your show is doing well, so congrats on that."

He shrugs, but I can tell he's pleased. "*Hunted* is pretty sweet. But movies, man. That's where I *really* want to be."

Inwardly, I cringe. He's clearly new to this and doesn't know yet that he shouldn't say stuff like that in public, not at this stage in his career. All it takes is one loose-lipped bystander—or that PA adjusting the back of his hoodie—to go to the press and suddenly there's some big story about how ungrateful Tanner Berg is, how he's ready to leave the show that just so recently made him.

Warning Tanner about that in public would just draw attention to it, so I just laugh lightly, like I know he doesn't really mean it. "Well, luckily you can do both. Great job on that last take, by the way. Your reaction to my line about your mom's death was seriously moving." I mean it, too. The kid's pretty good.

"Dude, thanks," he says, flipping his hair back the moment the stylist steps away. "I thought it was the shit, too. But Troy is all pissy about it."

The shit? God, this kid makes me feel like I'm a hundred years old. Kind of like Ivy does sometimes.

Also, he should probably learn not to bad-mouth the director so openly, either.

"Um, well," I start, glancing over at Troy, who is slumped down in his chair glaring at the playback on the screens around him. "He's got a lot going on. Filming usually gets a little stressful around this time."

And that's even when a director *isn't* dealing with the very public fallout from the Comic-Con debacle.

"Yeah, well, I think the dude could stand to lighten up. Speaking of which, you know about that new club out here, right? It's called Hustle, I think, and it's the shit. Like—"

Tanner doesn't finish telling me what exactly Hustle is supposed to be like, beyond "the shit," because Troy shouts for us to get back to our places for the next take.

I don't think I need him to tell me what Hustle is like, though. Trendy new clubs come and go, but deep down they're all the same. And I've seen way too many young stars lose themselves in them over the years.

I frown, but there's not time to say anything, and what the

hell am I going to say anyway? I don't even know Tanner. He flashes a peace sign—or does it mean something else now?—and heads over to the opening of the alley where Hemlock finds him.

I stretch my cramping quads out quickly—my trainer worked me extra hard this morning since I didn't get my daily workouts in LA—and jog back to my mark at the beginning of the sectioned-off street. I look to see if Blake is sitting out there watching me film, but then remember that he's got a phone interview with some British magazine right now.

The thought of more interviews tenses me up immediately. It was bad before, but after what happened at Comic-Con, after all that came out about Claire and the continuing negative press around the film and—

Blake's a pro, I tell myself. *He knows what he's doing. It'll be fine.*

Honestly, I'm just really glad it's not me being interviewed today.

We run through the scene several more times, and with each take in the sweltering heat, I am increasingly glad I'm not wearing Hemlock's standard plant-fetish leather. Instead I'm in linen shorts and a light cotton t-shirt. I'm Hemlock's alter ego Sabrina Kane today, discovering that her nephew, who she thought was safely in another state, is actually back in Miami.

Finally, Troy determines our little family reunion has hit all the right notes of shock (me), guilt (Tanner), protective anger (me again), and caustic fondness (both of us) to call it good. Though judging by his tone, it's more likely he called it because he got sick of arguing with the animal handlers over how long the two dogs being walked in the background of the scene should be out in the heat.

The dogs—both adorable Chihuahuas getting misted between every take—appear fine; it's the rest of us who are about to become puddles of sweat on a Miami sidewalk.

I turn for the chilled water that a PA brings me every few takes, but instead of a production assistant, there's Blake with that big sunny smile on his face, and a hand towel draped over his arm, my water bottle displayed like a fine wine.

"For the incomparably gorgeous and talented Miss Watterson," he says with a formal bow.

I grin. "I don't know which is more tempting for me to put my lips on right now, the water or the waiter." I take the water from him, and a groan escapes me at how icy cold it is. I want to rub this all over my body.

He laughs. "I think that question just got answered."

I'm too busy gulping down the water to laugh with him, but I lean in for a kiss shortly after; we smile against each other's lips.

I'm afraid to ask how the interview went, so I go for another scary question. "How's Ivy doing?"

Blake shrugs one shoulder. "I haven't gotten a chance to see her much, but she seems happy enough walking Costanza. I'm about to have Aaron install that computer tracking program, though, so we'll see how that goes."

That sounds like how she was when I saw her a few hours ago—happy enough. It saddens me how relative that seems now. But she was glad for the break from the hotel and her little brother, even if it meant that she was essentially under the constant supervision of even more eyes. And though she still heaved a number of aggrieved sighs in my direction, I actually got a few smiles from her and a joke about Costanza's terrible doggie breath.

I wonder if we should start bringing the situation with her up in our therapy appointments soon. We already had one since we've gotten back and have another scheduled in a couple days. I know these appointments are supposed to be about the problems in Blake's and my relationship, but our kids are obviously an important part of that, especially given the way Ivy's reacting to us getting back together.

"Speaking of Aaron," Blake says, pulling a card out of the back pocket of his shorts—he's dressed in regular clothes for the time being, since his next scene isn't for another few hours. "My assistant came through for us."

I smile at seeing the shiny American Eagle gift card. Blake's assistant, Cassie, informed us that Aaron had gotten at least one of his pairs of ruined pants from there. So we decided we owed him some new clothes, sooner rather than later, and had Cassie pick the card up this morning.

"Five hundred dollars, right?" I pause. "Do you think that's enough?"

"How many pairs of pants does this guy *need*?"

"Right. I need to remember who I'm asking," I say with a laugh. Blake has never cared much about fashion. He wears clothes that look good on him, sure (though honestly, he's Blake Pless, a Hefty bag would look good on him), but his daily wear consists of a rotation through a handful of casual outfits, shorts and light button-downs or t-shirts, and that's about it.

No matter how much money or fame he's achieved, he's still so down-to-earth, and I love that about him. I always have.

"Oh, hey, and there's Kelsey," Blake says, looking back over to where the actors are getting prepped for the next scene. Kelsey's sewing a button on the cuff of the pitch-black suitcoat that Bertram is wearing for his next scene, while makeup artists are alternately applying more last minute white body powder to his shaved head and blotting off sweat. If there's a better example of a Sisyphean task, I don't know what it is.

"Fantastic. She'll be so excited." Blake and I exchange a grin. Reason two for the gift card involves Kelsey.

I wave her over when she starts heading back to the wardrobe trailer.

"Hey guys," she says brightly, then frowns. "I heard about Comic-Con. Ugh. So sorry."

Sadly, that sympathy could be in reference to any number of things. I don't bother pressing. "Thanks," I say. "But we've got something for you. Or better yet, something for you to give to Aaron."

I hold out the card, and she raises an eyebrow.

"I'm giving him a gift card to a mall clothes store?" There's a hint of snarky judgment in her tone that reminds me all too much of Ivy.

It occurs to me that Cassie, Blake's assistant, is also in her mid-thirties. Maybe we should have picked someone younger to choose a gift card.

"You're giving him the opportunity to spend the day with you at the mall," Blake says. "While he gets new clothes, courtesy of us. And Costanza's weak bladder."

Blake's spin on it works wonders; Kelsey gets a sly smile on her face. "Yeah, okay. This could work." She chews her lower lip. "I think I even have the perfect line to use with this—I'll let you know how it goes."

"You'd better," I say. After grievously wounding our daughter on a daily basis, drawing negative press to the film, and learning that we inadvertently threw our old nanny to the internet wolves, it would be really nice to be able to make *someone* happy again.

Though I can think of lots of ways I could make Blake happy, given a few minutes alone in his trailer.

Since we're on the middle of a bustling film set at the moment, though, I settle for slipping my arm around his waist. He pulls me closer, even though my shirt is plastered to my back with sweat, and I probably smell like a swamp.

"Awww," Kelsey says, grinning at us. "You guys are the most adorable couple ever. And the best. Seriously. Thanks for this." She waves the gift card at us and heads off, her curls bouncing with every step.

"Do you think it'll work?" I ask.

Blake puts his other arm around me, so I'm pressed up against him. "Hopefully. If not, I guess we'll have to give up our dreams of starting that matchmaking empire and stick with acting. And being the most adorable couple ever."

"Mmmm." I'm enjoying the feel of his arms around me so much, I don't care that probably a dozen people are taking our picture right now. It can't be worse than the filmed makeout-turned-dry humping session they all witnessed a few weeks ago.

"Have you met Tanner yet?" I ask.

"Oh, the new kid. Yeah, I met him." From his tone, I gather he's not terribly impressed with Tanner. "I haven't seen him work yet. How is he?"

"He's actually got good instincts." I pause. "When it comes to acting."

Blake studies my face. "Uh-oh. What are you planning?"

"Nothing!"

He raises an eyebrow and I sigh. Good to see we can still read some things about each other so well after all these years, I suppose.

"Fine. I just thought I'd talk to him a bit. You know, give him some tips on the business. And the importance of professionalism."

He opens his mouth, but I cut him off before he can knock my plan.

"He seems like a nice enough kid. But he's really new to this, and he got big fast. I've seen so many stars like him go off the rails at their first taste of fame, especially if they don't have someone to guide them on how to handle it—"

"Like your parents, you mean." There's a sudden sharpness to his words that I know isn't directed at me.

But I feel the nick of them anyway.

"Yeah," I say, pulling back. "Like my parents. Who aren't perfect, but did keep me from becoming some coke-binging, paparazzi-flashing teen star train wreck."

He makes a little snorting sound. "Like you were ever going to be that. You're *Kim*."

Now neither of our arms are around each other; we aren't touching at all.

"What is that supposed to mean?" Though I know already. I'm Kim Watterson. Responsible. Rule-oriented. Not inclined to being spontaneous or wild.

"Nothing." He pinches the bridge of his nose. "I didn't mean—it's nothing."

Does that bother him about me? Has it always, or has dating

215

women who are more fun, more free, made him realize—

No, stop, I tell myself. *He loves me.*

"So you don't think I should do this."

His brow furrows. "No, I don't. He's not going to listen."

Maybe it's his flat tone, like there's not even a possibility he's wrong, or maybe I'm still stinging from his previous words about my parents, about myself, but my hackles rise even more. I feel like Roz, our one-eyed cat, when the dogs get anywhere near her.

"So that means I shouldn't even *try* to help? To give him some advice, maybe get him thinking about his longterm career?"

Blake flings his arms out to the side. "He's an eighteen-year-old kid who probably just wants to get wasted and sleep around. What exactly do you think you're going to be able to do here?"

I'm not actually sure myself, but the fact that Blake doesn't think I'm capable of doing anything to help . . . I clench my fists, feeling the bite of my nails in my palms.

"He respects me," I say—though I'm only partly confident that's what he meant by "totally legit," and I'm not going to admit that to Blake right now—"And maybe you don't believe I can help, but that doesn't mean I shouldn't try."

"Kim—" Blake starts, but I'm mad and hurt and not sure either of those emotions are entirely justified, and we're out here in front of so many watchful eyes, and I just can't right now.

"I've got to do my read-through," I say briskly. "Good luck with Ivy and the computer program."

Then I turn and walk through the bustling set crowd, forcing a smile so no one thinks anything is wrong.

TWENTY-THREE

Blake

I never thought I'd see Ivy so angry to be getting a computer back, even one that isn't technically hers. But as Aaron is setting it up on the side table in Kim's trailer, she lies on her back on Kim's couch with her arms crossed, looking like a vampire about to sit up in her coffin.

"This sucks, you know," she says.

"Yeah," I say. "It does."

Ivy makes a snarling noise.

"You sound like an angry poodle," I tell her.

She is clearly not amused.

"All right," Aaron says. "Computer up and running."

"And tracking my every move like I'm a criminal," Ivy says.

Aaron looks over at me. "Anything else?"

"No," I say. "Thanks."

When he leaves, having unboxed, plugged in, and set up the computer itself, then installed monitoring software so that everything that's done on it is recorded and reports are emailed to both Kim and me, Ivy lets out one of her patented zombie moans.

"Now the poodle is undead," I say. "That can't be good."

"It's not *fair*," she says half-heartedly, compared to her

previous attempts.

"Actually, I'm pretty sure this is the definition of fair. We told you to stop contacting Christopher. You continued to contact Christopher. Now we have a solution that allows us to make sure you don't contact Christopher while still doing your homework. Should we go over the rules one more time?"

"Why even ask? You're going to repeat them to me anyway."

"Good point. If you contact Christopher in any way, what happens?"

She scrunches down further. "You find out and take my computer away."

"If you disable the monitoring software or for any reason your session is not recorded, what will happen?"

Ivy deteriorates into a zombie poodle robot. "You. Take. The. Computer. Away."

"Right," I say. "And if you do any other unspecified things that we have not had the foresight to forbid you to do but which you reasonably could have foreseen that we would not have been okay with had we been asked ahead of time?"

"Ughhhhhh. My life is over." The zombie poodle robot melts into such a puddle that she half flows off the couch and ends up contorted in a position that cannot be comfortable, but which Ivy maintains out of stubbornness.

"Great," I say. "Good luck with that homework."

Ivy makes a noise that sounds like she might actually be dying, but I don't turn around. I'm pretty sure if she'd suddenly developed appendicitis or choked on anything other than her own sense of ennui, she'd have the sense to come out of there and make herself known before she died. I have to admit, I felt about as miserable earlier when I was being interviewed over the phone by that British reporter. She tried in about a dozen different ways to get me to admit that there was a deeper reason I called Kim my wife beyond my messed-up psychology. I tried not to sound like a zombie poodle robot as I explained over and over that there wasn't, but I'm not sure I entirely succeeded.

Outside my trailer, I find Kelsey leaning up against the side, her head cocked at a flirtatious angle, actually twirling her hair around her finger while she holds up the gift card in Aaron's direction.

"So," she says. "What do you say? Let's get you out of those pants."

I try not to laugh. I like to think I was more subtle than that when Kim and I were first working together, but then I remember the complete lack of surprise from any of the cast or crew when it became obvious we were sneaking out of each other's trailers every morning and making out behind the set pieces between takes. I'm pretty sure there were a few clues beyond our magnetic on-screen chemistry.

"If it gets me pants that don't smell like dog piss, I'm in," Aaron says.

Kelsey falters and they both look over at me, like they've just realized I'm standing there.

"Oh, hey," Aaron says. "Thanks, Mr. Pless."

"Call me Blake," I say. "And I'll pass your thanks on to Kim."

"Yeah, thank you," Aaron says again, and Kelsey gives me an excited grin behind Aaron's back.

I have no idea if Aaron is reciprocating her interest, but I'm not sure I *would* know, as I've never heard the kid say anything more than is absolutely necessary for his job. I'm not sure if he's just quiet in general or if he's nervous around me.

It used to drive me crazy the way the staff would treat me like I deserved some kind of reverence just because they'd seen me in movies. Now I'm so used to it that it's faded to a kind of background noise. But it still bothers me that I can't make real friends with the people I work with like I used to. There's always this distance, this sense that everyone is so busy freaking out that they're friends with *Blake Pless* that they forget I'm just a normal person.

In the early years, it was Kim who kept me from going completely insane from the dissonance and isolation. After that, I think maybe I did lose it for a while.

I take a deep breath and try to figure out how I'm going to fix what I said to Kim. I get why she's mad at me, but I didn't mean to imply that she's not capable of helping people. I just worry that she's going to get hurt, getting invested in a kid like that who, from what I've observed so far, is way more interested in getting wasted and enjoying his fame than in taking serious career advice.

Then again, I was that kid, once. Not so much the fame-seeking, partying type, but definitely the guy who fell into acting and didn't have a single clue what he was doing. I walk back toward the area where they're filming, hoping to catch Kim and apologize.

I may not think it's smart of her to try to save every stupid kid she works with, but I suppose I shouldn't fault her for the impulse.

It's the only reason she ever gave me the time of day.

TWENTY-FOUR

Kim

An hour after my little freak-out at Blake, I'm still upset. I don't blame him for the dig against my parents—god knows how many far worse digs he put up with from them until I finally had the guts to tell them that this was the man I was going to marry, and if they couldn't stop acting like assholes, they didn't need to be in our lives.

They made the effort, at least. I was pregnant with Ivy at the time, and the thought that they might be cut off from their future grandchildren was strong motivation to get them to cut the passive-aggressive bullshit. But it was clear they were never going to give their full approval to Blake, no matter how good a husband and father he showed himself to be.

I wonder how much of it was because they could never quite forgive me for breaking their rules. Regardless, things were never the same between my parents and me after that, which in some ways was good. They stopped trying to control me in every little thing; I stopped letting them.

To their (dubious) credit, they didn't rub it in after the divorce. Once, when I was in a particularly deep pit of self-pity, I confessed to my dad that I wasn't sure Blake had ever loved me. "I may not have liked him much," my dad said, "but anyone could see that man loved you, Kim." It made me cry at the time, but that one admission doesn't mean my parents will be thrilled to see us back together. Hopefully they know that my previous threat still holds—and when I finally bring myself to return their calls and talk to them about getting back together with Blake, I'll be sure to remind them.

My parents might have had too tight a grip on me, but some aspects of it were good for me. The guidance, the advice, the reminder of how fleeting fame and fortune can be if it's not properly maintained.

I don't expect to be Tanner's mom or anything—though he could probably use it, given how awful most showbiz parents are—but I've been where he is, and I've come out the other side, sane and successful.

Okay. *Sane* may be debatable. But compared to most teen stars, I'm a shining beacon of mental health.

I'm determined to talk to Tanner and prove Blake wrong about me.

"Hey, Tanner," I say, finding him sitting in a chair under a portable AC unit, going over the script for his next scene.

That's good. Responsible.

Or so I think until I get closer and realize he reeks of pot.

"Heeeey," he says, grinning up at me, the stoned sound to his voice removing any (slim) hopes that he just happened to wander past a few toking extras. "Kim. Good to see you."

"Yeah. Well. Hey." I'm suddenly unsure of how to start. Damn it, why don't I ever take a minute to prepare these things? "So you know I think you've got a lot of talent, right? I said that earlier."

He brushes back that flop of hair that just falls back over his eye again a second later. "Oh yeah. That was the shit."

"Right. Well—"

He leans forward. "You know, I think you're *way* too hot to be my aunt. Aunts aren't supposed to be hot."

Ugh. I try to keep from wrinkling my nose. It's not the first time I've been hit on by a co-star young enough to be my son, and not the first time said co-star has been high while doing so.

But even if Tanner is stoned, maybe I can get through to him a little. At least open the conversation.

"Um, thanks," I say, keeping my tone as friendly and yet unencouraging as possible. "I just wanted to say, I know what it's like to be a teen star. I was one, too. A loooong time ago." I try to emphasize that last bit. "I know how easy it is to get swept up in all of this. But it's important to—"

"You want a smoke?" He pulls a pack of regular cigarettes from his jeans pocket. I'm fairly sure he'd have a joint ready at a moment's notice, if I seemed so inclined.

"No. I don't smoke. And when it comes to pot, probably you shouldn't either, at least not during a shoot, you know? I know lots of people do way worse, but when you're on set, it's important to maintain a professional image—let people see that despite your young age, you can be trusted with bigger and more nuanced roles. If that's what you ultimately want, that is."

He nods slowly, his blue eyes serious. "Yeah, that makes sense." He puts the cigarettes back.

I smile, encouraged. He's listening to me. Should I leave it there for now?

I've never been good at leaving things there.

"Because I really think you have the talent to have a lasting career, and if you're open to some advice—"

He makes a snorting kind of laugh. "*Lasting*," he repeats, then gives me a significant look.

I blink. "Um, lasting *career*. Yes. But in addition to not doing drugs before scenes, you definitely want to be careful with how you interact on set with—"

"Hey, speaking of interacting, did you look up that club I told you about? Hustle? It's the shit," he reminds me. "They don't even *open* until 1 AM. I'm going tonight, getting super turnt. There'll be tons of girls."

He leans back in his chair, staring off into the distance

dreamily, like he's picturing it.

My brief wink of triumph is quickly becoming dismay. "Don't you have to be on set at six-thirty tomorrow?"

"Probably." The logistics of this don't seem to register.

"Won't that make it difficult to do your scenes at the top of your game? If you've been out all night partying?"

He looks mildly confused, but he doesn't say anything, so I continue.

"Maybe if you save Hustle for a night when you don't have to work the next morning—"

"Hey, okaaaaay," he says, as if something finally clicks into place. He looks me up and down in a way that makes my skin crawl. "I get it. Yeah. I mean, if you want to get with me, that's cool, you can just say it. Like, I don't usually go for way older chicks, but you're off the charts, like, you've been in *Maxim*'s top ten MILFs for, like, forever, and—"

"What? No!" I put my hands up, stepping back. "God, no, I am not trying to *get with you*. I'm trying to *help* you not to throw away your career before it's even started!"

"Whoa, fine," he says. "I'm just saying I'm into it. But, like, you'd have to chill a bit. I've got some stuff back at my trailer—"

"Oh. My. God." I shake my head. "Forget it."

Blake was right.

What the hell am I doing? I think, storming away, this time not even bothering to fake a smile. Why did I think I could change a single fucking thing for the better for this kid or this movie or my kids or—

My phone buzzes in my pocket. Probably my publicist, Tara, with another PR nightmare. I reluctantly pull my phone out, and my stomach lurches.

Not Tara.

It's Roger Huntley. My ex-boyfriend.

I can't imagine why he would be calling. We've maintained a distant friendship since our breakup, and so it's not like we never talk—or even occasionally meet for dinner to catch up, as the tabloids were so eager to jump on.

But now? He knows I'm on location filming, for one, but the bigger thing is he knows I'm back with Blake, which has to be a painful thing for him to learn. Not that I think he's not over me by now—it's been more than a year, after all. But the Blake of it all has to sting. Roger knew I was still in love with Blake during our whole relationship—he knew it even before I finally broke down and confirmed it for him. He held on, whether from desperate hope that this would eventually change, or maybe because he just wanted to be with me enough that he was willing to put up with it.

But I knew, especially by the time I turned down Roger's proposal, that my being in love with Blake—and only Blake—wasn't ever going to change. And Roger deserved more than being some consolation prize.

My thumb still hovers over the "accept" button. Is he calling to tell me how happy he is for me? I doubt it—Roger is more the type to send that kind of message in a text or email. And even if so, am I ready to handle that call? To wonder if he's really happy, or if he's someone else I'm hurting?

I wait too long; the call ends.

Then I see I've already missed a call from him, not twenty minutes ago, and I know that whatever Roger is calling about, it's not some well wishes.

Could it be something about his brother, the one with lung cancer? Are his parents okay? I'd be surprised if I was first on his to-call list, but we were together for three years, and I know his family pretty well. I also know how heartbroken he'd be if anything happened to them.

I call back immediately, ducking into an empty, people-free space between Bertram's trailer and the wardrobe trailer.

"Kim, hey," Roger says. "I was just leaving you a message."

He doesn't sound panicked or devastated, thankfully.

"Roger," I say. "I'm sorry I missed your call. It's—"

"Crazy busy on set, I remember." His tone holds a gentle,

teasing note.

"Yeah, well. Especially this one."

There's a pause so pregnant I think it might need a police escort to the hospital. "I mean, with the increased paparazzi and the bad press and—" I start.

Roger chuckles. "It's okay, Kim. You're back with Blake. That's got to be a bit of a whirlwind."

"That's for sure," I say with a light laugh of my own, relieved. He doesn't sound overly hurt.

"A good one, I hope."

"The being with *him* part, yes," I say, and that's the truth, no matter what else is going on. "It doesn't mean it's been entirely easy—at least the parts involving everyone else."

"Makes sense. I remember that, too."

I'm sure he does. As a well respected art dealer (and a young, handsome one at that, from a moneyed East Coast family) it wasn't like he'd had *no* experience with celebrity or press.

But dating Kim Watterson made him a household name, and I know, for him, that was generally more of a drawback than a benefit.

"Actually," he continues, sounding reluctant. "That's kind of why I'm calling, that part about other people's reactions."

Now I'm really confused. "What do you mean?"

He lets out a sigh, and I can almost picture him, leaning back in his chair at his San Francisco office—he started working more frequently there after our breakup—and tapping his pen against his knee. "Ivy called me."

My jaw drops. "What?"

"About an hour ago. I was pretty surprised to hear from her, obviously."

Obviously is right. Ivy and Roger got along well, but they were never particularly close—which was totally my fault. I kept the romantic and family pieces of my life as separate as possible, because deep down, I knew they'd never fit together, not after I'd ripped them apart.

226

Something I worry may still be true.

"Why did she call you?" I ask, still trying to wrap my brain around this.

There's a bit of a pause. "It seemed like she wanted me to try to win you back."

"*What?*" I know I keep saying this, but I can't imagine why— Oh wait. Of course.

I groan, even before he says the next part.

"She told me that you were, and I quote, '*super* unhappy,'" he says. "That you didn't really want to be back together with Blake because you were really still in love with me." Another pause. "That you have been all this time."

There's a hint of sadness in that last bit, though he says it wryly. I doubt Ivy meant to hurt Roger with this little stunt, but she couldn't have salted that wound better if she'd tried.

"Oh my god, Roger." I press my palm to my face. "I'm so sorry she did that. She's been . . . resistant to the idea of Blake and me together, trying everything to convince us to break up. I never thought she'd do something like *this*."

"It's okay. Really. I just thought you should know." He chuckles again. "She's a pretty good little actress herself, though. There were tears on your behalf and everything."

"I bet there were tears, but they certainly weren't on *my* behalf." I rub my forehead. What the hell are we going to do about Ivy?

"Well, even so, I wasn't particularly inclined to believe her story. And I'm glad to know that's all it is."

"It is, Roger. I'm sorry. Blake and I—it feels so right to be together again." I hope that's not too much, too hurtful. But it's true, and I'm guessing Roger knew that long before he made this phone call.

"That's great, Kim. I'm really happy for you and for Blake." He sounds sincere, and my heart lightens. "Even though it hurt like hell when we broke up, I know it was for the best. For you and for me. I'm glad for both of us that you were brave enough to do it."

His words bring tears to my eyes. I always hated what I did to Roger, how he got tangled up in my mess. And though I can't take that back, either—so many things I can't take back—at least he doesn't blame me for cutting him free of it.

"Thank you," I manage. "I mean it."

"Of course," he says. Then, in a brighter tone: "I'm actually dating Theresa now. For the last couple months. It's been going really well."

"Theresa from your office?" I remember her from a trip we took to San Francisco. She was a museum curator he'd recently hired for acquisitions, a cute brunette with a wicked sense of humor. I really liked her, even though it was clear she was fighting a pretty big crush on Roger. "I could tell she had a thing for you!"

He laughs. "I know, and I didn't believe you. But I should have known better. Kim Watterson is always right."

"Don't forget it," I say, smiling. "So you're happy, then?"

"I truly am," he says.

"That's wonderful," I say, and it's like this weight I didn't even know I'd been carrying for the last year is gone.

We don't end up saying much more before ending our call—I'm not in a great place for small talk, and Roger's never been much of a small talk person in general.

Then I hurry to find Blake, growing more upset with each step.

Blake is talking with Sarah Paltrow, nodding along to something she's saying about the script, when he sees me. He quickly finishes the conversation and heads over.

"Kim, I'm sorry about before," he starts, but I shake my head. Probably we need to talk about all of that, but right now I can only focus on one thing.

"Ivy called Roger," I say.

Blake blinks. "What?"

I'm glad I'm not the only one with that reaction.

"I just got a call from him. Apparently, she told him I was 'super unhappy' with you, and that I was really in love with him, and he should try to win me back."

Blake looks dumbfounded for the barest of seconds, then his mouth snaps shut. "She did *not*," he says, but he's not actually denying what happened. Just pissed, like I am.

"Yep. I can't—for her to do that, I just—" I'm at a total loss for words.

Blake grabs my hand. "Let's talk to her, now."

We get into the trailer, and there's Ivy, sitting at her computer, working on her reading assignments, looking for all the world like the same girl who only months ago I would have trusted completely.

What has happened? Is this just growing up? Or did we—did I—mess this up somehow?

"Ivy." Blake's sharp tone immediately makes her spin around in her chair. "What is it going to take to make you stop disobeying us like this?"

"What do you mean? I'm just doing my homework." But she looks down, picking at her nails.

"Roger," I say. "You called Roger, and you told him I was still in love with him. And that I was unhappy with your father."

She presses her lips tightly together but doesn't deny it.

"Setting aside how you broke a rule to use a phone at all, how could you do that? Didn't you even think about how that might affect him? Did you think that would actually work?"

She glares at me, then at Blake, and then back at me again. God, this girl can glare. "Maybe I thought it would. I don't know, maybe you *are* still in love with Roger. I don't know, because you don't tell me anything."

I gape. "I—what on earth are you talking about? You know I'm not in love with Roger. I told you that when we broke up. What . . ."

"Dad says there's some reason you got divorced, and it's important, and it's what made you unhappy, but you don't want to tell me."

My knees feel weak all of a sudden.

"Ivy—" Blake's face pales, and he looks back at me. "That's

not what I said."

I swallow, sitting down on the couch, my hands shaking.

The stress of everything collapses in on me like a dying star.

"I should get to know what's really going on. It's my life, too." Ivy folds her arms.

She's right, I should tell her. I should have told her a long time ago, but I can't. I just can't.

I can't breathe around the thoughts racing through my brain unchecked, the ones that say that it'll all be broken, all of it, irreparably. And when she knows, when everyone knows, when they see that I'm not fit to be their mother, to be Kim Watterson, film actress, to be Blake's wife—

"Ivy," Blake says in a steely voice. "Go walk Costanza. Now. We'll talk later."

I can't even look at either of them, can't do anything more than sit here, hugging my knees and trying not to completely fall apart.

TWENTY-FIVE

Blake

When Ivy leaves, joining Aaron and Costanza outside—who will jointly make sure she doesn't do anything stupid—I make sure the door is locked. Kim is in no shape to be interrupted, and we clearly need to talk about what's happening. Ivy's reading assignment is still up on the computer facing the room, but given how mad she is, I don't think she's going to be back to do homework any time soon.

"I'm sorry," I say. "I shouldn't have even told her that much, but she was asking how I could know things would be different this time, and I felt like she needed some kind of reassurance. I didn't want to tell her the whole truth, because that's yours to tell her when you're ready, but—"

Kim holds up a hand for me to stop. "It's fine."

But it's clearly not fine. She's folded up into a shape that resembles one of those origami frogs, and her breath is so shallow she's almost panting.

"Kim," I say. "Talk to me."

She shakes her head and hunches down further into the couch. "Ivy's right. I should tell her. I need to tell her. What kind of mom am I that I haven't told her?"

I move closer and put a hand on her shoulder. "You're the

231

kind of mom who is still working stuff out."

"Yeah," Kim says. "And I never seem to get it right, do I?"

My heart breaks, and I run my fingers down her cheek. "None of us do. We're all just working through it."

"Sure," Kim says, but her shoulders are still shaking. She turns away from me, curling up into a ball like a possum. "You're probably right. Give me a minute, and I'll be ready to do . . . whatever it is we're supposed to do next. Could you check if the shoot is on schedule?"

I freeze, anchored to the spot. I immediately think that she doesn't want me here, that I should turn away and do as she asks and assume that I'm just in the way.

I've made that mistake before, so many times. It terrifies me that I might get it wrong now, but I can't do that to us again. "You're doing that thing," I say. "That thing where you push me away."

Kim looks up at me, horrified, and I hate myself for accusing her of that. She hasn't *gone* anywhere, and I have no right to make her talk to me if she doesn't think I can—

"You're right," she says. "I'm sorry."

She's quiet for a moment, breathing slowly and deliberately, and I think this may be some kind of treatment that she's learned in therapy. I realize, then, that I don't know the first thing about her treatment. I know she takes medication and has done therapy, but other than that—

"Does breathing like that help?" I ask.

She nods. "Yeah. It's a focusing technique. It keeps me grounded in the moment. My therapist says that anxiety is about the future, it's about all the things that might happen. But here in the moment, nothing terrible has happened yet. I haven't driven you away again yet. I can still change it."

Oh, god. I get down on the floor, kneeling in front of her, and take her hands. "I'm not going anywhere. I'll never do that to you again. Never."

Kim's face crumples and tears leak out of her eyes. "Maybe

232

you should. I'm broken, and I hurt our family, and I can't even tell my daughter the truth about why her parents got divorced."

"I'm pretty sure a lot of kids don't know the details about why their parents get divorced. Ivy's mad, but that doesn't mean she has a right to know everything about our personal lives."

Kim's voice is small. "Yeah, okay. But her mom having OCD is a big thing. It's her medical history. I'm going to need to tell her eventually."

I close my eyes. "But I had no right to push it on you like that. Ivy was asking me all these questions about whether we were going to get divorced again and why I left and how I knew it was different now. I thought it was important to explain it to her, but I also didn't want to tell her things that are yours to tell when you're ready." My voice breaks. "I'm sorry, Kim. I'm so sorry."

She shakes her head. "It's okay. I'm not mad at you."

"Maybe you should be," I say.

"Maybe. But I know how Ivy gets when she asks questions. She's a little interrogator sometimes."

I smile. "I don't know where she gets that."

Her lips tug up, and I sit next to her on the couch and pull her into my arms. "I love you," I tell her. "Whether or not you're ever ready to tell the kids about your mental health, I love you."

Kim squeezes me back, and I wish I could go back six years and react like this to some of the problems we had. But our therapist is right. I can't change the past. The only thing I can do is behave differently now.

"You were right about Tanner," she says.

I groan. "Oh, god, I'm sorry about that, too. You were just trying to help, and I didn't mean to suggest that you're not good at helping people—"

"I know. But you were right about him. He's not looking for someone to guide him through the perils of the industry. He just wants to get laid and get high."

"Yeah, well. That probably means he needs the guidance

more, because this industry is going to eat him alive."

Kim sighs. "I think I just feel so helpless about Ivy, you know? She's so unhappy, and I can't fix it. I can't make her see that she can't run off kissing older boys at twelve years old, that we're trying to protect her, not control her."

"She's not thrilled about the computer situation, either. She acted like she was literally dying."

"I keep going back to that whole thing about not taking responsibility for her happiness. But it's hard, because I *feel* responsible for it. I guess with Tanner, I just wanted to feel like I could help *someone*."

"I feel pretty helpless, too," I admit. "We're supposed to be her parents. We should be able to make this better, and we can't." Kim nods miserably, and we sit there in silence for a moment. "Is that how you felt about me?" I ask.

She looks at me blankly. "What?"

"When we first met. When I was new to the industry."

She's still not following me. "Did I think you just wanted to get laid and get high?"

"No," I say. "Obviously not. Did you think you needed to save me?"

"God, no," she says. "I had so much respect for you. You were new, yeah, but you were talented and professional, and you showed up and did your job and did it well. You already had it all together."

I'm not sure that's true, but I want to believe she means it.

"Did you think that's what I was doing?" Kim asks. "There was a reason I made an exception for you to my dating co-stars rule. Two weeks into shooting, you were my best friend in the world, and I wanted to be so much more, because of what an amazing person you were."

That's how I remember it, too, only about her. I don't know why it's so hard to hear that she felt that way too. "You really think it's because of my dad?" I ask. "That I'm uncomfortable with you saying those kinds of things?"

234

Kim nods. "You're incredible. You always were. But you never saw yourself the way I see you."

"From the sound of it, if I did, I'd be insufferable."

"I don't know," she says with a smile. "You're Blake Pless. I think you could stand to have a little bit of an ego."

I roll my eyes. "No way. The second I start feeling like I'm 'the shit,' as Tanner would put it, I feel like everything's going to fall apart. Like, as long as I know it's luck, maybe my luck will hold."

She's quiet for a moment. "You don't have OCD, but that line of thinking is really similar to what the disorder is like. You feel like if you just act a certain way, you'll be able to control things. But you can't, and if you keep pretending you can, eventually your efforts to control the universe start controlling you."

I don't know what to say to that. It takes me a minute to respond. "But you don't think I have it."

"No. But I think you can hurt yourself by telling yourself a story that keeps you in a bad place."

I hold my breath. "I'm not sure what other story to tell."

"Maybe," Kim says, "you're a guy who's had some lucky breaks, but who has worked hard to make the most of them. Maybe you've been lucky in your friends and associations—"

"And my wife," I add.

"—but it's *your own* intelligence and business sense and kindness that have gotten you where you are today. At least as much as luck. Because to really make it in this industry, you need a lot of both."

I can see what she's saying. "I suppose you're probably right, even if it doesn't feel that way."

She leans closer into me. "You know one of the hard things about the divorce? Not being able to tell you how proud I was of you for everything you've accomplished."

"I felt the same way," I say. "Every time I'd see one of your movies, I'd want to call you and tell you how amazing you were."

"You watched my movies?"

"All of them," I say. "But not in the theater, because I knew I'd get caught and it would end up on TMZ."

Kim smiles. "I watched yours, too. I love watching you work."

This feels pretty incredible to hear. "Yeah, okay. Maybe I can give myself a little bit of credit." I pause. "How'd it go with Roger? Are you okay?" I don't want to be jealous, and I'm not, exactly. More . . . sad that he got that time with her when it would have been me, if I hadn't been such an idiot.

"It went well, actually," she says. "He said he was really happy for us, and he sounded like he meant it. He's seeing someone new, so that's good."

I have a stupid question that I know I shouldn't ask, but I have to anyway. "You don't have any regrets, do you? About not marrying him?"

Kim looks at me in surprise. "No. Can you imagine what would have happened if I *did* marry him, and *then* you and I talked about everything that went wrong with us?"

I sit with that for a moment. "I like to think we would have been responsible, but I don't know."

"I don't know, either."

As wrong as that is to admit, it also feels good to know.

There's a long beat in which Kim chews on her lower lip, and then she blurts out, "Do you really think you'll be happy with me? I know I'm probably not as fun as some of the girls you've dated."

I gape a little, not sure where this came from. "You're absolutely the most fun of all the girls I've ever dated. Did I say something to make you think otherwise?"

She frowns. "When I talked before about my parents keeping me from falling into the celebrity party scene, and you said I wouldn't have, because I'm *Kim*. And you're probably right. I mean, I know I'm rigid and rule-following, and that doesn't usually equate to fun."

I pull back and look at her. "First of all, you being *Kim* is always a good thing. I love the responsible side of you. And I have more fun with you than anyone, ever. Remember that time when we drove up the state, stopping by movie theaters and going to see our own movies with random fans?"

"Ha, yes. Our security hated us for doing that, but we got some good press."

"We didn't do it for the press. We did it because we wanted to. And we had the most fun I've ever had watching movies."

"Then we had kids," Kim says. "I was never comfortable doing that with the kids."

"Me neither. But maybe sometime we could do that again, just you and me."

She gets tears in her eyes. "God, I love you so much."

That's something I will never get tired of hearing. "You do, don't you?"

"Have I not been clear about that?"

A lump forms in my throat. While we're being honest . . . "I took it wrong, I think. When you said you didn't want to get married again."

She squeezes my hand. "I said I didn't want to get married again *yet*—"

"And I thought maybe that meant you weren't sure about us. You weren't sure you wanted to be married to me again."

Kim's eyes widen. "No, that's not—"

"But I think I get it now," I say. "Tell me if I've got this right."

She closes her mouth.

"You do want to get married again," I say, "but not in the middle of all this. Our lives are a disaster, and it would be better to get married when our wedding can be free of that kind of stuff."

"Free of fear, too. I want to be married to you again, but I want to do it just because I love you, not because I'm afraid of losing you."

"And then the memory can be beautiful," I say, "and not messy."

Kim smiles. "Yes, exactly."

I grin back at her. "I'm okay with that."

"Yeah? Because if you're not—"

I catch her chin with my hand and shift her mouth close to mine. "I am. I want that memory, too."

Then our lips find each other, and our hands slip down to each other's waists, and we're pulling off our clothes like we did that first time in this trailer. I'm not sure who we're keeping waiting, but I don't care, because right now I need Kim in my arms. I need to feel how much she wants me, how committed we both are to each other.

We can do this. We *are* doing this.

I love Kim, and I'm going to keep on doing so for the rest of my life.

TWENTY-SIX

Kim

The next day, we're back to filming on the beach, which is a relief in some ways (if more physically demanding due to the sand). The street scenes in Miami made for some good shots, I'm sure—the bright signs and door frames, the red bougainvilleas climbing up the sides of the most mundane of law offices and hair salons. But the beach, though still hot and muggy, doesn't make me feel as trapped, penned in on all sides by people and problems. I can look out over the jewel-blue water, and for a moment, I can forget the constant, watchful eye of the cameras and hundreds of crew members.

It helps, too, that I feel a bit better after my breakdown the other day. After hearing from Blake again (how many times will I need to hear this?) that he loves me and wants to be with me, no matter how messed up I am. That even if Ivy is upset, I can take my time to get to a place where I can talk with her—with her and Luke, ideally, though probably in different, well-planned, age-tailored conversations—about my OCD and its contribution to all that went wrong.

That even if I never get to that place, Blake will still love me.

I will, though. I'll get there. The last couple therapy appointments have helped me feel even closer to that goal, especially with Blake by my side. I'll be able to talk to my kids. To my parents. Maybe even one day to the press, drawing attention to the non-stereotypical symptoms of OCD, things that are so easy to overlook and brush aside and bury you deeper day after day. It could be helpful to people.

But it doesn't have to be right now—though if I could, maybe Ivy would start talking to me again. Or maybe she'd be even more upset.

Right now there's enough to stress about, I decide—like, for instance, this movie.

"The timing is still off," Troy grouses. "Do we need another run-through with Ricky to get you all moving like you're not in fucking quicksand?"

I grit my teeth. I doubt Ricky, our stunt coordinator, will be able to change anything. We're all exhausted and emotionally drained and sick to death of shooting in this heat. My muscles are already burning from the half-dozen times we've run through this scene—especially my calves, protesting yet another take of sprinting through the sand in these insane high heels.

But this is what I get paid for, what keeps my ranch going. I trudge back to my starting mark, a block of wood painted with an X.

No buried treasure there, boys and girls. Just the place Kim Watterson may finally keel over and die, denied even the dignity of shorts that fully cover her ass.

"Dryden," Troy barks. "This time hold off on your line for a two-count. Bertram, Kim, that'll give you a little extra time to get in place, but if I don't see both of you hauling ass like you're trying to survive Pompeii, I swear to god."

He doesn't finish that threat—probably because there's not much realistically he can do to us. But a director's disappointment in my performance has always been a motivating factor for me.

Less so for Bertram, I think, who I can see scowling from his mark about forty feet away.

Troy's not done chewing us out quite yet. "And Tanner, I

need more from you than that idiot surprise face. You're seeing your aunt as Hemlock for the first time, and she's fighting to save you. Dig deeper."

Tanner tosses his drink back to the waiting PA without even looking to see if she's still standing there. "Dude, I don't even have any lines in this scene. What do you want from me?"

"I want you to fucking *act*. And stop checking out your aunt's tits. Can you manage that, or should I call The Disney Channel and get some other boy-band reject to fill this role?"

I cringe, though I'm feeling less sympathy for Tanner after our conversation yesterday. From what I can tell, he's not doing any worse than the rest of us, though he's definitely off his game a little—not a surprise, given he probably didn't sleep between Hustle and call time.

Troy's just extra pissy today, and I have a good guess why. Supposedly there's now a petition going around, started by "real comic book fans" to get people to declare that they won't see this movie, on the grounds of it being "a pure money grab by the studios"—as if there is any blockbuster film that couldn't be qualified this way—and "nothing more than a PR vehicle for Blake Pless and Kim Watterson, at the expense of real fans who care about the characters of Hemlock and Farpoint."

When I got the call from Josh about that last night, I was pretty pissed myself. I might not be a comic book fan, and neither is Blake, but I don't ever play a character I don't care about—even if they're nothing like me, even if they are a flat-out terrible person or, in this case, have a propensity for super uncomfortable fetish wear. I always find the human piece in them that I can connect to. The Sabrina Kane underneath the Hemlock façade.

I can guarantee that I care about her more than many of these so-called "real fans."

After three more takes, Troy's mood isn't getting any better, and when Peter Dryden suggests that all four of us—me, Bertram, Tanner, and himself—take a moment to re-establish our bond with a group Hug Connection, Troy tosses the script in the sand and tells us to take an hour break.

Thank god. I may be willing to run in these boots forever for my paycheck, but I'm not about to participate in *that*. I can see the headlines now: *Kim cheats on Blake in on set four-way orgy*.

I make my way back to the trailer, dying to take off these boots, even if it means I'm going to have to deal with Ivy pointedly ignoring me as she does her schoolwork.

I hear a muffled giggle as I draw closer, and catch sight of a mass of blond curls and two bodies pressed up against the side of my trailer—Kelsey. With Aaron, his hands in her hair.

Apparently our matchmaking scheme worked out, after all.

"Ms. Watterson," Aaron says, seeing me and all but dropping Kelsey. "Sorry, I was about to bring you your updated schedule, but I didn't realize the shoot was over, and—"

"No worries," I say, fighting a wide grin, especially as Kelsey is giving me a big thumbs up from behind Aaron's back. "We took an early break."

"Well, um," he says, looking around for his leather folder, then finding it on the ground where he must have dropped it when either he or Kelsey tackled the other. He dusts it off, his cheeks turning pink, and pulls out a sheet of paper to hand to me. "Two scenes got switched for this afternoon, and your massage therapist will be here an hour earlier."

My muscles weep in anticipation of that woman's magical hands.

"Oh, and Mr. Rios called," Aaron continues. "He said he tried your cell, but wanted to make sure that you called him as soon as you were done filming."

Uh-oh. That doesn't sound good. Especially since I just talked with him last night about all the negative press. What on earth more could have gone wrong since then?

"Okay, great," I say, though it's likely anything but. "Thanks, Aaron. I'll call him back now." I smile at both of them. "Have fun, you two."

Kelsey grins at me, and Aaron gives a sheepish smile back.

In my trailer, Ivy is typing away. Her earbuds are in, but she hears me open the door, because she swivels just enough to see it's me and then swivels back. Costanza lifts his head, smelling me, and then jumps up from where he was chewing on a rawhide bone near her feet. He full-body wags his way over to me, and I give him a big hug. "Hey, you happy boy," I say.

Then louder, to Ivy, "Hey, honey. How's the report coming?"

She doesn't respond. I sigh; I was expecting as much. I dig my phone out of my purse, and there it is—three missed calls from Josh and two from Tara. All in the last hour.

Shit. Something's definitely up.

I pause. No matter what it is, it can wait another minute. I should at least try with Ivy.

"Hey, Ivy, what do you think about you and I going out to lunch sometime this week? Just the two of us?"

There's a slight shift in her posture but not much more.

"Maybe on Sunday we can do some shopping? Or hit that wildlife refuge? I heard that they have—"

"No thanks," she says, no inflection in her voice. Still not turning in her chair.

My stomach sinks. I pet Costanza one last time and head into the bedroom to call Josh back. Costanza starts to follow me, but Ivy jumps up. "Work's done. Can I take him for a walk now?"

She doesn't sound excited about it. Probably she's just trying to get away from the trailer, if I'm going to be here. My heart aches at the thought, even though calling Josh back will be easier if I'm not worried about Ivy trying to listen in.

"Sure thing," I say, giving her a smile that she doesn't return.

She attaches the leash and tugs Costanza out the door without a backwards glance.

I sigh and call Josh's number.

He picks up after one ring. "Kim. Thanks for calling back."

"It sounded urgent. I'm guessing something more than another fan petition to thwart the movie."

"Yes, well." He pauses, but only a beat. "A video hit the internet about an hour ago. A video of you and Blake that appears to have been taken secretly in one of your trailers."

My knees go completely weak, and I drop onto the couch. "A video," I say, my throat dry. I can immediately think of the type of videos that get leaked like this, the type of video that would sell for huge amounts of money, especially of Blake and me. "Of us having sex, I'm guessing?" I'm not sure how I manage to keep my voice so even.

"Yes," he says, his tone one of extreme reluctance. "But that's only part of it. There's a whole conversation beforehand, and . . ."

His pause makes my already stuttering heart stop. Oh no.

"It's some pretty private stuff," he says gently. "About you having OCD, and about Tanner Berg, and your and Blake's relationship."

"Oh my god," I whisper. A sex tape is bad enough. Something I never wanted to be out there. Something I've been very careful throughout my career to make an impossibility.

But this . . .

"I'm so sorry, Kim," Josh says. "I know how awful it can feel to have your privacy violated like this. I get it from a business perspective, and I get it from a personal one. My wife had something like this happen to her awhile ago."

I nod numbly, though it's not like he can see me.

"I've already been in contact with Camilla and, of course, Tara, and we've got a multi-pronged plan in place. I can tell you about it now, or—"

"I—" I cut him off, but I realize I don't know what to say. Except this: "I need to talk to Blake."

"Of course," Josh says. "I'll email you the plan and keep you updated. In the meantime, you should contact security. They need to find the camera and check out the rest of your trailer for any other recording equipment. I'd call them—and I will, if you want me to—but it'll take me longer to reach the right people."

Just as he's finishing saying this, I hear the trailer door bang open, and Blake call out "Kim?"

I can hear the strain even in that one syllable. He knows.

"Yeah, I'll do that," I say to Josh.

Blake throws open the bedroom door, his eyes wide.

"I've got to go, Josh," I say.

"Okay. I'll keep you posted. We're going to take care of this in every way possible, Kim. I promise."

"I know," I say, because Josh and Tara and Blake's agent, Camilla, are all people who are incredibly good at their jobs and have helped celebrities through this stuff before. "Thank you."

But what about the things that aren't possible? The genie may be corralled, but he's not going back in that bottle.

What about my kids' reactions, and my parents? What about the world knowing the things about me and my marriage that I couldn't even tell those I love most?

I press end on the phone call and stare at Blake. He stares back. We're both in shock, not knowing what to say or do.

Get out of the bugged trailer, for one, a part of my brain tells me. *Get security, like Josh said.*

But instead I just stand there. "Everything," I say quietly. "It's all out there now. Everything."

Blake steps forward and wraps me in his arms, and I feel my muscles relax a little, even as my brain still sits in its numb stupor.

Not racing, like I'd expect. Not bombarding me with every terrible possible outcome. That's coming, I'm sure, but for right now, I'll take the numbness.

Blake just holds me. I want to rest my head in the crook of his neck, but I've got Hemlock's pointy crown fixed to my head with about hundred pins, and I don't think he wants any of that pressed against his jugular. So I settle for my forehead against his shoulder, my arms around his waist, and his around mine, his heart beating this steady rhythm against me even through the layers of his leather Farpoint costume.

Not a bad thing to settle for.

He pulls back enough to look me in the eyes. "We're going to be okay," he says. "You and me. No matter what."

And despite our sex-tape-slash-marriage-confessional now available for the world to see, for the first time since Blake and I got together again, I know this, deep inside. "We are," I agree. No hesitation. No fear, for once, not on that front. "No matter what."

His eyes close like he's so relieved he might cry, and he presses his lips to my forehead.

"Okay." He lets out a breath. "So we have a sex tape out there now." Then he laughs, like he can't help himself, and flops down onto his back on the bed. "A sex tape. Of us. *Of course* this would somehow happen."

I'm still numb, still waiting for the panic and all the OCD thoughts to sweep me under like a tidal wave, but I find myself smiling at his reaction. He's right. It's ludicrous, after how careful we've always been about this kind of stuff—never even sending each other naked pictures, let alone deciding to make our own personal porno.

"At least we've been working out," I say, and he laughs some more, and even though I can't join in, the sound of his laugh—even this sort of crazed "Oh my god, how is this my life" laugh—is so good to hear.

After a moment, though, he sits up, and his expression is serious again. "But everything else in it—God, we talked smack about Tanner and talked about getting married and Ivy and your OCD . . ." He shakes his head, then looks over at me. "How are you doing?"

I give him the most honest answer I can. "I don't know. You?"

"Horrified. And pissed. That was ours, all of it. Not anyone else's."

I get what he means. When you're a celebrity, especially at our level, so much of yourself—your life, your loves, your family—is for public consumption, whether you like it or not. So to have things you are able to keep private, things you fight to keep as just yours, at least until *you* decide to share them—that matters. It keeps you from feeling like you're owned by the world and their constant craving for headlines.

And now they know it all.

I rub my forehead. "Josh says we should tell security right away."

Blake nods. "Camilla said the same thing. That video, I watched just enough to see the angle, and god, the thing's pointed right at us. How did we miss a camera there? The only thing across the room there is—" He stops, his eyes widening, and it hits me at the exact same time it does him.

Shit.

Ivy's computer.

Ivy's computer.

We run into the main room, and Blake grabs the laptop. He swipes the track pad so the black screen turns into Ivy's background pic, a female pro-surfer riding the perfect wave. Blake checks a few things, and now I can feel my heart pounding harder, cutting through that numbness.

Blake groans. "The computer software that monitors what she's been doing has been turned off." He snaps the laptop closed, his knuckles so white against the silver of the computer, I think for a minute that he might throw it.

My throat is sandpaper. "Do you think *she* could have done this?"

"I want to say no," he says, and god, I do too—not the least of which is because oh my god, could our twelve-year-old daughter have actually *seen us have sex*, which is bad enough, and then decided to put it on the *internet* to punish us?

"She couldn't," I say, but I don't believe my own words. "She knows how we feel about privacy. She knows . . ."

I trail off. Because she knows that all of the things she's done lately are wrong, but she did them anyway.

Blake's expression is a thundercloud. "We need to talk to her. Now."

I agree, even if it means putting off getting security—which won't really be necessary, if it was our own daughter behind this. And if she is, then that's something I'd rather keep out of the press, if at all possible.

If it's ever really possible.

I feel more eyes on us than usual as we leave the trailer. People look up from their phones and tablets, conversations stopping awkwardly as we walk by. The video is spreading, everyone watching. Everyone knowing. Judging.

It's too much; my brain can't even take it in. I clutch his hand.

"Kim, Blake," Sarah Paltrow says, "Troy wants to get the next scene—"

"We need to talk to security," Blake says firmly. "And our daughter. Where's Ivy?"

Sarah pauses, then points over in the direction of catering. "When should I tell Troy you'll be ready?"

"We'll let him know," Blake says and tugs me after to follow.

I look back to see Sarah raise her walkie talkie, passing on the message.

That, of all things, starts to make my chest tighten, the panic setting in—like my brain can't handle the bigger issues, so it's decided to worry at this.

All these people working this movie—the crew, the cast, hundreds of people—need us to do our jobs. To do everything we can to make this movie work, to make it successful. And all I can bring them is delays and PR nightmares, and what if the movie tanks because of us, what if people lose their jobs and—

I force myself to focus on what's important right now—Ivy. We find her near the catering vans, just as Sarah had said. She's got Costanza on his leash, snuffling around for scraps, while she peers over the shoulders of some crew members with a tablet out.

"Ivy," Blake says. His voice is sharp, and Ivy wheels on us, her expression hard.

Is it guilt? Or just anger that this is out there?

Oh, god, the things we talked about. If she knows, if she

already knows, and I wasn't the one to tell her—

The crew members look between us and Ivy and quickly switch off the video they were watching, but not before I hear my own voice on it, though I couldn't make out the exact words.

"Come with us," Blake says in a low voice. Ivy follows behind us with Costanza, who happily bobs along, completely oblivious.

We get to Blake's trailer and go inside. Costanza smells another of his rawhide chews and leaps forward, knocking into the coffee table instead. A mostly empty Starbucks cup topples over.

I close the door behind us, but before either of us can say anything, Ivy beats us to the punch.

"How could you *do* that?" she asks. "You said all those things about Tanner!"

Tanner? I simultaneously want to laugh at the absurdity and shake some sense into my daughter. Of course our twelve-year-old would care most about the cute older boy involved.

"That's not the biggest issue here," I say.

Ivy's eyes are dark. "You think I did that, don't you? You think I put that video out."

Blake's voice is as deceptively calm as mine. "Did you?"

"Does it matter? You're not going to believe me anyway!"

"Try us," Blake says.

Ivy's lips purse as she glares at us, and my heart pounds.

"No," she finally says. "Why would I want everyone to see you guys being all *gross* like that? You don't tell me anything, ever, and you make my computer spy on me and then you blame me when it spies on you instead!"

"We're just trying to figure out the truth, Ive," Blake says. "If you say you didn't do it . . ."

She stares us down. "I. Didn't."

There's a long beat where both of us stare at our daughter, trying to read the truth from her beautiful, furious face.

I want to trust her. I do.

"Okay," Blake says, his voice softer. "Thank you. We'll talk more, okay? But you need to stay here while we go talk to security and figure out who did this."

Ivy's eyes cut back and forth between us, like she's waiting for more, but then she just lets out a sigh and drops down onto the couch. "Fine," she says.

We leave the trailer, and when the door closes behind us, I look over at Blake. "Do you think she's telling us the truth?"

He squeezes my hand, his eyes sad. "I don't know. I just don't know anymore."

TWENTY-SEVEN

Blake

I carry Ivy's computer between trailers to the security office. Camilla was right; I need to talk to them immediately and see if there's anyone who can take a look and figure out whether it was my daughter who did this.

There's a certain surreal quality to being aware everyone in the world knows about the darkest, hardest things that have happened to you. I know that Kim and I are going to handle this. I know that we're still doing better than we were before we started shooting this movie, because being with her through anything is better than being without her.

Ivy, though. I don't think she did it—I don't know where my daughter would have learned to simultaneously disable the monitoring software, set the webcam to surreptitiously record, upload the whole thing to the internet, and also cover her tracks.

Then again, she did want to know what Kim and I knew that she didn't. You can Google how to do basically anything, and Ivy's too smart for her own good.

Still, if she found out she'd taped us having sex, I would have expected her to freak out, but not put it online. It's not like I've been great at predicting Ivy's behavior these days, but the other stunts she's pulled weren't exactly the workings of a criminal mastermind.

I find Russ from security inside the trailer. He's already heard about the video and is on the phone with someone I'm guessing is with legal.

"Mr. Pless just arrived," Russ says. "I'll call you back."

I hand him the laptop. "The video must have been taken on that. It's my daughter's laptop. We had tracking software on it to keep tabs on her, but it's been disabled."

Russ nods. "Do you suspect your daughter of making the tape?"

I sigh. "No. But I don't have proof she didn't, either."

Russ opens the laptop. "I'll get Jo on this, see what she can find. It was in your trailer?"

"Kim's," I say. "Kim's assistant Aaron set up the computer, so he had access, but so did everyone in wardrobe and makeup and anyone who happened by." I stop, thinking of anyone particular who might have it out for us. Troy isn't pleased with anyone, but I'm not going to accuse the director on the set of his own movie.

"All right," Russ says. "I'll ask around and see if anyone saw anything. I'll get you a report by the end of the day."

By the end of the day. Because the internet moves at light speed, but regular investigations move at a crawl. "Okay. Thank you."

"I'm sorry this happened on my watch, Mr. Pless," Russ says. "I'll get to the bottom of it."

"It's not your fault," I tell him. I feel like it's mine for putting that computer there, for not thinking that we might be recorded, even in our own trailers. But what are we going to do? The hotel staff could just as easily have recorded us there. Or any of our assistants back home. Nowhere feels safe, and I hate that this is happening to my family.

I take a deep breath, heading back to the beach. The stunt people are rigging up a crane that is going to suspend Kim over the sand in some spell cast by Guidepost. They're scheduled to shoot her half of the scene first. I don't come in until later, but I still head in that direction. I need to find Ivy. Aaron is charged with keeping an eye on her whereabouts, and I need to ask him whether he saw anything in the trailer.

It's security's job, but I can at least try.

On the way over, I text Marguerite to warn her to keep Lukas inside today. The press is going to be whipped into a frenzy, and even with security on their tail, I don't want them getting swarmed. When I arrive where they're filming, I find Kim standing under one of the enormous sun shades, holding a VitaminWater and looking like she's about to cry. Troy stands over her, and while I can't hear what he's saying, I can tell by his body language that he's pissed.

Enough. Nothing that's happened has been Kim's fault, and I'm sick of Troy taking it out on all of us, but especially her. I jog up in time to hear the tail end of Troy's rant.

"—not about you," he says. "I know this is hard for you to understand, but we're making an actual *movie* here, and there are millions of dollars on the line. This isn't the time for you and Blake to get kinky in your trailer and get it leaked all over the internet."

"Troy," I say in a warning tone. Both Troy and Kim turn, and Troy looks like he's about to lay into me. "Back off," I tell him. "It wasn't Kim's fault about the video, and it wasn't mine, either. We're more upset about it than you are, so just leave it alone."

Troy glares at me. I've challenged his authority on his set, which is a big faux pas, even for an actor as well-paid as I am. But I'm done listening to him bully my wife—my *ex*-wife—and I'm done letting him make us scapegoats for things that are out of our control.

"Blake," Troy says. "You're not in this scene. Step away, and let us work."

"I will," I say in a low voice. "When you do."

Kim looks surprised, and I half expect her to snap at me for treating her like she can't take care of herself, but she actually looks relieved.

Troy doesn't say anything, just stalks off across the sand, and

I let out a slow breath.

"I'm sorry," I say to Kim, though I'm not even sure what I'm apologizing for.

"No, *thank you*," Kim says. "I know I should have told him off myself, but I feel so bad for the timing of all of this."

I put an arm around her. "Have you seen Aaron and Ivy?"

"No. Do you want me to help look for her?"

"Kim!" Troy shouts. "Get your ass in the harness!"

I glare at him. He sounds like she should have already been there, which she might have been if he hadn't delayed her by chewing her out.

"It's okay," I say. "I'll find her and talk to her. You can take a turn when your part of the scene is done."

Kim nods and trudges across the sand toward the crane. I watch her go, wishing I could take her away from all this and spend some time relaxing, just curling up and ignoring the rest of the world.

When filming's done, that's exactly what I intend to do.

TWENTY-EIGHT

Kim

The last thing I want right now, in the midst of dealing with my private life becoming even more public than usual, is to be suspended ten feet off the ground in a harness, flashing sizeable portions of my ass in Hemlock's booty shorts and fishnets.

And yet, here I am.

Troy calls out "action," and we run another take. I flail angrily against the invisible powers holding me suspended (which will be a lot more invisible when the thin cable holding me and the small crane it's attached to are edited out). Peter Dryden holds up the orb whose powers are keeping me in midair. He delivers his big villain monologue, chewing the scenery so much I'm surprised it doesn't give him indigestion.

I expect Troy to tell Dryden to tone it down a bit on the next take, but he doesn't, just tells everyone we're moving on. I'm not sure if Troy has given up on the notion of subtlety (not that there was much to begin with) or if he's just over the film entirely by this point. Neither of which is a good sign for the finished product.

I'm doing the best I can for this film, I tell myself, Troy's accusations still ringing in my ears. *That's all I can do. That's all anyone can expect of me.*

But with everything else going on, with all the information that's now known to everyone in the world, when anyone with a cell phone out might be watching me even now have *sex* with my ex-husband—I feel even more responsible to get this one thing right. And somehow even more helpless.

I hang there, still suspended, as Troy calls for the actors in the next part of the scene—Blake and Tanner. Blake disappeared for a while looking for Ivy, but he's back now. He jogs to his mark on the sand where he's going to teleport in—conveniently almost directly under me.

"Did you find her?" I ask.

He shakes his head. "I think she and Aaron took Costanza for a walk. I texted him to bring her to us as soon as they get back." He looks up at me, and he must notice I look worried. "She can't run off. If the perimeter is keeping the reporters out, it can sure as hell keep her in."

That is true. The paparazzi can be even more creative and tenacious than Ivy, and we haven't seen security throwing anyone out yet today. Ivy is here, probably sulking and whining about how awful we are.

Lucky Aaron. I'm not sure what gift card to buy him for having to put up with that.

Blake squints up at me. "I like the view."

"I bet you do," I return. But our banter is forced. We're both too worried about Ivy, and the fallout from the leaked video, and the multiple missed calls from my parents and even his parents.

"Maybe I should teleport us both out of here," Blake says. "Spend the next few weeks in Belize—one of those little bungalows, remember?"

I do. God, that was a nice two weeks.

"Or that animal sanctuary in Utah," he continues. "I could see if my dog-walking skills have improved."

"I think you're going to see that back home in a couple

weeks," I say, my smile less forced now. "But yes. Yes to all that. Get us out of here, Farpoint."

He opens his mouth to speak, but Troy's booming voice—he's using a megaphone now—cuts him off. "Tanner Berg! Where the hell is Tanner Berg?"

Sarah runs up and says something to him, and Troy looks like he might be about to throw the megaphone in the sand and kick it a few times for good measure, but then just wearily rubs at his forehead. "Five minute break," he announces loudly. Quieter, but still loud enough that I can hear him, he says to one of the PAs, "When you bring Tanner, bring his assistant too. She'd better have given him the updated fucking call sheet."

Of course Tanner would fail to show up on time for his scene. He's probably sleeping off last night. If he'd been willing to listen to me even the tiniest bit—

"It's not your fault he's screwing this up," Blake says, and I glare down at him, even though it actually feels nice that he can read me so well. Also, my glare must not be as potent as Ivy's, because Blake gives me a knowing smile back.

"No, it's definitely his fault," I agree with a sigh. "I just wish I could've helped. And that the whole world didn't now know exactly how we feel about his screwing this up."

That's definitely not the worst of the things they know, but it's still hard for me to even think about the rest.

"Blake! Kim!" a woman's voice calls, and we turn to see Kelsey jogging towards us through the sand, her cheeks flushed and her hands clenched into fists—she looks about as happy as Troy when he almost toddler-tantrum-stomped his megaphone. Other people have turned to look, too, and she cringes, lowering her voice as she stands right next to Blake and shoves a cell phone at his face.

Blake takes a step back. "Kelsey, what the—"

"It's Aaron," she growls. "That son of a bitch. He's the one who leaked that video of you two."

"What?" I'm flailing in midair for real now, trying to get a look at the phone that Blake is now holding.

"I found it on his phone after we—" She purses her lips, like she's considering, then shrugs. "After we had sex in the wardrobe closet."

"You found the video?" Blake looks confused. "Maybe he was just watching it."

"No, I found all his gambling sites. Dude's a straight-up addict, like, deep in debt. I always thought he must have been texting some girl or something, as much time as he spends staring at that thing, but no. Online poker. And he sucks at it."

I blink. Aaron did always seem to be doing something on his phone, but that's not super rare nowadays. "Kelsey, you got all of this from one post-sex peek at his phone?"

She smiles slyly, clearly proud of herself. "No. I had a suspicion from the one post-sex peek at his phone. The rest of it I got after I locked him in the closet and took his phone with me."

I gape, and Blake stares at her for a minute, then shakes his head. "Okay. But do you know for sure it was him? Just gambling a lot isn't evidence of—"

"The email! It's right there!" Kelsey says, taking the phone back from Blake and then swearing. "Sorry, the screen went blank." She swipes at it a few times. "But here, look! It's the email confirming the receipt of it by this dude at *Stars Today*."

Blake looks at the phone, and once again I flail to see, my gut twisting in a way that has nothing to do with the harness wrapped too tightly around it.

"Shit," Blake says. "Yeah, it was him. God, we should have known." He looks up at me. "He was the one who set up the damn software in the first place."

Anger floods through me. "So we'll go to security," I say. "I'll get down from this stupid harness and we'll—"

"Wait a second," Blake says, and his cheeks pale. "Kelsey, you were just with Aaron. But he was supposed to be watching Ivy. You didn't see her anywhere, did you?"

Kelsey gives him a weird look. "Um, no. I definitely would not

258

have been hooking up with Aaron with your daughter hanging around."

Oh, shit. If Ivy's not with Aaron . . . "Maybe she's still in the trailer. I mean, we told her to stay there—"

Blake's eyes cut back and forth along the bustle of crew members waiting and prepping for filming to begin again. "She wasn't there when I checked."

Blake was right, though. She won't have managed to get off the set. Though if she did somehow turn into Houdini and manage it, she could be anywhere in Miami by now, and—

"What do you mean, you can't find him?" Troy yells at a woman I'm pretty sure is Tanner's assistant. He's not using his megaphone, but he doesn't need to. We can all hear him. "Where the fuck did he go? Somebody find that fucking kid!"

Blake and I meet eyes, realization dawning on us both simultaneously.

Tanner is missing. Ivy is missing.

Our daughter is off with some druggie, sex-crazed older boy. Because she's mad at us. Because she thinks he's cute.

And no matter how wise to the ways of the world she thinks she is, she has no idea how much danger she could be in.

I can't breathe. I can only twist in midair.

Blake looks up at me. "I'm going to find them," he says, and all I can do is nod. He takes off at a run, and I see him grabbing crew members and giving them orders to help with the search.

"Blake, where the hell do you think you're going?" Troy calls, but Blake storms off, a couple crew members going in different directions.

I need to get down. I need to find our daughter, too. This beach is so big, and there are so many trailers and places to hide. And if Tanner was with her, they might have been able to get off set, and oh my god, they could be anywhere, they could be—

"Kim?" Kelsey asks, her eyes wide with worry. "Should I go looking?"

"Yes," I say. I can't fall apart now. Ivy needs me. "You can

259

come with me." I turn to the stunt guy operating the crane. "Set me down right now."

He nods and reaches for the machinery, but Troy must have heard me and stomps over. "Don't you dare lower that crane. We'll have to reharness her, and that'll set us back even more."

"My daughter is missing," I growl, though I'm not sure how fearsome it can really be with me dangling in the air. "I need to find her."

"You need to do your damn job," Troy says. "After all the shit you've pulled, you owe it to—"

"No," I say, cutting him off. My blood is boiling. "I am not responsible for this film. I am not responsible for the bad press or the paparazzi or the videos of me and my husband that get leaked against our will. I am responsible for showing up and doing my job—which, with very few exceptions, *I have done* and done damn well. But more importantly, I am responsible for taking care of my family, and that will always come first. If you continue to have a problem with that, I will walk off this fucking set and not look back."

Troy's cheeks are bright red, his mouth gaping. Kim Watterson doesn't rock the boat. She's not a diva. She's professional, does her job, and is respectful, always. She takes the weight of the whole project on her shoulders and doesn't complain even if it crushes her.

Kim Watterson has spent her whole life doing this, and Kim Watterson is *done.*

"If you don't stay up there and film this scene," Troy sputters, "You'll be in breach of contract, and I'll send every goddamn lawyer the studio has—"

"Just try it, Troy. And let me know who the studio heads are more likely to find dispensable. Will it be me and Blake? Or will it be *you?*"

Troy's mouth presses into a line so tight his lips disappear, because he knows.

We're Watterpless, and no producer is going to back him

over us.

"Let me down, *now*," I order the stunt guy, and he presses the button, not even looking at Troy as he does so. The cable lowers, and as soon as my heels hit the sand, I'm fumbling to get the harness off. Kelsey helps me.

Troy says nothing, just glares.

Once, I would have panicked from that glare alone. From the disappointment of someone in a position of authority over me. From the disappointment of the crew watching me, from the fans who will have more reason to worry about the movie.

But right now, all I care about is my family.

As Kelsey and I dash off to join the search for Ivy, I tell myself that I will never let anything—not my fears, not my OCD, not my sense of responsibility for everything and everyone around me—get in the way of putting my family first ever again.

TWENTY-NINE

Blake

vy and Tanner aren't in any of the trailers, though I do find the closet that Aaron's trying to break out of and send security in that direction. The rest of the team fans out over the section of beach that's supposed to be cleared of people. I walk along the surf because I can move faster on the firm, wet sand, scanning both the water and the shore for any sign of them. They could have gone the other way, and I'm getting close enough to where I can see news vans parked that I'm afraid they must have, when I spot a set of cabanas this side of the press line.

If Tanner took Ivy in one of those, I'm going to kill him. I'm going to wring him by his scrawny neck while he wriggles like a worm. I sprint toward the cabanas, trying the doors, calling Ivy's name, until I find one that's unlocked.

The scene I burst in on is different from the one I imagined, but still horrifying. Ivy is lying in a hammock in one of the cabanas licking fudge brownie off her fingers, while Tanner reclines on the floor next to her, looking up at her legs. He turns his lazy gaze to me as I storm in, and Costanza lifts his head from the corner where he's speculatively sniffing a paper bag that I'm guessing contains the rest of the brownies.

I snatch the bag and tower over Tanner. "What the *hell* do

you think you're doing with my daughter?"

Tanner holds up his hands. "It's okay, man. We're just hanging out."

"Dad?" Ivy says. She looks at me with bloodshot eyes, but I'm the one who sees red.

Pot brownies. They're eating pot brownies. Tanner gave marijuana to my daughter.

I pick Tanner up off the floor by the shoulders, just to get him away from Ivy, but once I've got him, I slam him against the cabana wall.

"What the hell do you think you're doing?" I shout again, this time right in his face. "With *my* daughter?"

"It's cool," Tanner says. His eyes aren't focused properly, and I hold him against the wall with an arm on his throat.

"No," I say. "It's not cool." I'm ready to press down harder on his throat, but Russ and two other security guards must have heard me shouting, because they arrive at the door.

"Blake," Russ says. "Take it easy, okay?"

I look down at Tanner. I want to murder the kid, but I clutch the paper bag in my free hand and decide I'm going to do him one better. I'm going to prosecute his ass from here to prison for giving drugs to my underage kid. Every news outlet in the country is going to run this story. I've worked with a lot of assholes, but never one whose career I wanted to end.

Tanner's changed that, and by god is he going to regret it. I step away from him. "Get him in custody," I say. "And call the police. He's been feeding pot to my twelve-year-old, and I want it all in a report. Got it?" I thrust the bag at Jo, one of the other security people. "And get this tested for drugs. If I don't get a *detailed, airtight* summary, I will hold you personally responsible."

Jo takes it, wide-eyed. I'm generally regarded as easy to work with. But not when someone messes with my daughter.

Tanner holds up his hands. "Naw, man. I didn't do anything. You should try those brownies, though. They're the shit."

Tanner is the one who's a shit, but I manage not to go off on him again while Russ escorts him out of the cabana. This is completely going to ruin Troy's shoot today, and probably he'll have to recast Tanner or write him out of the rest of the scenes, which will be a disaster.

But I don't care. I just want the kid away from Ivy.

Another security guard tugs Costanza out of the cabana. He's started whining, probably from all the yelling, and I'm beginning to wonder if he wouldn't have been better off back at the ranch, attachment issues notwithstanding.

I kneel next to Ivy, who rolls away from me and almost falls out of the hammock. I grab her, but she wrenches back and manages to land on her feet. "Leave me alone, Dad," she says. "You're ruining everything."

"The only thing I'm ruining now is your buzz." I want to ask her if she knew what was in the brownies, but I'll save that for later when she's sober.

Oh, god. My twelve-year-old is high. How did I not protect her from this? How do I suck *this much*?

"Ivy," I say, moving around the hammock toward her. "Seriously. I need you to come back to my trailer and lie down."

"What do you care!" Ivy screams at me. She stumbles backward and trips onto a lounge chair. "You don't care what happens to me! You didn't care when you left Mom, and you don't care now that you're back together, and you won't care next time you leave, either! Just go away, Dad. Just leave me alone. Everything's easier when you're not around."

I stare at Ivy. I don't want that to sting, but it does. My own daughter doesn't want me around, and we used to be so close. Like an idiot, I thought we'd always be able to talk. I take a step back.

No. That's wrong. It doesn't matter if she wants me around. She's my daughter. She's stuck with me. And so are Kim and Luke, for that matter. Kim told me things would be easier if I wasn't here, and listening to her was the worst mistake of my life. She wanted me to fight for her, and I should have, for all

264

three of them.

I'm damn well going to fight for them now.

"I'm not leaving, Ivy," I say. "I'm not leaving you, or your mom, or your brother. I'm your father, and I'm never leaving any of you again."

Ivy looks at me for a moment with red eyes.

And then she bursts into tears.

I reach down and scoop her up, lifting her into my arms and carrying her out of the cabana and down the beach. I can hear shouting behind me—we're within sight of the press line, and I know there are going to be pictures of this.

But I don't care. Let them take pictures of me taking care of my daughter. Let them be ready for the legal trouble Tanner's just landed himself in.

This is my family, and no matter what hits the news, I'm going to take care of them.

Whatever it takes.

When I get back to the trailers, Kim runs up to me. "Blake! When I got out of that stupid harness, I went looking for her, but I couldn't—oh god, is Ivy okay?"

Ivy has her eyes closed, which is good, because I don't want her talking where other people can hear. "Yeah," I say. "She'll be okay. Let's take her to my trailer." On the way there I catch sight of Aaron, who's being led by security in handcuffs. I hear sirens, and I hope the police get here soon, because they're going to be taking reports for hours.

But first, I need to get my daughter somewhere safe. Kim opens my trailer for me, and I take Ivy straight back to the bedroom and lay her on the bed. "You get some sleep, okay, Ive?"

Her eyes are still closed, and she nods lethargically, as if she used all the energy she had to scream at me, and now is drifting off in a haze. When Ivy's safely closed in the room, Kim grabs my arm. "What happened to her?"

"She's high," I tell her. "Tanner fed her pot brownies. Our *twelve-year-old* was given *marijuana*." I realize I sound like the

265

oldest, squarest adult on the block right now, but I don't care. Kim looks equally horrified, and together we crash on the couch in the main room.

"Oh, god," she says. "You're sure that's what it was?"

"She was pretty out of it. So I hope that's all it is. But I gave the brownies to security, and they'll get them tested." I shake my head. "I want to prosecute the hell out of Tanner. Do you have a problem with that?"

"No," Kim says, then winces. "But it'll be public. Do we really want to put Ivy through that?"

"We can't protect her from everything. I obviously did a shitty job of protecting her from this, but I can't let that little asshole get away with it."

Kim nods and lowers her head into her hands. "How could we let it get this bad?"

"I don't know. I'm not sure she took the drugs on purpose, but still, running off with Tanner like that—" God, I have no idea what we're going to say to her now. "I don't know how to talk to her about how dangerous that was without making her feel like it would have been her fault if he'd done something worse to her. I don't want to teach her that some guy taking advantage of her is her doing, no matter what bad decisions she makes. But I also want her to *stop making these decisions*, damn it."

Kim grabs my hand and holds tight. "Me too. I don't know how to talk to her about it either."

I close my eyes. "We're in this together. So if we mess it up, at least she's got both of us."

Kim nods again, and we sit there like that until the police come knocking on the door to take our statement. And while I feel like Ivy deserves a better father and Kim deserves a better partner, and they all deserve not to be only just starting to heal from the damage we did all those years ago, I know this: what I said to Ivy was true.

I'm never going to stop fighting for them again.

THIRTY

Kim

Both Blake and I take the next day off work. After everything that happened, our family needs it, and even Troy doesn't complain—at least not where we can hear. Considering all the legal ramifications of the things that happened on his set yesterday, he's wise not to. Not that we blame Troy for either Aaron's illegal recording of us or for Tanner giving our underage daughter drugs, but right now he doesn't know that, and I don't mind making him sweat a little if it gets us the space we need.

I'm just not sure how to best use that space, now that I have it.

I sit at the table in the kids' hotel room, sipping a cup of coffee. We gave Marguerite the day off, and Blake took Luke out for the morning to give me and Ivy a chance to talk, but Ivy is curled up in her bed, a motionless mound under the covers. She's slept quite a bit since yesterday, and I don't know if she's still sleeping or just avoiding me.

I can't blame her if it's the latter.

My phone buzzes, briefly startling Costanza out of a deep sleep near my feet. I sigh before looking at it. I don't want to deal with PR statements or legal steps or even Helene's concern that the cats at the ranch are beginning to band together to stalk the ducks.

But it's not any of those things. It's from Bertram, and it's a picture of me from my rant yesterday that must have started circulating the internet, with the cable and crane photoshopped out. I'm suspended in midair, my hands on my hips, my hair catching a fortunate gust of (sweltering) breeze, a take-no-prisoners kind of determination on my face.

I look like a badass woman who can and will take on anything for those she loves. Not just Hemlock, either—me. Kim Watterson.

A text follows right afterward: *Well done, Kimberly. Well done.* My heart swells.

Then another text: *Now if you could use your powers to get me out of the karaoke duet I drunkenly agreed to perform with Dryden when this bloody film is over, you will truly be saving the day.*

A laugh bursts out of me, and I start to text back, when I hear Ivy's voice.

"Is that a text from Dad?" She's sitting up in bed, her hair a tangled mess.

"No, it's Bertram." I pause. She's never cared who texts me before. "Why do you ask?"

She shrugs, pulling her knees up to her chest. "Because Dad makes you laugh like that. You laugh a lot more now."

I'm not sure how to respond. She's not wrong; I *have* laughed more in the last few weeks than in years before that, even though things have been stressful and often terrifying. I settle for the truth, something I should have been better at all along. "Being with your dad again brings me a kind of happiness I thought I wouldn't ever get back. It's a different kind of happiness than I get from being your and Luke's mom—not more, not less. Just different. And I need both, you know? To be my most happy. It's not like—"

"I get it, Mom," she says, and there's a hint of that teasing tone she always takes with me when I overexplain something to the point where she wishes she'd never asked the question in the first place. "Dad already said, like, the same thing."

"Yeah, well, your dad's pretty smart. Especially when he agrees with me."

Her lips quirk up, just the barest ghost of a smile, but it's so good to see.

"How are you feeling?" I ask.

The smile disappears, and she picks at the blanket. "Okay."

"Do you want anything to eat? We have cereal, or I can order room service or—"

"I'm not hungry." Her cheeks turn pink. "Anymore."

She clearly remembers her bout with the munchies last night after we got her home. Normally Ivy is the slowest eater in the world, picking at her food like she needs to consider each and every bite. Her frantic consumption of two full bags of Funyuns might have been amusing had it not been because she was a stoned twelve-year-old.

I decide not to press it, though. She's talking, sort of, and besides, that's a conversation Blake and I want to have with her together. But there's one that I owe her on my own, one that is long overdue.

My throat tightens, my pulse picking up. I try to think of the Kim in that picture Bertram sent. I'm not always her, but I know she's there. I know I *can* be.

I stand and walk over to Ivy's bed, sitting next to her. She doesn't scoot away, but she doesn't move closer. "So, the video," I say. "You saw some of it, obviously."

She looks surprised. She clearly didn't expect me to start with *that*.

"Yeah." She wrinkles her nose. "Not the sex part. Because ew."

At least that's something. I don't want to think about the sheer amount of therapy seeing her parents' sex tape would require. Just knowing there *is* one is bad enough.

Her voice grows quiet. "I really didn't post it. I didn't even know about it until I heard people talking."

"We know," I tell her. "It was Aaron. He sold it to pay gambling debts."

Ivy looks alarmed at this, and I let it soak in without comment. It's probably good for her to know that kids don't have a monopoly on making truly stupid decisions. "Did you see the part of the video where I talked about having something called OCD?"

Her eyes narrow, her chin jutting out, and my heart squeezes. "That's what you didn't want to tell me about."

"I was afraid to," I admit. "I shouldn't have been. But I spent a long time being afraid to tell anyone. I was afraid people would think less of me. I was afraid *you* would." Tears sting my eyes. "But I should have told you, anyway. I should have tried better to explain what happened when I knew you were old enough to understand it."

Ivy's hard expression remains, but she looks down at her hands.

"Would you like me to tell you what it is?" I ask.

"It's a sickness in your brain," she says. "It messes up the way you think sometimes. Like depression, like my friend Maia's mom has."

Now I'm the surprised one, and she looks a little self-satisfied. "Tanner let me use his phone, and I looked it up. I read a bunch of things about it." Her smug look slips. "I know that was breaking another rule."

It is, but one I'm not about to scold her for.

"I'm not glad you broke the rule, but I am glad you already know some things about it." I put my hand over hers. Her fingers are almost as long as mine now. I remember when she had those chubby little baby fingers, forever smeared with peach jam. I remember how she would wrap those sticky hands around one or two of my fingers, holding on tight. Trusting me to keep her safe, to show her the world.

I long to feel her grasp my hand like that again.

"Is that what made you guys get divorced?" she asks. "Dad said you were unhappy for reasons that had nothing to do with him."

I nod. "Neither of us knew what was wrong at the time. We

didn't know much about it. But it made life really difficult for both of us."

"It made you afraid," she says, studying me. "I remember you being afraid of things. Like when you took down my curtains. I remember you telling Dad they would hurt me. And I was mad, because those were my princess curtains, and they matched my bedspread."

My heart cracks open. I remember that too, how she cried. Like when I cut her hair. "The OCD made my brain think the curtains might strangle you somehow. I knew it didn't make sense, but I couldn't stop thinking about it. I couldn't stop being afraid."

"Are you still afraid?"

It's a good question, and one that's not easy to answer. "Not of things like curtains, usually. Mainly because I take medicine and go to therapy. But I still feel afraid sometimes, just like everyone does. And I still have irrational thoughts, but now I know better how to handle them."

She pauses. "Are me or Luke going to get it?"

It hurts to think she has to worry about this, that I might have passed this on. "Neither of you have any signs of it yet. And I don't think you will, but if you do, we'll be able to figure it out much sooner than I did. And we'll get you the help you need right away, and you'll be fine. The medicine and the therapy are really good stuff."

She purses her lips and looks up at me with those beautiful, deep hazel eyes of hers. I think she's going to have another question, but instead she squeezes my hand, and it takes my breath away. "I'm sorry, Mom. I bet that was really scary. And sad. Especially when Dad wasn't living with us anymore." She blinks and looks down. "I remember you being really sad when you thought I wasn't looking. Both of you."

Tears leak from the corners of my eyes. "Thank you, honey. It was. Scary and sad. But I always had you and Luke, and I was so grateful for that. I am always so grateful for that."

Ivy leans into me—not a full hug, but god, it's wonderful. I press my lips to the top of her head. We sit there for a moment, saying nothing, just breathing together. Until Ivy speaks up again.

"Can I have some cereal now?"

I chuckle. "Sure thing."

We pour bowls of Rice Krispies, and I cut up some strawberries to add in. We sit at the table and eat, and Ivy asks some more questions about OCD, and even though it's still not the easiest thing to talk about, it's easier than I thought it would be.

I'm clearing my bowl from the table when Blake and Lukas arrive. Ivy is still slowly picking at hers, as usual, her Rice Krispies turning into a soggy mush.

" . . . And then the dragon swoops down, and the whole castle is about to be on fire," Luke says as the door swings open. "Wooooosh!" He flings his arms up for emphasis. Costanza jogs over to them at the sound of Luke's voice and nearly knocks Luke over.

"That does sound pretty intense. And you want *me* to be in this movie? With all these dragons and stuff? Sounds dangerous." Blake grins at me, then sees Ivy at the table. He raises his eyebrows.

I try to communicate with a smile that things are going . . . better. For the moment, at least.

"It wouldn't be a real dragon, Dad," Luke says, scratching Costanza's head. "They use computers."

"Well, that's good." Blake pulls out a chair and sits down at the table. "Hey, Ive. How're you feeling?"

She avoids meeting his gaze and speaks around a spoonful of cereal. "Good."

Blake's smile slips; I know how it hurts to have her not even want to look at us.

"Mom and Ivy should be in it, too," Luke offers. "And Costanza. But especially Mom, because she knows what she's doing."

Blake laughs. "Yes, she definitely does." He squeezes Ivy's

arm and says to us, "Luke has decided his Lego castle adventure would make a good movie. I think he's probably right."

"We'll need to have Peter Jackson over for dinner again," I say, giving Lukas a hug before he runs off to his corner of the room, Costanza bounding at his heels (and then crashing into a stack of Ivy's books).

"Obviously," Blake says, but his eyes cut back to Ivy. There's a moment of awkward silence—well, silence punctuated in the background by Luke making blaster noises with his Star Wars Legos.

I'm trying to figure out how to bring up the things we still need to say to Ivy, but she sets her spoon down with a heavy clunk.

"I'm sorry," she says, mostly to her cereal.

Blake and I look at each other, wide-eyed. Did Ivy just apologize? Of her own accord? And sound like she *means* it?

"Okay," Blake says slowly. "For what?"

It's an honest question. She's had plenty to apologize for over the last several weeks.

Ivy's cheeks are bright red. "For sneaking off with Tanner," she says, barely above a whisper. "And eating the brownies when I knew they had drugs in them."

A knot forms in my gut. She hadn't told us yet if she knew, or if she'd really thought they were just plain brownies. The idea that my twelve-year-old knowingly took drugs is terrifying.

Then again, she's confessing to it, when she could easily have lied. And she's clearly ashamed; that's something. I pull out the chair and sit down again, forcing myself to breathe evenly.

"Thanks for apologizing," I say, then exchange a glance with Blake. Neither of us knows how to handle this perfectly, how to say just the right thing.

But we're in this together.

"You know why we were so worried, right?" Blake asks. "About you running off with Tanner? About the drugs? About running off to meet Chris at Comic-Con, and . . . all of it?"

She sucks in her lower lip. "Because it wasn't safe," she mumbles.

We've talked to her before about sexual assault—we even mentioned it again after Comic-Con, so I know she knows why exactly it wouldn't be safe. But that clearly didn't stop her this last time.

"I know it seems not so dangerous sometimes," I say. "It seems like you could be in control of the situation—and sometimes you can, and it ends up fine. But the problem is, the more dangerous situations you put yourself into, especially with these older boys, and god, *especially* with drugs, the more risk there is that you could really get hurt. And we love you so much, Ivy. We're your parents, always, and we want to do anything we can to keep you safe."

Her lower lip quivers, and I reach out and grab her hand resting by the spoon, glad that she doesn't pull away.

"If you did get hurt, though, if some boy did take advantage of you, it wouldn't be your fault," Blake says. "No matter if you took drugs or not." He glances over to Luke, who is obviously not paying the slightest bit of attention to any of us and is now singing an orc battle song he made up a few days ago. And I know what Blake is going to ask. He lowers his voice. "Did Tanner . . . do anything to you? Did he touch you, or . . . or hurt you in any way?"

Ivy shakes her head, and relief nearly makes me dizzy.

"No." She shifts in her seat uncomfortably. "I liked the way he looked at me at first, but then I didn't really like it anymore. It felt weird."

Ugh, I bet. I want to punch that little punk. And I can tell by Blake's expression he feels the same.

But Ivy doesn't need that from us.

"I know what that feels like," I say. "And it can be scary."

She looks up and meets my eyes, and I can tell I got that right. She was afraid and didn't totally understand why. I squeeze her hand tightly.

"I didn't like the way it felt, either." Her voice is a whisper.

"The drugs. Like, I thought I did, but then I just . . . didn't know what was going on in my brain, and everything felt wrong."

God, I definitely know what *that* feels like, and not because of any pot brownies. My poor baby. I just want to hold her and never let go.

"That makes sense," Blake says, and he puts his hand on her back. "I'm so sorry that happened to you." He sighs. "The truth is, we can't protect you from everything, as much as we wish we could. But the rules are there to protect you from as much bad stuff as possible. And it's all because we love you so damn much. You get that, right?"

She nods, and tears trickle down her cheeks. She brushes them away furiously with her free hand. Blake pulls her in close and she leans into his chest. She's squeezing my hand so hard it hurts, but I'm not going to complain about that, ever.

"That love doesn't change, even with Dad and me being together," I say. "It won't change when we get back home, and Dad lives there with us. It won't change when we get re-married. We will always, always love you *so much*."

"And me too!" Luke chimes in happily from his pile of Legos on the other side of the room. I guess he started listening at some point, after all.

"You too, Lukey," I say. "Both of you. You guys are our world. This family, all four of us, together. That's what matters."

Luke starts singing the battle orc song again, lost in his Lego adventure.

Ivy sniffles and sits back up. "So you guys are getting married again?"

"We haven't set a date yet," I say. "But yeah. And I'd love it to be soon."

I'm not sure if it was the events of the last day, or me finally standing up for myself and my family, or maybe that picture of a Kim able to face her fears, but I'm not afraid anymore that the wedding will be about anything but us.

I could marry him today, happily.

A smile spreads across Blake's face. That smile like sunshine that I want to see for the rest of my life. "Me too," he says. He glances at Ivy. "I know you might not be happy about that, but—"

"It's okay," she says. "I'm okay with it."

"Yeah?" I can't hide my surprise.

She nods. "You should get to be happy again. Even if it's still gross to know you two have sex."

Blake laughs. "Yeah, well, knowing your parents have sex is kind of unavoidable, but we'll do our best to not let any more of it get recorded, so no one has to *see* it."

She wrinkles her nose, but smiles despite herself. "Thanks."

And it's in that smile that I can see that she really is okay. That she's going to be okay with us as a family—that really, she'll be better than she knows, because Blake and I together and happy will be better parents than we were miserable and apart.

She sighs, resigned. "So I'm guessing there's still consequences to talk about, but can I take a shower? I smell gross."

"Sure thing," Blake says. "And when it comes to consequences, that apology and taking responsibility goes a long way to making those lighter, you know."

She brightens again. "Really? Because if I could get even *supervised* phone time again—"

"Shower," I say with a laugh. "Then we'll talk."

She gives us each a hug, lingering just enough that I know she's doing it because she needs it, not just for our sakes. Then she leaves to go shower, and I fling myself into Blake's arms.

He doesn't seem to mind, holding me tight. "That went well, don't you think?"

I nod against his chest. "Yeah. And she and I talked before you got back—I think it's all going to be okay. I really do."

"Yeah, me too." He tilts my face up to his. "Did you really mean that about getting married? Because if you're not ready, that's totally fine. We can—"

"I meant it," I say. "I'm not afraid of the memory being

anything but perfect, no matter what. You'll be my husband again, and I want that more than anything."

"God, so do I." He takes my face in his hands and kisses me, and I melt against him, against the incredible feeling of those lips against mine, cradled by the knowledge that this man loves me as much as I love him. That he always has and always will.

We're going to make this work. Our family together again. *Us* together, for the rest of our lives. Nothing is more perfect than knowing that.

Though the thought of getting to marry Blake all over again comes pretty damn close.

And I've got a plan for that.

ACKNOWLEDGMENTS

There are so many people we'd like to thank for helping make this book a reality. First, our families, especially our incredibly supportive husbands Glen and Drew, and our amazing kids. Thanks also to our writing group, Accidental Erotica, for all the feedback.

Thanks to Michelle of Melissa Williams Design for the fabulous cover. Thanks to everyone who read and gave us notes throughout the many drafts of this project—your feedback was so greatly appreciated.

And a very special thanks to you, our readers. We hope you love these characters as much as we do.

Janci Patterson got her start writing contemporary and science fiction young adult novels, and couldn't be happier to now be writing adult romance. She has an MA in creative writing, and lives in Utah with her husband and two adorable kids. When she's not writing she can be found surrounded by dolls, games, and her border collie. She has written collaborative novels with several partners, and is honored to be working on this series with Megan.

Megan Walker lives in Utah with her husband, two kids, and two dogs–all of whom are incredibly supportive of the time she spends writing about romance and crazy Hollywood hijinks. She loves making Barbie dioramas and reading trashy gossip magazines (and, okay, lots of other books and magazines, as well.) She's so excited to be collaborating on this series with Janci. Megan has also written several published fantasy and science-fiction stories under the name Megan Grey.

Find Megan and Janci at www.extraseriesbooks.com

The Extra Series

The Extra
The Girlfriend Stage
Everything We Are
The Jenna Rollins Real Love Tour
Starving with the Stars
My Faire Lady
You are the Story
How Not to Date a Rock Star
Beauty and the Bassist
Su-Lin's Super-Awesome Casual Dating Plan
Ex on the Beach
The Real Not-Wives of Red Rock Canyon
Chasing Prince Charming
Ready to Rumba
Save Me (For Later)

Other Books in The Extra Series

When We Fell
Everything We Might Have Been

Made in the USA
Coppell, TX
01 April 2022

75884610R00163